The Non-Linear Flow
Of The Universal Tides

Michael Gary Wirth

Cover photographs courtesy NASA/JPL-CalTech & Dennis Elemma

Published by Leafen Egg Creations
Edison, NJ 08817

ISBN: 0615894798
ISBN-13: 978-0615894799

For my father Gary who never got the chance to read this but I'm sure he'd be proud if he did.

CONTENTS

ACKNOWLEDGMENTS

Where to start? This book would never be possible if not for the encouragement that I received from the people around. First and foremost, to my mother Deborah, without whom, I literally wouldn't be here to write this. Also to my sister, Alison, ironically also without whom I wouldn't be here. Thanks for jumping into that pool all those years ago, sis.

To my wife and partner, Lauren, the woman that lifts me up when I need it and knocks me down a peg when I get too cocky. Over the last 5 years of writing this book, I lost interest in finishing a number of times. But you encouraged me to jump back into it to finish my goal so I can create something that I can be proud of and for that, I can never thank you enough.

This book would also never be possible without the feedback of my early readers. Your contributions helped me to mold my original concept into the story it became. So a special thanks to Jack Chambers, for allowing me to bounce ideas off of you. To Ben Jacoby, for getting me out of the house and being my afternoon writing buddy. To the Veroni brothers, Michael and Tommy, for the feedback you've both given me. To Robb Orr, for all of your encouragement and inspiration. And to my beta readers Danny Gonzalez, Herbert Rodriguez, Kimberly Chadwick and Nicole Bresner, just for caring enough to want to read the book.

Now, on to the next one.

PROLOGUE

Jehoel pumped his legs, winding his way through the streets of the city. His sandaled feet slapped against the pavement, orchestrating a vibrato in the quiet air. Beads of sweat formed on his forehead, rolling down into his face, blurring his vision and stinging his eyes. He raised his hand to wipe away the perspiration and turned his head. He couldn't see his pursuer behind him, but that didn't mean he was safe. Knowing the man that was following him, Jehoel would have quite a chase ahead of him.

The sun peeked out over the horizon, creating long fingers of light that reached out across the metropolis. Under normal circumstances, New Eden was a beautiful, sprawling city. Silver discs stood atop thin risers, making the buildings look like glimmering, metallic sunflowers. The streets shimmered in the growing sunlight from the moisture left over from a recent rainfall.

Jehoel reached the corner of an intersection, stopping just long enough to let a large truck pass. He snapped his head in both directions, looking for the safest escape route. Despite the dawn breaking, the city was still mostly dark, making it difficult for Jehoel to see where he was running. When he first saw his attacker, he knew that there would be trouble. Out of instinct, he set off in a sprint, with no consideration of where to run to. All that mattered was that he ran. He went about two blocks before realizing where he might be able to hide. He knew that security at this time would be light so there may not be anyone there to protect him, but it was his best choice, given the circumstances.

1

Turning sharply, Jehoel cut down a dingy alleyway between two buildings. His foot fell in a puddle and slipped out from under him, sending him tumbling into a group of metal garbage cans. The cans fell to the ground in thunderous applause, spilling trash everywhere. Jehoel pushed himself up out of the garbage, a rather unpleasant substance squishing between his fingers. Ignoring what the stuff on his hand may be, he headed for the alley, cursing under his breath for giving his pursuer the opportunity to catch up to him.

Erupting from the other side of the alley, Jehoel spotted his destination. Had he the breath to do so, he would have sighed in relief. Instead, he ignored the stinging in his ribs and his pounding heart and continued to run, hoping to close the small gap between him and the tall golden building before he collapsed.

From the corner of his eye, Jehoel noticed the shadows flicker and dance. He turned his head toward the distraction, realizing that one of the shadows was growing. Looking up, he saw a figure in the air, a winged man descending upon him. Though the sight of a man with wings wasn't abnormal to someone in Jehoel's line of work, at that moment he was filled with a feeling of intense dread. Jehoel made to sprint, to escape the shadow but it quickly cut left and swooped down, blocking his path.

"Why did you have to make this harder on yourself?" the man asked. He reached out to Jehoel, a silent offer of assistance. "Just come along with me and I can promise you this will go a lot easier."

The man looked down on Jehoel, a shining example of contradictions. The kindness of his words held a sinister motive. His hand was outstretched in friendship, but he desired to inflict pain. It was all a shock to confront as Jehoel once considered this man a friend.

"Why are you doing this, Nathaniel?" Jehoel asked through labored breaths. He barely heard the words over the sound of his heart beating in his chest. "What do you want from me?"

A wicked grin grew across Nathaniel's face. "Oh, Jehoel. It's not you we want."

Jehoel blinked rapidly as he looked up at Nathaniel, his eyes widening as he realized the meaning behind his words. A sudden flash of light filled Jehoel's vision and a pain spread throughout his skull. He dropped to his knees as the world around him grew fuzzy. Struggling to look up at Nathaniel, Jehoel's head suddenly became too heavy for his neck to hold.

Nathaniel reached down and grabbed him by the arms, pulling him ungently to his feet. Jehoel could hear the sound of footsteps approach him from behind, but he paid it no mind. He flopped his head to the side, his eyes facing Nathaniel's general location.

"You'll never find it, Nathaniel," Jehoel said, his words slurring like a lifelong alcoholic. "I made a promise long ago. I intend to keep it."

Nathaniel reached his hand under Jehoel's chin, squeezed his cheeks and gave his head a playful shake. A smile spread across his face, seeing the amusement in the sight of Jehoel's flared lips and dilated pupils. "We will see, old friend." Nathaniel chuckled and released Jehoel's chin, slapping his cheek playfully.

Through the haze of the concussion, Jehoel thought he heard a second laugh among Nathaniel's. A higher pitched laugh, tinged with a hint of sadism. A woman's laugh.

Jehoel shook his head and focused his efforts. He needed to send a message, needed to alert someone about what was happening. But the pain fractured his concentration, made it difficult to reach out to Michael and the others. Luckily there was something else that he could contact. Something with which he had an even stronger bond. If he could move it, he may be able to prevent Nathaniel from finding it.

So he opened a doorway.

CHAPTER 1

My eyes glazed over as I read through the hundredth paper of the day. The essay began like all of the others before it and would no doubt end the same way: dry and filled with emotionless facts. Granted, I expected this outcome when I assigned my class a 1,000-word essay on the interstellar trade policies of the Zeb-Klemmich system. I knew that I would be presented with the same thing as I had been in previous years; a regurgitation of the information delivered during my lectures with very little added interpretation or insight. Yet this year, the task of grading these papers felt even more tedious, most likely due to my impending retirement just months away and my antsy, anxious feeling. Glancing sideways, I eyed the stack of remaining papers and sighed. I leaned back in my chair and wiped the fatigue from my face, pulling at the length of my beard absentmindedly.

A knock broke my reverie, my head snapping toward the door. I smiled, welcoming the sudden distraction. Reaching down, I grabbed my *Universe's Greatest Watcher* mug (a gift from the graduating class of, oh, so many decades ago) and drained the remnants of coffee, gagging as the tepid liquid hit the back of my throat.

I placed the mug back on the desk and closed my gradebook. Pushing myself up from the chair, I strolled to the door as a second knock rang through my office.

Pulling the door open, I was met by Galgaliel, one of my oldest friends. I met Galgaliel during our first year with the Grigori.

4

Our heads were filled with wild dreams of becoming full-fledged Watchers. We hit it off immediately, our passions reflected in each other, to the point that we were barely apart. Though over the years our aspirations have changed, with me becoming a teacher and her opting for a career with the AHM, our friendship never faltered.

Looking at her as she stood in the doorway, I could tell this wasn't a joyous meeting, her face a mixture of trepidation and uncertainty.

"What's wrong?" I asked. Her eyes shot to mine, barely recognizing my presence. She raised her thumb to her mouth and began to chew on her fingernail, a habit I knew too well. She brushed past me into the office, taking the seat in front of my desk. I closed the door and returned to my own chair, crossing my hands on the desktop.

I watched as she fidgeted in the chair, crossing and uncrossing her legs nervously. She dropped her hand to her knee and left it there for a moment before raising it to her mouth and working the thumbnail again. Her other hand tucked a tuft of brown hair behind her ear, her bright blue eyes darting around the clutter on my desk. Despite her agitation, I wanted to allow her to broach the conversation and her reason for visiting, but if I waited any longer, I would need more coffee.

"What can I do for you, Gal?" I prodded.

Galgaliel placed her hands on the desk, her eyes focusing on my face. She leaned in closely and I felt the warmth drain from the room.

"It's Jehoel, Metatron. He's gone."

"What do you mean 'gone'?"

"Exactly that. He's disappeared. I just got word from Gabriel that Jehoel was supposed to report in this morning, but there's been no sign of him." She leaned back in the chair, returning to her thumbnail chewing.

My eyes shot to the bay of clocks along the top of my walls, finding the clock for New Eden. "It's a few minutes after noon. He can't have been missing for that long."

Galgaliel shook her head, allowing a tangle of curly brown hair to fall to her face. "That's not like him, you know that. Jehoel is one of the most dependable angels in the squad. He wouldn't just disappear like that."

Though I wasn't personally acquainted with Jehoel, he did have a reputation of being trustworthy. I've never heard of him shirking his responsibilities. I began to understand the nature of Galgaliel's fears.

"I need to ask you a favor," Galgaliel asked, scratching her face, eyes falling back to my desk. "Can you…"

I leaned back in my chair, a smile playing on my lips. "You want me to find him."

She lifted her eyes to mine and nodded.

Dragging my hand down my face, I sighed. It was way too early and I had way too much to do to deal with something like this. There could be any number of reasons for Jehoel to go dark, many of which would require a security clearance that I didn't have to understand. But how could I refuse Galgaliel? My gaze lingered on her, examining the worry on her face. Sure, there could be a reasonable explanation why Jehoel didn't check in, but I trusted Galgaliel's gut. If she felt something was off, I believed her.

"Come with me," I said, pushing myself up from the desk. Galgaliel rose and followed me down the short hallway in the back of my office. The walkway had gone into disuse in recent years, becoming a storage area of textbooks, old papers, and just about anything that I wished to forget. A haphazardly stacked pile of banker's boxes shook as I rushed by. I stopped, raising my hands to steady their teetering. Satisfied that it would remain standing, I continued down the hallway, Galgaliel right at my heels.

I looked up at the large, oaken door that stood at the end of the hallway. Carved a few years after the beginning of time, the sight of it was enough to captivate me, no matter how many times I've seen it. The intricate scrollwork that ringed its frame contained the alphabets of every known language in the universe. Within the border were a collection of figures, beautifully carved in the wood. Winged men floated near the top of the door, high above the scene of a phalanx of people kneeling in praise of them. In the center of the door were two men locked in battle, one ringed by the power of light, the other engulfed in darkness. The two stared at each other, neither allowing their resolve to falter, knowing the outcome if it did. As I looked upon the scene, I felt a faint shudder flow through my body. Brushing the feeling aside, I reached out and grasped the knob.

A dull wail screamed from the hinges as I pushed the door

open. The door hadn't been opened in years so I was grateful the hinges didn't just give out and drop the door to the floor. The room smelled of dust and mildew, a smell of age and wisdom. I stepped into the room, waving my hand in front of the lightbox on the wall. The overhead lights kicked on, casting the room in a soft, orange glow. Galgaliel followed me into the room, carefully closing the door behind her. My eyes fell upon the single item in the room, a pedestal that rose beautifully from the center of the floor.

I strode toward the pedestal with careful, deliberate steps. I could feel Galgaliel stepping closer to me, her blue eyes watching me carefully, but I tuned her out. Using the Oculus was a difficult task, a task which I was out of practice. It had been years since I used one in an official capacity, not since I became headmaster of the School of Grigori where my days had been filled of teaching others to use its abilities to oversee universal events. A wave of memories flooded over me, memories of before my time as a teacher. I wondered for a moment if I would still be able to tune into the mystical energies and find what I sought before realizing that I had been one of the oldest Watchers left. Using an Oculus was second nature to me.

So why did I feel so nervous?

Inhaling deeply, I closed my eyes and narrowed my focus. I raised my hands and placed them on the cold, glass sphere, feeling pinpoints of heat permeating my hands. Focusing on the warmth of the globe, I collected it into a bundle and tuned my inner vision into the right areas. I wasn't sure what I was looking for so I made a broad sweep on the city of New Eden.

Minutes passed to no avail. Jehoel was nowhere to be found. I widened my search, looking into other districts, when I felt a sudden pull. It was a strange sensation; not often did an event go out of its way to draw an audience. But in my time, I had learned that when this did occur, it was wise to follow it. So I allowed the pull to take me through a great distance across the galaxy. As my mind drifted through the abyss, I wondered what could have been so important to draw me there.

The birth of a new messiah and with it, a religion that would engulf a nation?

A great civil war that would tear planets to pieces?

The next great scientific discovery?

The thought of witnessing a fantastic event in the universe

excited me. I watched over the shoulders of students as they witnessed events such as these, wishing that I had the luxury of being the Grigori on scene. Finally, after all of these years, I had the chance to be back in the game.

Imagine my disappointment when all I found were two men in a fishing boat.

CHAPTER 2

Matt Woods placed his fishing rod against the side of the boat and leaned out over the water. When he first spotted the shining thing in the river, he quickly dismissed it, assuming that glow came from the sun's reflection off of an old soda can. But the more he looked at it, the more he realized that the shiny spot was moving through the water erratically, in ways that soda cans generally do not. That, coupled with the fact that the sun usually doesn't penetrate more than a few inches of the murky blackness of the Arthur Kill, made Matt realize he was looking at something of interest.

"Hey, man," Matt said, motioning to the water. "Come take a look at this."

Aaron Sheehan lifted his floppy canvas fisherman's hat from his head and wiped the sweat from his face with his forearm. "Did you find the fun you promised me?" he said, sarcasm dripping from his words. Replacing his hat, he laid the fishing pole on the floor of the boat. Reaching into a red, flip-top cooler, he grabbed a bottle of beer, twisted off the cap and took a long chug. He sighed loudly as the cool taste of the India Pale Ale faded from his tongue.

As Aaron rose to his feet, he could feel a river of sweat run down his back, leaving a long, dark streak in his Outer Banks Egyptian cotton Polo. He did not react well in the heat, having been blessed by his stout Irish heritage with pasty skin. Despite the thick layer of SPF 70 he slathered on his face that morning, Aaron could feel his skin reddening by the moment. He stepped across the boat as a large cloud floated past the sun. Aaron sighed, relieved to have a moment of peace from the harsh rays.

"You complain more than my grandmother," Matt quipped, shooting a quick glance back at Aaron. Unlike his friend, Matt enjoyed being in the outdoors. Besides fishing, Matt loved to hike, camp and rock-climb, instead of burying his nose in a book like his long-time friend. But Matt had the build for those activities, carrying a well-built, muscular frame. Even his chestnut skin allowed him to tan with ease, which made being out in the sun for long stretched of time tolerable. He was always adventurous and full of energy, making him the perfect foil to Aaron's introvertedness.

"Just look down there," Matt continued, pointing into the water.

Aaron took another long swig of his beer and leaned over the side of the boat. He stared down into the river, expecting to see a plastic shopping bag or an old shoe or something similarly un-Earth-shattering.

His expectations could not have been more wrong.

Under the water was a fish. This, by itself, would be completely normal. But this was not just any fish. It was a fish that glowed brighter than the taillight of a '57 Ford Fairlane. Except the fish glowed green instead of red like the taillight of a '57 Ford Fairlane.

"Well, that's interesting," Aaron said, his eyes never leaving the aquatic oddity. For the first time since they left the dock that morning, his mood lifted.

"What is it?" Matt asked.

"It's a fish."

Matt rolled his eyes. "Yes, I can see that. My question was more along the lines of 'why is it glowing?'" The cracking in his voice belied his fears of an underwater toxic waste spill. He wondered if he was going to wake up in the morning with a third arm or a platypus tail.

"It's called 'bioluminescence'," Aaron said. "It's a naturally occurring phenomenon in simple-celled creatures that live in very deep water." He crinkled his brow as he stared at the fish darting through the water. "But it usually only happens in jellyfish and plankton. Nothing as complex as a fish as large as that."

"So is it some kind of mutant fish?"

Aaron shrugged. "Or a completely undiscovered species." A thought tickled the back of his brain. He pictured himself making waves in the Marine Biology industry, the discovery of a complex bioluminescent creature turning the ideas of aquatic wildlife on its head. He began to script the acceptance speech he would give when he was presented with an honorary PhD from the University of Phoenix or some other prestigious school.

The pair stood in silence as they watched the fish dart playfully beneath the water like a…well, like a fish.

Suddenly, the fish turned and swam quickly downstream.

"It's getting away," Aaron shouted. "Follow it!"

Matt spun on his heels and hopped into the driver's seat of the boat. He turned the key on the dashboard and the engine roared to life. Cutting the wheel to the left (or 'port' as it would be referred to in boating terms), he jammed on the accelerator. The small cuddy cabin cut through the water like a thresher through a hayfield, following the tiny green spot.

Aaron found himself lying on the floor of the boat, a wave of pain crashing through his head. Pushing himself up on his butt, he grimaced at Matt.

"A 'hold on' would have been nice," he said, brushing the puddle of beer from his shirt. Matt smirked, his eyes never moving from the fish. The boat jumped over the waves, kicking up a fine mist of saltwater. The spray stung Matt's eyes but he ignored the pain, refusing to blink for fear of losing sight of the fish.

"No, seriously. I think I may have a concussion," Aaron said from the back of the boat (or 'stern' if we decide to keep with our nautical theme), his polo now completely soaked with sweat *and* beer.

Matt heard the words but made no acknowledgement of them. He raised his arm and wiped the water from his face.

As the distance between the boat and the fish decreased, Matt eased off the accelerator. Not wanting to spook the fish any more than they already had, he brought the boat to a stop. They lilted from side to side in the choppy water as the fish circled playfully a few feet away.

Matt slowly rose from the driver's seat. "Move," Matt whispered to Aaron, shooing him away like an irritating fly. As Aaron slid from the seat of the red pleather bench, Matt lifted the seat, revealing a deep storage box. He grabbed the aluminum handle of the fishing net and, grasping it with two hands, extended the telescoping shaft..

"Seriously?" Aaron asked. "That's how you're going to try and catch it?" He lowered the seat of the bench and sat, watching as Matt leaned over the side of the boat.

Matt dipped the blue mesh net into the water and inched it closer to the fish. "Unless you have a better idea…" he muttered, allowing his thought to trail off. He pushed the net further into the water, lining it up with the fish. The water was dark and murky, making it difficult but the light from the fish illuminated the mesh just enough for him to see.

Suddenly, the fish turned toward the surface and looked Matt dead in the eye. Matt stared at the creature, frozen. Moments passed as the two locked themselves in a battle of wills, neither willing to concede. But the fish was the first to break, spinning abruptly and swimming deeper into the water.

"Dammit!" Matt shouted, throwing the pole to the floor of the boat.

Still rubbing the back of his head, Aaron picked up the net and placed it on the seat beside himself. "Told you that wasn't going to work."

"Shut up, please," Matt replied. He plopped himself in the driver's seat and reached down to grab a bottle of beer. He twisted the cap off and drained half of the bottle in one gulp. Matt was as eager to catch the fish as Aaron, though for less loftier gains. Ever since his father caught the 87 pound tuna off the coast of Maryland six years ago, Matt ached to out fish him. He figured a glowing fish would easily trump a tuna of any weight. Matt sat in silence and finished the beer as thoughts of bragging to his family and friends faded from his mind.

Aaron watched as Matt swirled what was left of his beer around the bottle. He looked down at the net on the seat beside him. "What else do you have in here?" he asked, rapping on the side of the bench.

"Fishing stuff, mostly," Matt said, his eyes transfixed to the bottle in his hand. "Tackle boxes, rods, some old diving equipment."

Matt froze, his head slowly tilted backwards. He looked up at Aaron, a sly smile stretching across his lips.

CHAPTER 3

Aaron spent four years studying English Literature in college. Given his love of reading, he felt that a degree in English Lit would be the right move out of high school. Now that he was pushing 30, Aaron wondered why anyone would allow an eighteen year old to make decisions about the rest of their life. He regretted every moment of the teaching job he took, trying to make high school freshmen understand the differences between *Great Expectations* and *The Great Gatsby*. He regretted not following a different path in life, a path that would give him the chance to study the world, not just words.

Slipping into the black neoprene diving suit, Aaron felt a tingle of excitement flow through his body. He considered the insanity of diving into the deep, dark waters of the divide between New Jersey and Staten Island in search of a mysterious, glowing fish but quickly pushed his hesitations out of his mind. He lived a dull and dreary existence since he moved out of his parents' house seven years earlier, playing it safe at every turn. For once, he was going to embrace the crazy. He looked down at Matt and watched as he finished checking the connections on the diving tanks.

"It's been a while since they were filled," Matt said, "so I'm guessing we have forty, maybe fifty minutes of air."

Aaron grabbed the tank and slung it across his back. He snapped the latch around his waist. "Is that gonna be enough time?"

Matt shrugged as he picked up the second tank. "Depends

on how far the fish is. If we can't find it within twenty minutes, we'll need to turn back."

Aaron nodded and hooked the mouthpiece around his neck. Looking out along the lengths of the Arthur Kill, he felt his stomach flip in anticipation.

When most people hear about the Arthur Kill, which usually isn't very often, they generally think about the Outerbridge Crossing and the Staten Island area of New York. Though the river is lined with ports, most boaters choose the Arthur Kill as a pushing off point on their way to a different destination. Murky waters, flotsam, and some of the ugliest fish in the universe, the Arthur Kill isn't the ideal place for a mid-afternoon fishing trip. But Matt was willing to put up with it considering the low rents in the area.

While fishing in the Arthur Kill is possible and even, at times, relaxing, swimming there was a risky venture. Matt rose to his feet and secured the diving tank to his back. He looked down at the brown, choppy water, his mind returning to the stray thought of oozing radioactive waste. "Maybe this isn't such a good idea," he muttered.

Aaron looked over at Matt. "Don't be such a baby. You know what you're doing. We'll be fine."

Matt inhaled deeply and nodded. He knew that Aaron was right, that he was close enough to an expert at diving. One of Matt's favorite summer activities was to jet down to the Jersey Shore and partake in a few diving courses, as well as other water-related sports. He was comfortable both on and in the water yet he couldn't shake the clutching fingers of nervousness he felt in his chest. There was something about the scene that bugged him.

Shaking his head, Matt reached up and slid the diving mask over his face. The heat from his skin fogged the glass and cast the world in a vignette, making everything look like the sample photos on the walls of the local *Glamour Shots*. He leaned into the bench and grabbed two heavy flashlights, hooking one onto his diving suit and handing the second to Aaron. He then pulled out a handful of Glo-Sticks and slid four into a pouch at his waist, giving Aaron the rest. Bending down, he picked up the fishing net from the bench. He unscrewed the blue plastic head from the pull and clipped it to a carabiner attached to the body harness. He then slid a bulky yellow watch onto his wrist, fastening it securely.

Stepping up onto the seat of the bench, Matt sat on the edge of the boat. He pushed the breathing regulator into his mouth and exhaled, releasing a short *hsssss*. He looked down at his wrist and pressed a button on the diving watch. It beeped and the display flashed rapidly. After a moment of this, the screen showed a countdown from forty minutes. Matt closed his eyes and relaxed his body. Leaning backwards, he fell into the river.

The sudden shifting of weight caused the boat to lurch, forcing Aaron to grab the back of the driver's chair and steady himself. He looked out over the side of the boat and waited for Matt to reappear. A moment passed before Matt's head broke through the surface of the water.

Aaron placed the regulator in his mouth. He took a deep breath, cringing at the acrid taste of the canned air. As he stepped up onto the bench, he could feel the weight of the breathing tank throwing his balance off. His body leaned to the side. He grasped the side of the boat to keep him from falling over but this only caused the boat to rock, knocking him off balance even more. Despite Aaron's best efforts, the rocking boat won out and he tumbled head over feet into the river, kicking up a splash of grungy black water as he disappeared beneath the surface.

Matt's regulator hissed erratically as he laughed at Aaron's plunge. Shaking his head, he sank beneath the water and unclipped the flashlight from his belt. He pressed the button, unleashing a beam of light that cut through the blackness of the river and nearly doubling his three-foot field of vision. Turning to his right, he spotted Aaron floating listlessly beside him. Catching Aaron's attention, Matt pointed the flashlight at his wrist, indicating that they had wasted nearly three minutes of oxygen. Sweeping the flashlight downward, he pivoted his body downward, kicking his way toward the riverbed.

As Matt swam deeper into the river, the cloudy water began to clear, allowing him to make out different shapes farther below. The rough, rugged outlines of large rocks, sandy hills, and sunken garbage became clearer. Squinting through the facemask, Matt surveyed the underwater terrain, wondering if he would find the chewed through corpse of an old-timey gangster wearing cement shoes. He was in the middle of deciding what type of suit the gangster would be wearing when a brief flicker caught his attention. Turning, Matt spotted the fish's green glow.

The light was faint but there was no way he could mistake it. Not many things this far down into the river would have their own light source. He stared, enraptured by the far off glow as Aaron swam up next to him. Feeling his friend's presence, Matt pointed the flashlight in the direction of the fish. Aaron turned his head and together, they watched as the fish swam in tiny little circles, darting in and out of a decomposing suitcase. It fluttered upward a few feet before making a sudden turn and shooting down toward the riverbed, disappearing into a crack in the foundation of the Outerbridge Crossing.

Tugging the flashlight from his belt, Aaron clicked it on, focusing the light on the old cement foundation. He kicked his feet, propelling himself toward the crack. As he neared the base of the pier, he swung the flashlight's beam around the area, examining the hole in the ground. Below him, he could see the green speck shrinking as the fish made its escape. Aaron grabbed the edge of the crack and pulled himself down. As his head disappeared into the hole, he felt a hand clasp his shoulder. He looked back and spotted Matt, stern-faced and shaking his head.

Matt understood what Aaron was thinking; the problem was he didn't think it was a very good idea. Though he was willing to dive below the river to chase the fish, climbing through a crumbling pylon was beyond his scope of rational. His mind returned to the decomposing-body-in-cement-shoes idea. Matt hoped Aaron would read the message in his face, warning of the danger.

Aaron looked up at Matt and closed his eyes somberly, nodding slowly. He clicked his flashlight off and clipped it to his belt. He reached into his pocket and pulled out one of the Glo-Sticks, cracking it in both hands. Giving it a quick shake, he turned back toward the hole in the pier and disappeared into the pylon.

Matt watched as Aaron's flippers kicked their way downward, the bright, orange light casting creepy shadows on the walls. He inhaled deeply and checked his wrist watch. Ten minutes had elapsed since they dropped into the river. Shrugging, Matt climbed down into the hole, promising himself to only continue for another ten minutes, even if it meant dragging Aaron back to the surface.

CHAPTER 4

Aaron held the Glo-Stick at arm's length, using the cylindrical lantern to guide his way through the hole. The crack in the foundation was tight, allowing him just enough space to wriggle through, but that wasn't the most dangerous part of the ordeal. Rusting rebar jutted from the crumbling concrete pylon, creating a forest of hazards for him to navigate through. Braches of old metal swiped at him as he swam by, just barely missing his diving suit. Despite the danger, Aaron continued on, winding his way through the crack as best he could.

Looking ahead, Aaron noticed the color of the walls begin to darken. As he approached, he could see the end of the concrete pier spill over into a passageway below. Aaron looked back and spotted Matt's flashlight inching its way through the crevice. Aaron placed his hands on the edge of the concrete, feeling the cracks in the wall. He worked the Glo-Stick into a gap, letting it stick out just enough to illuminate the opening. Turning back, Aaron stepped out of the crevice and dropped into the passageway.

Falling through the riverbed, Aaron pulled a second Glo-Stick from his pocket and activated it. His eyes quickly now to the pitch blackness around him, the bright flash of light stunned him for a moment, forcing him to turn his head. As his eyes adjusted, he looked around the passage, examining the faint outlines of river plants living along the walls. He reached out and grabbed one of the plants, stopping his descent. He jammed the Glo-Stick into the wall. Looking up, he spotted Matt's flashlight beam. It was brighter this time, assuring Aaron that Matt was getting closer. He shoved himself against the wall and continued to drop through the passageway.

Lighting a third Glo-Stick, Aaron spotted a school of tiny fish flitting around his head. He reached out to touch them, causing the fish to break formation and scatter in all different directions. Aaron watched as they swam around him, eventually reforming their original pattern. He reached out again, dispersing them a second time. He chuckled to himself, so engrossed in his little game that he failed to notice the passageway open up to a large cavern.

Aaron kicked his feet gently and hovered over the massive cave. A clean, white light emanated from the floor, pulsating steadily. Aaron's eyes watered as he stared down at the cavern beneath him. His vision hadn't yet adjusted from the sudden change in brightness but Aaron was so engrossed in the wonders beneath him that he couldn't avert his eyes.

Hearing a watery *thunk* behind him, Aaron turned to find Matt emerging from the crack in the ceiling, his face twisted into a grimace, rubbing his forehead. Aaron threw his head back and laughed into his breathing apparatus, a thick stream of bubbles flowing up through the water. Matt reared back to throw a punch at Aaron but succeeded in merely throwing himself back an inch and a half.

Shaking his head, Aaron ignored the attack. He pointed downward. Matt aimed his flashlight into the cavern but the beam was quickly engulfed by the pulsating light from below.

The cavern walls were covered in a variety of colorful flora, from blue to pink to green to silver. Schools of fish chased each other through the water. A large fish with long, pointed teeth lunged at the smaller fish, catching one in its jaws. It turned and swam away, a look of contentment in its eyes.

Aaron floated at the mouth of the cavern, stunned by the discovery of a hidden tunnel beneath the Outerbridge Crossing. He looked around the cave, absorbing the wonder of it. Shadows passed over his body, cast by the hundreds of fish swimming across the light from the sphere. Aaron turned to find Matt swimming beside a large, multi-colored fish with translucent fins, the pair somersaulting through the water. Looking down, Aaron squinted through the throngs of fish, staring at the sphere below him. Aaron flipped and swam toward the light.

As Aaron grew closer to the sphere, he could feel a strange sensation flow through his head, like a ringing at the base of his brain. He pushed himself through the water, kicking his feet harder and harder as he got closer to the light. With each inch, he could see the sphere growing larger, much larger than he first assumed it to be. The light also grew much brighter the closer he got, forcing him to squint and allow his vision to adjust.

Aaron stopped just above the sphere. Floating gently, he gazed down at the ball of light, unable to pull his eyes away. A shiver ran through his body and the tingling in the back of his head turned into a crackle. His skin rippled, as if all of the hair on his body did the Wave like at a baseball game. But he ignored all of these feelings and circled downward and around to the base of the sphere.

Placing his flippers on the floor of the cavern, Aaron noticed a strange shimmer at the core of the ball. The edges of the sphere undulated and the color of the light shifted, growing darker. Aaron's heart thumped as an inexplicable feeling of anxiety washed over him. He inhaled deeply, steadying his emotions. As his heart slowed, Aaron noticed the sphere settle.

Odd, he thought. Stepping forward, he raised his hand toward the sphere. His fingertips brushed the surface of the sphere, causing it to ripple. The nervousness rushed back into Aaron's chest as the sphere's light shifted again. He jumped backward and the rippling settled.

It's reacting to my presence, he thought. *This is magnificent.*

He looked up and scanned the cavern for Matt, spotting him on the far end of the cave playing with the rainbow fish. Shrugging, he inhaled deeply, the bitter air burning the back of his throat. Aaron closed his eyes and counted under his breath, stepping forward with each number.

One.

The sphere's light shimmered, shifting from a pure white to a dingy yellow.

Two.

A surge ripped through the sphere. It pulsated quickly, stretching outward, threatening to tear through its own skin. The light darkened further, shifting to orange, then to a deep red.

Aaron paused a moment, pinching his eyelids tight. A

wave of nausea bubbled in his stomach. He took in a deep breath, fighting back the urge to heave. Exhaling, he lunged forward, ignoring the final count.

His hands broke through the outer layer of the sphere, burying his arms to his elbows. Streams of light erupted from the ball, shooting out across the cavern. The water thrummed and vibrated, increasing the pounding in Aaron's head ten-fold. Rearing his head back, Aaron screamed into his breathing regulator, engulfing his face in a cloud of bubbles. His body grew weak from the pain, giving out on him. He collapsed but his body remained locked in place by his arms trapped within the sphere.

Matt felt the pressure in the water intensify before he noticed the change in the colors around him. He abandoned the rainbow fish and flipped in the water, turning his attention to the floor. A beam of light struck him in the face, blinding him. He shook his head, chasing the stars from his vision. Looking down, he stared through tears in his eyes at the pulsating sphere. It took a moment for his eyes to adjust and the spots to scatter before he noticed the slumped, black figure next to the giant ball. Blocking the light from his eyes, Matt watched at the sphere slowly expanded, swallowing Aaron inch by inch.

CHAPTER 5

Sweat oozed from Matt's pores as he swam the distance between him and Aaron. A cold chill shot up his spine as he watched his friend being engulfed by the sphere. Matt's breath ran ragged with anxiety as he propelled himself through the water, kicking his legs as hard as he could. He didn't know what would convince Aaron to immerse himself in a giant ball of light but he certainly feared the outcome if he couldn't get to him in time.

Matt sliced his arms through the water, his attention focused on Aaron's crumbled form. He struggled to see through the bright light of the sphere and the haze in his facemask. As he grew closer to Aaron, a thick, black shadow passed in front of his face. A rush of water pressed against his body, pushing him to the side.

Matt circled downward, changing his path. He swam a few feet before the shadow appeared again. Matt stopped and reared back, switching his attention to the top of the sphere. Long, black tendrils poked out from the ball, whipping around the length of the cavern, feeling the rocky walls and ceiling. He watched as one of the tendrils slapped the rainbow fish, ensnaring it, and dragged it back to the sphere. His heart jumped in his chest and his throat seized. Forcing energy into his shaking legs, he pressed his way toward Aaron.

Bolts of lightning flashed behind Matt's eyes. His chest slammed into the floor of the cavern and a massive weight pressed against his back. He placed his hands on the ground and pushed himself up but the weight increased, forcing his body back into the silt. He struggled to breathe as the weight crushed his chest against the rocky floor. Turning his head to the side, Matt struggled to see what held him down, afraid to find that a large boulder broke free of the cavern ceiling. But he couldn't get a decent vantage on the object. He wiggled his body to scoot across the ground. He managed to move a few inches before he felt himself being dragged backwards.

Matt looked at the sphere and spotted the long, dark tendril extending toward him. Looking back, he saw the end of the tentacle undulating a few feet from him.

What the hell is this thing? he thought to himself. Looking ahead, he saw that the sphere of light continued to extend farther, nearly touching Aaron's face.

Matt inhaled as deeply as he could and held his breath, reaching his arms far out before him. He searched the riverbed with his fingertips, finding a small crevice in the floor. Digging his fingers into the crack, he exhaled, forcing as much air from his lungs as he could and pulled himself forward while turning onto his back. He watched as the tentacle thrashed across the cavern, searching for its lost prey. Ignoring the pain in his chest, Matt kicked up from the floor, moving away from the tendril as fast as he could.

Matt spun his attention back toward the sphere, making a mental note of his state. His chest hurt and his head throbbed, but he could move and, more importantly, breathe. He watched as the sphere engulfed Aaron's face, feeling a sudden surge of fear well up inside him. He kicked his feet harder, hoping to close the gap quicker.

Matt winced as he collided with Aaron, the pain washing over his entire body. Wrapping one arm around Aaron's waist, he reached up and plunged his hand into the sphere, grabbing Aaron by the face. He pulled, trying to free Aaron from the grip of the sphere with no success.

Dropping lower to the ground, Matt wedged his feet against the riverbed. Putting all of his weight into his legs, he pulled again. He strained against the hold of the sphere and Aaron's body began to budge.

A quiver flowed through the outer layer of the sphere. It expanded sharply, quickly wrapping them both in its light before it contracted and released them. Aaron and Matt tumbled backward over each other, floating away gently.

Free from the sphere, Aaron's eyes snapped open. He looked around the cave. He watched as the sphere shrunk smaller and smaller, robbing the cave of its light. Shriveling to the size of a pea, it disappeared, plunging Matt and Aaron into total darkness.

CHAPTER 6

A bright flash erupted from the Oculus, forcing Galgaliel and me to avert our eyes In the few moments it took us to turn back, the two men had completely vanished from the screen. The flowing plants were settled, the fish swimming serenely as if nothing had been there to disrupt their play. My face pinched in disappointment and confusion as I stared down at the scene. I found Galgaliel wearing the same expression.

"What happened?" she asked. "Where did they go?"

It had been a long time since I was asked questions like these. And it had been even longer since a time I could not answer them.

Understanding this next part requires a little background knowledge of the tools at hand. The Oculus is a specialized tool that came about when the inhabitants of the planet Talgon discovered a strange, ethereal glass. Unfinished Talgonian glass is generally not very impressive, with its dull luster and milky white color, but it does have a peculiar quirk: it vibrates. It took the Talgonians quite a while before they realized that the vibrations can be manipulated. Once they did, however, a small sect of Talgonians used the glass to fashion a device, the modern Oculus, and with it discovered a host of inhabited worlds in the universe. As the Talgonian's knowledge of the universe expanded, so did their mission.

To monitor all events that affected the universe on a grand scale.

The Talgonian sect made an effort to communicate with the new worlds they discovered and invited more and more beings into their fold, which led to the creation of the Grigori. The Brotherhood of the Grigori carry on the principles set forth by our Talgonian ancestors by documenting all of the universal milestones and passing that record along to our offspring.

One feature of the Oculus is that it can be finely tuned, adjusted to dial into any specific world or event. Changing the scene from one world to another is easy; a lone Grigori like myself can do that at any time. I placed my hand on the Oculus, hoping that it had simply gone out of tune. Closing my eyes, I tried to realign its vision, but when I looked back at the scene, nothing changed.

Stepping forward, I grasped the occulus with both hands and focused my concentration on the surge of energy we witnessed. All energy has a unique signature, a pattern that sets it apart from everything else and there was something strange about this flare-up. Something…familiar. The feeling I got seeing that powerful discharge was like singing along to a song that you haven't heard in a long time; you know the tune and the words are on the tip of your tongue but you just can't seem to get it right.

"What's going on?" Galgaliel squeaked at me. I raised my hand, shushing her. She bristled at my brusqueness but ignored it. I was too close to allow anything to break my concentration.

The energy tugged at me, drawing me into its path. Loosening my control, I put my awareness in neutral and allowed it to take me along for the ride. It's a strange feeling, not being in control of your consciousness. Like that moment before you fall asleep, when your brain is molding the real life events that happen around you into your dreams. In the past, this was a feeling I grew used to, having succumbed to it a number of times, but I now understand how surreal this feeling is.

I followed the energy through the cosmos, past different sectors of the universe. We moved so quickly that stars and planets whizzed by me, their colors blurring and melding together. I looked around, trying to get my bearings but the speed made it impossible to recognize anything. Minutes passed, or at least it felt like minutes. Time had become irrelevant.

Finally, the energy began to slow. Stars and shapes came into view. Looking down, I spotted a small blue planet with fluffy white clouds circling the world's atmosphere. From way up high the planet looked calm. Serene.

The energy dragged me down toward the planet. As we passed through the atmosphere, I watched the sprawling cities slide in and out of view. We flew over oceans and I watched the waves crashing into each other. A grey and white bird *cawed* at me as I floated across his path.

Without warning, the energy stopped. I hovered above the ocean, miles away from anything. No cities, no people, no animals (well, except for the fish, probably). I looked down at the water and squinted, trying to peer through the murky black water.

As I stared below me, a tiny blue light came into view. The light grew larger and larger, quickly expanding to three, five, ten times its original size. I felt uneasy staring at the light, a wave of nausea building up inside me, but couldn't tear myself away from it. As if it were pulling me towards it.

A massive flare of energy ripped the ocean's surface, crashing into me. It jarred my concentration and sent my consciousness reeling. My body shuddered and flailed backwards, shooting through the lightyears of space. By the time my awareness merged with my brain, I was sprawled out on the floor like a drunken college student. Galgaliel knelt beside me, cradling my head.

"Metatron? Metatron, are you OK?"

I blinked the stars out of my eyes and looked at her face, flush with worry. Grunting, I nodded an affirmative to her question. This seemed to alleviate her concern

Galgaliel slowly rose, helping me up from the floor. I dusted myself off and straightened my tunic as she turned to the Oculus. She stared at the glass, watching the ocean waves lick each other, looking for any signs of activity. "What was that?" she asked. "Do you think this has something to do with Jehoel's disappearance?"

I considered her question. So far today, two unexplainable things had occurred, and it wasn't even lunchtime. I had no idea what was happening, or what repercussions we would face from it, but if these two events were unrelated, it was one heck of a coincidence.

"I don't know," I said. "But I need to speak with Michael. At once."

CHAPTER 7

Aaron's heartbeat slowed as he floated gently in the dark. He watched a school of tiny glowing fish scurry past him, unaware of what just happened. His body ached, his legs felt like jelly and he had a strange tingling sensation in his arms. He inhaled deeply, his heart finally reaching a normal rhythm.

Reaching down, he unclipped the flashlight from his belt. He clicked the button and it sprung to life, cutting a swath in the underwater blackness. He swung the beam toward the ceiling, looking for the entrance. He spun around, hoping to catch a glimpse of the orange Glo-Stick. A tingle of anxiety flowed through his body as all he saw above him was solid rock.

The flashlight fell on a small opening in the ceiling at the far end of the cave. Aaron breathed a sigh of relief. Turning, he pointed the flashlight toward Matt, finding him floating quietly in the water, his limbs motionless. Aaron's anxiety kicked into full gear as he swam to Matt's side. He looked at the watch on Matt's wrist and watched it count right past 54 minutes. He shined the flashlight on the gauge attached to Matt's air tank.

The needle had dipped clear past the red zone.

The anxiety turned to fear. *He's almost out of air*, he thought. *My friend is drowning.*

Aaron wrapped his arm around Matt's chest. He kicked his feet, mustering as much energy as he could and swam toward the hole in the ceiling.

Aaron slinked through the opening, his arm locked around

Matt's chest. He wound his way through the tight corners of the tunnel, sensing that something was off. The twists and turns he remembered, but they somehow seemed to be easier this time. He recalled dodging jutting metal and rusty rebar earlier, but now everything seemed to be more natural. What was most odd was that he didn't find any of the Glo-Sticks he wedged into the rocks. Maybe he could buy that one or two of them slipped free and fallen, but all of them? That didn't make sense to him.

Aaron shook his head upon realizing how unimportant a few missing Glo-Sticks were given Matt's situation.

Reaching the crack in the ceiling beneath the bridge's foundation, Aaron dropped the flashlight and forcefully lifted Matt toward the opening. He remembered his friend struggling by himself to wiggle his way through. *How am I supposed to get him through as dead-weight?* he asked himself, frowning at his poor choice of words.

Grabbing him by the chin, Aaron positioned Matt's face in front of his and slapped him. Not hard, mind you, as it is difficult to slap anything hard underwater. But the slap was enough to rouse Matt slightly. His eyes fluttered and he showed signs of recognition. He looked at Aaron, then at the crack, then gave Aaron a nod.

Matt reached his arms through the crack and placed his hands on the riverbed. Weakly, he pulled himself up, struggling as his air tank caught on the rocky ceiling. Aaron squeezed the plastic clip on Matt's chest and swam around behind him, pulling the tank from his back. The tank sank like a rock to the bottom of the tunnel and Aaron shoved Matt up through the hole. He kicked his way toward the surface, his chest quivering as he swam.

Wasting no time, Aaron slithered through the ceiling into the river. He pumped his legs and propelled himself upwards, grabbing both of Matt's arms as he passed. *Save your strength, man. Just concentrate on staying alive.*

Aaron looked up and found everything engulfed in darkness. He wondered how far down they had gone. How long were they down there? What time was it? They set out fishing early that morning, and it must have been just after noon when they dived into the river. However, as he scanned the surface of the water, or what he thought was the surface, it looked like the middle of the night. Could they have possibly been under water for hours?

Matt's body began to spasm. Aaron struggled to retain his grip.

Almost there, was the last thing Aaron thought to himself before he realized that Matt's body had stopped moving.

CHAPTER 8

Aaron crested the surface of the water like a dolphin in the Gulf, pulling Matt closely behind him. He grabbed Matt's mouthpiece and yanked it from his face, allowing air to circulate into his lungs. Matt helped the process through a regimen of wheezing and inhaling, allowing his lungs to inflate like a carnival balloon.

Aaron smiled as Matt coughed and hacked.

"Why did I take the empty tank again?" Matt asked through shallow breaths, his mouth contorted into a frown. Aaron laughed and slapped Matt on the back.

Aaron turned his head around the river, squinting in the dark. Through the haze of the creeping blackness, he barely saw anything.

"Where's the boat?" he asked.

Matt cursed. Loudly. And repeatedly. Having been in such a hurry to catch the fish, he had forgotten to anchor the boat. With all the time they spent underwater, it could have drifted off and been miles downriver. "Dammit!" he said again for good measure.

"We lost the boat, didn't we?" Aaron asked.

Matt nodded. "We'll have to swim back to shore."

"Do you have the energy for that?" Aaron asked.

"Don't have a choice, do I? I could stay here, but that doesn't seem like much of a plan." Matt looked down at the watch on his wrist and pressed a button on the side. The digital display blinked and changed, switching to compass mode. Matt stared at it for a moment, struggling to read the display in the dark. He pushed a second button, casting the face of the watch in a pale green glow. "That way," he said, tilting his chin.

And they swam.

*   *   *   *   *

Pulling himself up on the wooden dock, Aaron unstrapped his airtank, allowing it to drop to the ground with a metallic clang. He crouched down and extended his arm to Matt, grabbing his wrist. He dragged him up from the river to the dock before dropping to his knees panting.

Matt lay face down on the dock, his heart beating wildly against his ribs. His arms and legs burned and his body convulsed as he breathed. He could feel the edges of the wooden planks dig into his skin but he ignored them. Making the pain go away would require moving and that was the last thing he intended.

A shiver ran through Matt's body, prickling his skin with goosebumps. As the pain in his body subsided, he could feel the cold settling around him. Tilting his head back, Matt squinted through the night air. A fog had rolled across the neighborhood, engulfing everything in a thick, white mist. He turned to the left and looked out over the parking lot.

"Where's my truck?" His throat was dry, causing the words to crack as he spoke. The parking lot was nearly empty, the only occupant a tan Toyota with fogged windows rocking rhythmically. There was no sign of Matt's pick-up truck or his boat trailer.

"Wonderful," Matt continued. "First the boat, now my truck." He dropped his head to the dock, smacking his forehead against the wood.

Aaron slipped the flippers from his feet and rose. A stiff breeze blew across him, giving him the shivers. Though he didn't fault Matt for being upset at the loss of his truck, he lamented not having a set of dry clothes. Or even his shoes, for that matter.

"Come on, man." He bent over Matt and grabbed him gently by the arm. "Let's find a phone and call a cab. We can report the truck stolen once we get changed."

Matt grunted an agreement as he allowed Aaron to help him to his feet. He looked around the empty parking, hoping to find a pay-phone of some sort. Though it had been years since he last saw a pay-phone in town, he figured that something *had* to go right for him at some point. As he looked around, however, a

31

strange feeling washed over him. "Does everything look...different to you?" he asked.

Aaron turned and looked out at the parking lot. His eyes passed between the old, dilapidated buildings, the wilting trees, and broken streetlights. Though the scene reminded him of the city they left from that morning, it did seem different. The full-bloom Compacta bushes that lined the streets, buds popping into red and brown flowers, had been replaced with grungy garbage cans, trash spilling over their edges onto the broken sidewalk. Two large apartment buildings rose high into the night sky, casting a looming shadow over the rest of the neighborhood, replacing the row of cozy, Colonial-style homes that had been there earlier.

Aaron turned back to Matt, his brow crinkled in confusion. "You're right. Could we have drifted downstream?"

Matt shrugged. "I hope so. At least it will give me a chance to get my truck back." He looked at Aaron. "But it figures there's not a pay-phone in sight."

Turning toward a side-street, a bright pink and red glow caught his attention. Matt squinted through the mist, trying to read the tall, glimmering letters on a neon sign, spotting the word *Peachez* above an old run-down building.

CHAPTER 9

As I rushed down the hallway to the elevator, my brain worked overtime thinking of the best way to explain the things Galgaliel and I witnessed in the Oculus. Hundreds of different possibilities came to mind to justify the sudden disappearance of the two fishers but somehow none of them seemed to fit. I hadn't been able to truly figure out what happened yet I had a feeling it was somehow tied to Jehoel's disappearance. And if I was right, then it was information that Michael needed.

Reaching the elevator, I jabbed the button on the wall, pushing it multiple times for good measure. I stroked my beard and shifted from foot to foot, waiting for the elevator to arrive. Looking up, I watched as the lighted numbers decreased steadily. My anxiety grew and my patience waned; I thought technology was supposed to make our lives easier. Closing my eyes, I took a deep breath. The elevator bell dinged and I hopped into the car, pressing the button for the top floor.

I was just as impatient inside the elevator as I was while waiting for it. When the elevator reached the top floor, I rushed from the car and down the hallway, stopping at the large door at the end. I took another deep breath to calm my nerves. Reaching up, I ran my fingers through my hair, straightening the tangled mess on my head and face. As I flattened a few stray wrinkles in my tunic, I looked up at the brass serpent's head knocker at the door, shaking my head at Michael's unique sense of humor.

Three loud bangs echoed through the hallway as I clapped

the knocker against the door. The door swung open and a force beckoned me to enter. I found Michael sitting behind a large oak desk, a young seraph hovering next to him. The seraph fished out gauze and tape from a first aid kit laid out on the desk and attended to Michael.

"Are you OK, sir?" I blurted, rushing to his desk, the concern in my voice evident. It had been a long time since Michael was in the forefront of a battle, longer still since receiving an injury. To see him in such a state was unsettling.

Michael shook his head and smiled modestly. "I'm fine, Metatron," he said. "It comes with the job." The seraph wrapped a length of gauze around Michael's wing, causing him to wince. He turned to the seraph and shot him a look of annoyance

"Be careful," he growled through clenched teeth. The seraph nodded, his face contorted into silent fear. Michael turned back to me, his clear blue eyes burrowing into mine. His stare could pierce the hardest of men, compelling them to spill even their most carefully guarded secrets. His eyes alone had the power to get whatever he wanted, but they became a more powerful tool matched with his face, those chiseled features and sharp angles, a cross between a Michelangelo sculpture and an Abercromie and Fitch model.

Michael waved his hand, dismissing the seraph. We sat in silence as the young angel gathered his first-aid kit and exited the office. As the door closed quietly, Michael's eyes returned to mine. "I take it you've heard about Jehoel."

Nodding, I told him of my visit from Galgaliel. Michael listened intently as I shared the story of the humans and how they stumbled upon a dimensional rift. He watched me, expressionless, as I related the entire underwater tale to him.

As I finished, Michael leaned back in his chair, cringing as his injured wing pressed against the hard wood. His eyes narrowed as he stared at me.

"Why are you coming to me with this?"

The question confused me. "Well, I understand that you have your hands full with the disappearance of Jehoel, but if these two men aren't sent home, it could have disastrous effects on the dimensional stability."

Michael shrugged, his lack of interest unwavering. "Again, why come to me? You have more than enough power to lead two wayward humans back home. Take care of it."

I felt my face flush. For decades, this has been a point of disagreement between Michael and me. My current predicament is my own fault, really, for not expecting this conversation to take this turn. I cleared my throat. "You know I cannot do that, General."

"Ah, yes," Michael said, leaning forward. He folded his hands on the desk and glared at me. "Your silly little oath."

Here we go...

"It's a shame that all the power you Grigori possess is wasted on you Grigori," he said, his mouth twisting into a sarcastic grin. "It can be put to such better use elsewhere."

I sat in silence as Michael assaulted me with insults. His words rolled off my back. It was no use arguing with him; his opinions on the subject of my mission were too strongly negative. He enjoyed belittling my oath, but even after all of these years, I refused to let him see my anger. Instead, I bowed my head respectfully.

"Thank you for your time, General," I said before rising from the chair and turning toward the door. I could feel Michael's eyes gloating silently as I exited his office.

* * * * *

I waited for the elevator doors to close before I allowed myself to fume. The entire walk back to the Ocularium was spent muttering in anger. How dare Michael mock the oath that predates the Angelic Service itself? The Grigori, my people, have faithfully helped to maintain order in the universe for eons, documenting events and ensuring that history lives on despite every inevitable change. Without us, countless civilizations would have been lost, completely forgotten, once they reached the extinction stage. But Michael allowed his hubris to cloud his judgment, and he failed to see just how the Grigori served the Angelic High Military. I mean, the angel hours saved by not having cherubim off on reconnaissance missions alone is worth something.

Most of my anger had been released by the time I returned to the Ocularium. As I passed through the doorway, Galgaliel looked up from the Oculus, immediately recognizing the irritation on my face.

"What happened" she asked. I explained the full conversation I had with Michael, right down to the last insult.

She stared at me in silence, watching as my red face

changed to its regular color. "Maybe he has a point."

As one of my oldest friends, I expected Galgaliel to empathize with my point of view. She should have understood my feelings, having to endure such an insult against myself and my people. It came as a shock to hear her side with Michael.

"How can you agree that I should break my solemn oath?" I asked, turning my anger on her.

Galgaliel shook her head and smiled consolingly. "That's not what I meant, Metatron. Maybe Michael is right in the sense that leading these two men home should be a quick and easy solution."

"Yes, but you know that I can't just pop down there, take them by the hands and say 'I'm taking you home.'"

Galgaliel's consoling smile grew, belying a curious idea.

"I didn't say *you*."

CHAPTER 10

Aaron stepped carefully on the ragged broken sidewalk, heading for the glowing pink oasis down the street. He looked up at Matt, recognizing the frustration in his face. Aaron ignored him, not wanting to rile him up any more. He turned his attention to the night sky and watched as a thin cloud floated past the moon.

He tugged at the damp wetsuit clinging uncomfortably at his body, bunching up in a few places he'd rather not have overstuffed. Looking down at the storefronts, he hoped to find an all-night clothier, some place he could purchase a fresh pair of slacks and a nice button-down shirt. But all he was met with was a row of "Closed" signs, dashing these hopes. In the end, it wouldn't have mattered anyway as his wallet had floated away in the bottom of Matt's boat.

They rounded the corner into the club's parking lot. It was nearly empty, with only the random Honda Civic and Ford Explorer parked almost between the lines. The pink neon sign towered over the lot, its light illuminating the building in a garish hue. Music poured from the building, oozing from its walls and filling the quiet night air with the rapid fire *boom boom boom* of the newest Top-40 song. Matt placed his hand on the door handle and felt the vibrations from the music shake throughout his body.

As he opened the door, Matt was instantly assaulted by the harsh dance music and a wave of cigarette smoke. His eyes teared as the smoke momentarily blinded him. A coughing fit washed over him, burning his already aching chest. He stood at the doorway waiting for Aaron, waving the smoke away from his face.

"You all right?" Aaron asked.

Matt nodded between coughs. He stepped through the threshold of the doorway and was met by the sight of three scantily clad ladies gyrating on poles while a gaggle of men watched, throwing money at them. Aaron kept his attention on the bar, sliding a stool out for himself, feeling uncomfortable with the idea of objectifying women. Matt, on the other hand, had no shame, and joined the other men in the ogling duties.

"Do you have to stare like that?" Aaron asked.

"Yes. Given the night we had, I deserve a little distraction. Besides, they like it."

"How do you figure that?"

"Well," Matt responded, "if they didn't like being stared at by a bunch of strange men while dancing around in their underwear, then they wouldn't be dancing around in their underwear in front of a bunch of strange men."

Aaron shrugged, unable to argue with Matt's logic. He waved his hand to attract the bartender. As she walked over to them she raised an eyebrow, spotting their wetsuits.

"What'd you boys do, jump ship?" she asked, the corner of her mouth twisting into a coy smile. Matt turned to her and answered with a mock laugh.

"Can we just get a couple of beers please? Oh, and I need to use your phone."

She reached under the counter and pulled out a heavy black telephone. "The phone you can have. But the beers... Sorry guys, but you'll need to prove that you can pay for those."

Aaron turned to Matt and cocked his head. Rolling his eyes, Matt unzipped the front of his wetsuit and reached inside. Pulling out a black, metallic wallet, he pressed a button on the side and it sprung open. A wad of folded bills dropped onto the bar.

"Good enough," the bartender said, sliding over toward the beer taps.

Matt picked up the phone's handset while Aaron unraveled a few of the bills, sliding them across the bar. The bartender returned with two mugs filled halfway with an amber liquid and topped with a thick, white foam. Aaron grabbed one of the mugs and sipped the beer, coughing on the taste of stale ale.

Matt listened to the dulcet tones of the Muzak version of

Michael Bolton's "Love Is A Wonderful Thing". Or at least he thought it was a Muzak version. It could have been the original. As he listened to the music, his eyes floated around the club, settling on a petite brunette, dressed in tight, black, Lycra shorts and an equally tight, equally black, and equally Lycra halter top sashaying her way toward them. He reached for his mug but Aaron grabbed his wrist. "Don't drink that," he warned.

Matt shot Aaron a questioning glance when the bartender appeared before them. She placed a finger on the receiver button of the phone and grabbed the handset from Matt.

"You do not belong here," she said.

Matt's head swung around to her, his face twisted in irritation. "What the hell? I was trying to make a phone call."

The bartender stared Matt down without acknowledging his words. Her eyes bore into him for what seemed like an eternity. "You should not be here," she said. "Neither of you." She looked at Aaron who met her gaze with a slack-jawed wonderment.

"Listen, lady," Matt said, his voice dripping with disdain, "you may have a nice rack but you have no right to throw us out of here. Our money is just as good as anyone else's in this joint. If you have a problem with us, then get us another bartender." He reached for the handset but the bartender slid the phone away from him.

"No, you don't understand" she said, a friendly smile spreading across her face. "I mean I am going to take you home."

Matt looked up at the bartender, his mind awash in salacious thoughts. "Now we're talking," he said, rubbing his hands together.

Aaron shook his head. He had no idea what was going on, but clearly his thinking had differed greatly from Matt's. The bartender glided through the opening of the bar and stood before the pair, her hands extended, beckoning them. "Come with me," she said, "and everything will become clear."

Matt hopped to his feet and grabbed the woman's hand, a grin nearly splitting his skull in two. Aaron was skeptical of the offer. Though Matt had heard the promise of sexually explicit activities, Aaron wasn't so certain that that was what the bartender meant by "taking them home." Deciding that both he and Matt had the physical ability to subdue the small woman if things turned sour (or at least Matt could), he stood from his barstool and sighed.

"Fine, then," Aaron said. "Let's go."

The bartender smiled and took their hands, slowly turning toward the door to lead them from the bar.

The trio stepped through the door of the run-down building into the cool, evening air. The bartender looked left, then right, carefully eyeing the empty street. Without warning, her chest burst into flames, a fire quickly engulfing her head and torso. An ear-piercing screech shattered the quiet of the city. Aaron and Matt scrambled away from the bartender as the fire spread throughout her body, reducing her to ash.

"Jesus, man, do something!" Matt shouted, his voice cracking with fear.

The bartender's screams slowly faded from the air, replaced by the sound of a shrill laughter. "Dear boys," a voice said, "you won't find Jesus anywhere near here."

CHAPTER 11

The smell of burning flesh turned Aaron's stomach, forcing him to double over and retch. His heart beat rapidly and his chest heaved as he released the stale beer all over the sidewalk. He wiped the speckles of vomit from the corner of his mouth and looked toward the sound of the laughter, never expecting what he saw.

The woman was strikingly beautiful. She had a head of long, red hair that tumbled over her shoulders, the thick curls bouncing with each step she took. Her hazel brown eyes flitted between Aaron and Matt, watching them closely. Dark red lips curled up at the edges giving them a maliciously flirtatious smile. She wore a long white dress that shimmered in the night air, reflecting the colors of the neon lights overhead, bathing her in a pinkish-orange aura.

"Did…did you do that?" Matt asked cautiously. His voice wavered, the heat emanating from the bartender's smoldering body making him uneasy.

The woman gave them a warm smile and batted her eyelashes playfully. "Of course I did, honey," she said. "And you should thank me for it."

Aaron stared at her. He glanced down at the charred remains of the bartender before looking back to the woman. "But how..? Who are you?"

"My name is Lauren," she said, gliding toward them. Her gait was slow and gentle but underscored with an air of aggression.

"That woman was sent here to hurt the two of you." Her voice had a faint Southern twang, like a displaced Georgian, making her seem sweeter and less threatening than her actions would imply.

Matt stepped back as Lauren strode towards him. "I think you should answer the other question first," he said. "How did you set that girl on fire from fifty feet away?"

Lauren's grin grew, a wide smile across her face. Her white teeth glimmered in the neon lights. "Honestly, that's not all that important. What is important is that the two of you leave."

She waved an arm above her head and grimaced at the two men. A loud *whoosh* erupted from behind them, and Matt felt a strange breeze tugging at his back. He turned to find that the air had split, revealing a large rift. A purplish mist flowed from the tear, slinking towards him. He froze, shifting his attention from the hole in space to the dangerously beautiful woman walking his way and wondered how a day of fishing could turn into this.

The sound of Lauren's cackle rose above the roar of the mid-air vacuum. She thrust her hands out from her chest, releasing a harsh wind from her palms. Aaron braced his feet on the ground and leaned into the gale, defying the force of the attack. Matt tried to hold himself against the onslaught but his legs were still weak from the swim. He fell to his back, twisting his body as he hit the pavement. He scrabbled around the ground, his hands searching for a crack or a divot or anything that he could hold onto to prevent himself from being pushed into the vacuum. His body slid across the pavement, the intense wind shoving him into the hole. Aaron watched in horror as Matt disappeared through the rift and into the swirling ether.

Aaron turned to Lauren. "Why are you doing this?" he shouted, lifting his hand to shield his face from the wind.

"It's just a job, sweetie," she replied. "Don't take it personally." With a twitch of her hand, the air pressure doubled, knocking Aaron backwards through the portal. As he disappeared into the abyss, the rift stitched itself together. Lauren lowered her arms, her cackle slowly drifting off into the silence of the city. She turned and walked off into the deserted street. Raising her hand, a pillar of fire reached down from the sky and encircled her. As the flame disappeared, Lauren was gone, returning the city to its calm and eerie silence.

CHAPTER 12

A piercing screech filled the air as Galgaliel reappeared in the Ocularium. The smell of smoky barbecue wafted through the room as her body convulsed on the floor. I rushed to her side and cradled her head, trying to calm her, to force her eyes to focus on mine. After a moment, the seizures began to subside and Galgaliel relaxed.

"What happened?" I asked. I couldn't understand why she was back so quickly. Our plan was conceived in haste, but it was solid. Gal would find a vessel on the planet and entice the two men back with her so she could help them find their way home. Only a few moments had passed before she reappeared.

"It's Lauren," she said, sitting up in my arms. "I found them and offered to take them home when she came out of nowhere and torched my vessel."

I felt my face contort into a grimace. This was very bad news. "But if Lauren knows about the travelers, does that mean he does as well?" Galgaliel shrugged, rubbing her temples.

We assumed the travelers' appearance had been an accident; after all, it wouldn't have been the first time an unsuspecting soul had fallen through the Universal Barriers. But could it be that Lucifer had orchestrated the entire event? That he pulled them through to set some kind of "Master Plan" into motion?

Pushing the thought to the side for a moment, I rose and helped Galgaliel up. She wobbled on her feet, her body suffering from the effects of being forcefully removed from that other world. In order to confront the travelers, she needed to obtain a vessel, a human form. Finding and inhabiting a vessel is stressful by itself. But to be abruptly torn from that body by a burst of hellfire? The disorientation she was going through was so strong I was surprised she was even able to stand up. Not to mention it had destroyed that poor girl in the short shorts.

Steadying her on my arm, I pulled a chair closer and lowered Galgaliel into the seat. I rushed off to my office to fetch her a glass of water. Standing in the center of the room I realized that I had no sink in my office, nor clean glasses for that matter. Grabbing the mug of cold coffee from my desk, I rushed back to the Ocularium and handed it to her. She took a sip, released a slight cough and sipped again.

"Will you be OK?" I asked.

She nodded uneasily. "Yes, I think so. I just need to rest." She took another sip of tepid coffee.

"Do that. Please tell Michael about Lauren's involvement as soon as you can." I turned back to the Oculus.

I watched as Lauren confronted the travelers, cornering them against a building. My stomach churned as my eyes fell to the smoldering body of the woman between them, the woman that Galgaliel inhabited. I pushed the thought out of my mind, hoping that Lauren's actions would help us to understand Lucifer's goals. She didn't appear to want to harm them; if she did, they would be as dead as Galgaliel's vessel. My jaw dropped as she used the Hellfire to open a rift in space and push the travelers through it.

My theory about Lucifer's involvement began to make more sense. He could be trying to create chaos among the dimensional fold by introducing these two men into worlds where they shouldn't go. The ensuing chaos would help Lucifer build his strength for…whatever he has planned. But it could be that Lucifer had a more specific idea for the travelers. Either way, whatever happened would prove disastrous.

When Lauren disappeared, I used my abilities to analyze the energy signatures left behind. I was able to identify Lauren's trail easily, having dealt with Hellfire in the past. But the other doorway was different somehow. It contained traces of Hellfire but there was something else there. Something just under the surface. As before, I tugged at the strings of this energy field and followed it to the other end. And as before, it pulled me through the reaches of the universe.

CHAPTER 13

Matt spun head over feet through the nexus between worlds, losing all sense of direction. His senses were assaulted by strange shapes and outrageous colors. The sound of nothing whooshed past his ears, deafening him. The place smelled like a mixture of summer nights and stale cheeseburgers. His arms and legs would tingle before going completely numb. Matt could taste the afternoon beers at the back of his throat as they threatened to break free of his stomach. He swallowed hard, doing his best to keep the vomit down. Concentrating all of his effort to see where he was headed, he willed his eyes to focus on one point. Unfortunately, that point was a jagged, rocky beach, and it was headed toward him at an incredible speed.

Matt landed face first in the sand. Tears filled his eyes as the pain spread throughout his body. The impact of the fall knocked the air from his lungs and he struggled to catch his breath. He lay on the ground for a few moments, allowing the air to circulate in his lungs. He moved his body little by little, verifying that it was still under his control. Satisfied that the pain wasn't unbearable and thankful that he hadn't broken anything, he pushed himself up on his backside.

Sighing, Matt rolled his head, relieving the tension in his neck. He looked at the nexus in the sky above him, watching the pink and purple clouds slide across each other. As he stared, a tiny figure materialized in the center of the nexus, growing larger and larger by the second. Recognizing the figure, Matt summoned what remained of his energy and leapt to the side just as Aaron crashed onto the beach. Matt shuffled over to him and rolled him onto his back, feeling his neck for a pulse, sighing as he found one.

Matt placed his hands on his knees and slowly rose to his feet. The pain in his body was tolerable but he still felt short of breath. Inhaling deeply, he coughed as the air burned his lungs. His mouth tasted strange, as if he licked a rusty pipe. Each ragged breath he took hurt more and more. Matt's vision went blurry and the world around him began to spin. He fell to his knees in the sand, realizing that for the second time in one day he was suffocating.

Falling sideways onto the ground, Matt fought to keep his eyes open. His breaths became shorter and shorter, every tiny movement causing intense pain. He could feel the unconsciousness overtaking him.

As Matt's mind drifted, he noticed movement out of the corner of his eye. He craned his neck to look at a small, black vehicle pulling up beside him and Aaron, the outline of a man's head just slightly visible in the windshield. A moment passed and a long, metallic tongue stretched out from the side of the truck. A creature, clad in a dark grey bodysuit, walked down the tongue and turned to them. His face was covered in a respirator, making him look like the villain in a B-movie sci-fi flick.

The man stood over Matt and stared down at his unmoving body. Matt lifted his head to look up at him, straining to see the eyes behind the mask but the effort of the movement sapped the remaining energy from his body and the world faded into blackness.

*   *   *   *   *

Aaron awoke to a pounding in his head. He felt groggy and hungover, exactly like the morning after his twenty-third birthday when Matt introduced him to the wonder that is a Jaeger-Bomb. He opened his eyes slowly, afraid of the mess he would be greeted by but all he saw was an unfamiliar metallic ceiling.

The throbbing intensified as he pushed himself up on his arms. His face felt heavy and the air tasted funny. Reaching up, Aaron felt a heavy mask attached to his face. Grasping it, he pulled it up over his head and dropped it to the floor next to him.

Aaron looked around the room, wondering where the hell he was. The small metal room had no windows or doors that he could see. Judging by the way the room shook, he could tell that he was in a vehicle, like some kind of RV. A row of cabinets lined the top of the walls. Each cabinet door had a tiny touchscreen in the bottom corner which Aaron assumed was some kind of fingerprint scanner. A thick, black pipe ran the length of the ceiling, a white ring painted every few feet. Aaron traced the pipe to the rear of the vehicle, where it ended just above a closet full of grey bodysuits.

Looking next to him, Aaron spotted Matt lying on a small cot. Matt's face was covered in a mask similar to the one he was wearing. Aaron watched as Matt's chest rose and fell slowly but steadily.

Aaron stepped off his cot and walked to a shiny chrome toolbox in the back corner of the vehicle. Pulling on the drawer, he revealed a collection of tools, most of which he recognized. However, a few of them he had never seen before. Reaching in, he grabbed something that looked like a screwdriver, except far pointier and deadlier. Holding it closer, he noticed a small button on the side of the handle. He pushed it and flinched as two metal prongs erupted from the tip.

"Glad to see you're awake."

Aaron jumped at the voice, dropping the tool back into the drawer. He spun around on his heels and was greeted by a pair of jovial eyes watching him from the rearview mirror.

"Didn't mean to scare you," the man continued.

"No, no it's fine," Aaron replied, waiting for his heart to slow. "I assume you're the guy who helped us."

The man nodded, his thinning hair bobbing in the mirror. "I'm James, and I'm just glad I was in the area. Any other day and you and your friend'd be dead."

Aaron inched toward the front of the truck and settled himself into the passenger seat. Looking out the front window, he watched as a strange world came into view. The ground was covered in soft, purple sand, gently fading away into the horizon, creating the illusion that it was covered in one of those fuzzy blankets you use to wrap a newborn baby. Large, craggy rocks dotted the landscape, jutting up at different angles. A brown haze hung in the sky, obscuring the light from the stars above, casting the landscape in a creepy semi-darkness. Only the strongest and brightest stars were able to permeate the atmospheric smog.

"Aaron," he said, extending his hand to James. He grasped

it firmly, the size of his hand surprising Aaron.

"Where are we?" Aaron asked, leaning forward in his chair to stare up at the sky.

"The Numian Sea. Just on the outskirts of the Wasteland. What were you and your friend… uh…"

"Matt."

"…Matt doing out here without equipment?"

Aaron sighed, trying to work out the best angle to his story. He considered telling James the truth about the glowing fish, the redhead who can set people on fire from ten yards away, and their tumble through a vortex that can't be described without the aid of a hallucinogenic drug, but decided that being labeled a lunatic by the guy who just saved his life wasn't worth the hassle. "I wish I knew, James."

The minutes ticked by as they rode in silence. Aaron ignored the awkwardness in the truck, choosing instead to look out at the alien world unfolding around him. James kept his vision straight ahead, turning the wheel every now and then to recalibrate the truck's route. He reached up and flipped a switch on a control panel above his head. A vent fan whirred to life, circulating warm, stale air through the truck's cabin. James sighed and turned to Aaron.

"Your friend gonna be OK?"

Aaron looked back at Matt. "Yeah, he's fine. He's breathing, at least." As he turned back to the window, a shimmer on the horizon caught his attention. Squinting, Aaron stared at the speck as it came into view.

Rising up over the horizon was a tall, metal spire. As they drew closer, Aaron saw that the spire erupted from the center of a multi-building complex, each squat, little box emanating out from a central promenade. The buildings were interconnected by a network of thin, glass tunnels. Aaron could see tiny black shadows passing across the bridges, bringing to mind the ant farm he has as a child. He was dumbstruck by the sight of the sprawling, futuristic compound.

James cut the steering wheel to the right and the truck quickly changed direction. Before them, a row of loading bay doors came into view. Aaron watched as one of the doors slowly rose, allowing a flood of yellow light to flow out. James angled the truck toward the open door, reducing his speed, rolling gently into the building.

Dozens of trucks lined the inside of the loading bay, each facing outward toward their respective doors. Judging by the identical nature of the fleet, Aaron assumed the truck he rode in looked exactly like the rest. He wondered what the designation of James' truck was. "Niner-Fourteen." Somehow, that sounded right to him.

James shifted the truck into park. Aaron reached for the door handle, ready to exit the vehicle.

"What are you doing?" James asked urgently. "You gotta wait until the door closes."

Aaron grunted, acknowledging the advice. He placed his hand on his lap as the metal bay door shut with a loud *clunk*, followed by the high-pitched hiss of air pressurization. Aaron noticed James reach for his door handle and felt it safe to follow suit. He swung the door open wide and turned back toward Matt. "Wake up, man," he shouted. Reaching back, Aaron pulled on the breather mask and released it, letting it smack him in the face. Matt's eyes snapped open and his head shot up. He blinked at Aaron a few times before reaching up and removing the mask. "Where the hell are we?" he asked with a slight shiver.

"Come on," Aaron said, jumping down from the vehicle, Matt following closely behind. Though hundreds of question kicked around his head, he kept them to himself.

James circled the rear of the truck and spread his arms wide. "Welcome to Janus, fellas."

A loud clang caught Aaron's attention and he looked up at the far end of the room. A metal door opened, revealing the form of a tall, slim woman. Her hands were clasped behind her back and she wore a dark blue uniform, immaculately pressed and spotless. She walked with an air of authority, each step taken with confidence. Long, sky-blue hair flowed freely from a baseball-cap style hat. A large pistol hung at her right hip.

The woman reached the end of the metal staircase and turned toward them. Aaron noticed that a silver badge was pinned to her chest and her shoulders were decorated with identical rows of three silver stars. Aaron knew that the stars denoted her rank and dredged his memory for what three silver stars signified. General? Major General?

She looked at James and smiled. "Welcome back, James,"

she said.

"Thank you, 'Lana," James replied. "It's good to see you." His smile increased as his eyes scanned the length of the woman's body.

The woman turned her attention to Aaron and Matt. "Who are your friends?" she asked.

"Oh, these two? Don't know. Found them out in the Wasteland. They was on the brink of death when I picked 'em up."

"Is that so?" she said. Her eyes narrowed as she placed her hand on her sidearm.

Aaron held his hands in front of him, trying to portray himself as non-threateningly as possible. "No, no," he said. "It's not what you think." He took a step toward her, realizing his mistake as soon as the woman pulled her pistol from its holster.

"Don't move," she shouted, shifting the weapon between the two of them. "Not one more step!"

Aaron took a giant step backwards in an attempt to redeem himself. He looked at Matt and saw him kneeling on the ground, his fingers interlaced behind his head. "What are you doing?" Aaron asked.

"Trying not to get shot," Matt replied, his eyes never leaving the woman.

CHAPTER 14

Aaron and Matt sat in a small room surrounded by blank white walls, which gave the room a sterile, cold feeling. The metal folding chairs they sat on were hard and uncomfortable. The matching table, which separated them from a third, unoccupied chair, was unstable, wobbling whenever Matt rested his arms on it.

Across from them, a long mirror ran the length of the wall. Though Matt had never been in a room like this before, he knew from all the police procedural shows he watched that they were in an interrogation room.

"What did we get ourselves into?" Matt asked. Placing his elbows on the table, he buried his face in his hands. The table made a *thump-thump-thump* noise as he shook his head in frustration.

Aaron did not answer, his concentration focused on the back of his hand. Having been stuck in the room for over an hour, he passed the time by playing Connect-The-Dots with the freckles on the back of his hand. So far, he made a duck, an elephant, and a '64 Plymouth Belvedere wagon.

Though they may have been incarcerated, at least they were given clothes and the opportunity to change out of their diving suits. One of their guards had brought them some old mining clothes; gray pants worn so thin that they were practically mesh and a pair of plaid, button down shirts. Matt wondered what the purpose of the plaid was in the mines, but he kept those thoughts to himself. Having the used clothes was much better than walking around in neoprene.

The door opened, snapping Aaron from his Connect-The-Dots trance. Matt lifted his head from his hands and turned to the blue-haired cop standing in the doorway. Her eyes flicked between them, but Aaron noticed they seemed somehow less intense, less distrustful.

Maybe James explained the situation to her, he thought to himself. *Maybe time allowed her to cool down.*

The officer pulled the unoccupied chair from under the table and slowly lowered herself into it. She removed the hat from her head and placed it on the table. Closing her eyes, she shook her head, causing the cascade of bright blue hair to wave behind her. She folded her hands in front of her and steadied her eyes on Aaron.

"My name is Twilana Salizar. I am a representative of the Janian Task Force."

Aaron studied the woman seated before him. He didn't want to like her. They were under arrest by her command for the crime of being unarmed in a large vehicle storehouse. But as he stared into her eyes, two large, purple discs looking back at him, he found himself somehow attracted to her. Maybe not attracted physically but… Well, yeah, attracted physically. But there seemed to be more to it than that.

Twilana continued. "I…" She inhaled deeply, holding her breath for a moment. She dropped her eyes to the table, her thumb worrying at a spot on her hand. "I need your help," she said, exhaling.

Matt shook his head, unsure if he heard her correctly. "Wait, wait, wait. How are we supposed to help you? You've arrested us."

Twilana looked between the two men, carefully considering the words she was about to say. "Shortly, our council representatives will engage in what they call 'peace negotiations' with our neighbors. However, the negotiations are a farce. The Lacertidae want our mines, our cities, and our complete surrender. And our leaders are willing to give it to them for a cut of the profits."

Matt looked down at his hands, a grin spreading across his face. "And?" he asked. His leg shook nervously, wobbling the table as his foot beat rapidly on the floor. The smile quickly turned into a scowl. "What does this have to do with us?"

"James told me how he found you. How you appeared out in the Wasteland, almost 30 miles from any outpost," she said. "Nothing human can survive out there for that long with no protection or breathing apparatus. You must be capable of incredible things."

Matt leaned toward Aaron. "Who is James?" he whispered.

"The guy who saved our asses," Aaron answered.

Matt nodded, remembering the chubby guy in the vehicle depot. He turned back to Twilana. "You didn't answer my question."

Twilana leaned back in the chair, folding her arms across her chest. "I would like you to stop the negotiations." She raised her hands and curled air quotes around the word 'negotiations'. Aaron smiled at her sarcasm.

Matt failed to see the humor. "What, you want us to be your little private hit squad?" Matt made no attempt to hide the irritation in his voice.

Twilana took a deep breath, steadying her anger. As the leader of the Janian Task Force, she was not accustomed to being spoken to with such a lack of respect. But considering the favor she approached them with and how she was asking them to risk their lives, she was willing to put her pride aside and deal with Matt's tantrum. She smoothed the wrinkles on her sleeves, allowing a moment of silence to pass between them.

"As I have stated," she continued, "I believe you have the abilities to help me against the Lacertidae. But more than that. I have learned that the two of you are ghosts."

Matt and Aaron looked at each other. Matt leaned back in his chair, swiping a hand down his face. Aaron's body stiffened, his back rigid.

"We did a search of everything we could. Fingerprint. Retinal scan. Even DNA. As far as anyone is concerned, neither of you exist. So you ask me why I need your help? It's because I need someone that cannot be traced."

More silence. Aaron leaned forward, folding his hands on the table. He bowed his head and spoke softly, preventing an imaginary audience from overhearing their conversation. "If we help, what's in it for us?"

Twilana tilted her head toward him and smiled. The tension in her eyes relaxed slightly. She was glad they were beginning to be reasonable. "You will receive my gratitude, and the gratitude of a divided society."

Matt shot up out of his seat, the metal chair clattering as it tumbled end over end on the concrete floor. "That and a nickel will buy me a jar of spit," he shouted, slamming his hands on the table.

Twilana's smile faded, her face hardened. Her satisfaction turned to anger and the irises of her eyes swirled, changing color from the deep violet that entranced Aaron just moments ago to a mean dark gray. Matt watched as the colors shifted and his anger turned to confusion. He straightened his body and took a step backwards.

Aaron placed a hand on Matt's arm. "Relax," he said soothingly, hoping to defuse the situation. As he spoke, his gaze never left Twilana's face. He recalled the attraction he felt for the woman before and found it intensifying. He shook his head and looked up at Matt. "Please sit down."

Matt sighed, turned to pick up the chair. He sat down and ran his hands over his face before folding them on the table in front of him. He tried to avoid making eye contact with Twilana, hoping to ignore the swirling miasma of her eyes, but he found himself sneaking a peek or two.

"Excuse my friend's outburst," Aaron said with a chuckle. He squeezed Matt's shoulder and gave him a gentle shake. Turning back to Twilana, he continued. "You see, we aren't from around here. That's why you can't ID us. The thing is, we don't even know where *here* is. But we would like to go home. So…if we help you, will you help us?"

The gray in Twilana's eyes slowly faded back to their original deep-violet. Her anger and composure relaxed. She pondered Aaron's request and nodded. "I will do what I can," she said.

Aaron smiled and looked at Matt. "See? Everything will work out fine."

Twilana rose from her seat, folding her hands behind her back. Her countenance went completely stoic. No anger, no acceptance. She turned and studied her reflection in the mirror. "We don't have much time," she said. "You will need to stay here for now. I will supply you with weapons and equipment. When the time is right, the doorway will be open, and you will be left unguarded. Then, you will make your move."

Matt's agitation came bubbling back to the surface. "That's your plan? 'Make your move?' This isn't our move, lady. We have no idea what we're doing here!"

Twilana turned abruptly and slammed her hands on the table. It wobbled hard and slid a few inches across the floor. She leaned in, pushing her face close to his, forcing him back in the chair. Her eyes were slits, her jaw clenched so tightly Matt could see the fibers in the muscles of her face.

"You have no idea what you owe me." Her words came out in a hiss. "My superiors wanted to execute you on the spot. I chose a more diplomatic approach. If you don't want to help me, then I will allow them to put you to death. However, according to your friend here," she motioned to Aaron, "with my help, you have a chance of returning home. And the only way you will get my help is to do what I ask. So might I suggest you reconsider your current stance."

Matt stared into Twilana's eyes, watching once again as the anger swirled the colors of her irises. He swallowed hard, struggling to release the sudden bulge in his throat. "Yeah, sure. OK."

Twilana righted herself, running her hands down her uniform. "Excellent." She turned and reached her hand out toward a small black panel on the wall.

"Just one more thing…" Aaron said.

Twilana stopped, tilting her head slightly to acknowledge his voice.

"How will we know the right time to move?"

"You will know." Her words were steady. She placed her hand on the panel. A thin, green light emanated from behind the screen. A buzz filled the air and the door disappeared into the ceiling. Twilana passed through the threshold as the door quickly dropped to the floor.

Matt sat in silence, willing his heart rate back to normal. Aaron stared at the door, a goofy grin on his face. Rubbing his hands, he turned to Matt. "This is so cool."

Matt looked at Aaron, his eyebrows narrowed into a V. *What?*

Aaron read his expression. "We get to be a part of a war."

Shaking his head, Matt placed his elbows on the table. Resting his chin in his hands, he replied, "You're sick, you know that? You do realize we're gonna die here." Matt's voice was flat and despondent. No excitement. No enthusiasm. No happiness.

The exact opposite of Aaron's voice.

"Come on," Aaron said, sounding as chipper as a school girl on a first date. "We aren't going to die. We just need to help with the negotiations between these Lacertidae guys and her people. How hard can it be?"

Matt raised his head, mouth agape, and stared at Aaron. "Did you *not* hear her? 'Weapons'. 'Unguarded door'. 'Make your move'. She's allowing us to bust out of here, but it's not for peace negotiations."

Aaron considered Matt's point before shrugging his shoulders. "What choice do we have? If we say no, they'll execute us. At least this way we have a fighting chance."

Matt leaned back, draping his right arm over the back of the chair. His eyes remained unfocused for a moment, then two, studying the wall's poor paint job. Aaron leaned forward and snapped his fingers to get Matt's attention. Matt looked at up him.

"Well, I'm always down for a bad idea."

CHAPTER 15

"You know it doesn't have to be this way," Nathaniel said. He sat on a small wooden bench in the corner of the room, picking the dirt out from under his nails. He looked at Jehoel, his eyes stern and unwavering. "Just give him what he wants and you don't have to deal with any more of this."

Jehoel's barely conscious body was chained to a wall. His face was covered with bruises and blood dripped down his chin, pooling on the floor by his feet. His chest was misshapen, the by-product of quite a few broken ribs. His wings were tied to the stone wall by a length of barbed wire, so tightly that it prevented him from even flexing them. After hours of being bound like that, the muscles in his wings had grown numb but every move sent a wave of pins and needles surging through them, adding to the discomfort of the beating he was taking. Jehoel lifted his head and looked at Nathaniel through swollen eyes.

Nathaniel pushed himself to his feet. "Yeah, I didn't think it would be that easy," he said with a smile. He turned to the Demon and nodded.

Not the most intelligent group in New Eden, the Demons are a gang of men who are sought after for their brute strength. Most of them work in labor-intensive jobs such as construction or beverage delivery, while some of them earn a living as bouncers in the city's hot nightclubs and seedy bars. This particular Demon was already in Lucifer's employ as security at The Devil's Den, a hole-in-the-wall strip club Lucifer owned. Liking his style, and his ruthlessness, Lucifer gave him a promotion.

The Demon's muscles rippled under the black tank top as he drew back his fist and buried it into Jehoel's abdomen. Jehoel's body lifted with the impact, a crackling noise came from his chest as the tiny shards of broken bones rubbing against each other. His lungs quickly evacuated, leaving him gasping for air. The Demon brought his fist back again and delivered a brutal punch to Jehoel's cheek. A tooth flew from his mouth across the room, a fresh stream of blood dribbled down his body.

"Why?" The word was barely audible, spoken between desperate gulps of air. But Nathaniel heard it. He stopped pacing and looked at Jehoel.

"Why? I've told you already. We need to know where the…"

"No," Jehoel continued. "Not that. Why you? After what it did to you. You were…like…brother…"

The anger flashed behind Nathaniel's eyes, recalling the moment his life changed forever. With two strides of his long legs, he was in front of Jehoel, his face only inches away from the prisoner's

"You have no idea what it was like!" Nathaniel's emotion was raw, his fury intense. "I was broken, bleeding. My wings had been torn from my back. Michael called the retreat and left me there to die. Him and his cronies just turned their backs on me like I was some…some…like *trash* that wasn't needed anymore."

Jehoel's head slumped. Nathaniel grabbed him by the chin and lifted it so that Jehoel's eyes saw nothing but Nathaniel's face. A wad of spittle began to foam at the corner of Nathaniel's mouth, but he paid it no attention.

"What it did to me was *nothing* compared to the betrayal I faced at the hands of my 'brother'," Nathaniel continued. "But Lucifer found me. He gave me another chance. Gave me my wings back, even. And now, Michael… Gabriel… All the rest. They will know what it's like to be beaten and left for dead." Nathaniel pushed Jehoel's face to the side, causing the bound angel to wince. Stepping back to the stool, he gave the Demon a slight nod. The Demon stepped in and delivered another blow to Jehoel's face.

"So let me ask you again, Jehoel," Nathaniel said, reclaiming his seat on the stool. "Where is it?"

CHAPTER 16

The minutes ticked by in silence as Matt and Aaron sat in the interrogation room. Matt's eyes darted around the room, unable to focus on any one spot. He tried to keep his mind occupied, to not think about the favor Twilana asked of them. But his distractions would prove limited and he felt the nervous apprehension settle in the pit of his stomach. He agonized over their decision, unsure if they made the right call, choosing to fight in someone else's war. Logically, it was the only choice they had if they wanted to get back home. But a part of him worried that getting home wasn't an option.

He pushed himself up from the chair and padded his way toward the mirror, his bare feet slapping against the concrete floor. He stared at the mirror, squinting into the smooth glass. "So, any ideas on how we can get home?" Matt asked. Placing his hand on the glass, he traced an outline of a person, head, shoulders, and chest, letting his finger trail off past the break between the mirror and the wall.

"What are you talking about?" Aaron asked, his face scrunched in confusion.

"When you told Twilana we'd help her," Matt replied, placing his face against the glass. He put his hands on both sides of his eyes, blocking out the light. "You said she needed to help us get home. How do you think that will work?"

Aaron stared at Matt, watching as he looked through the mirror. Hearing the question, he realized he hadn't given it any thought. Here they were, stuck in a place that he had never heard about, surrounded by people that could apparently do things that no human could possible do. He knew that they got here somehow, so there must be a way back.

"What if we went back to the place James found us? What if there was some kind of hint there as to how we could get back home?"

"Maybe," Matt replied, half ignoring the question. He rapped his knuckles against the mirror three times, rattling the Plexiglas. "Hello!" he shouted, pausing a moment for a response. When he received none, he leaned back. "I suppose that could work," he said, looking over his shoulder. "At least it's a start." Matt exhaled deeply, creating a fog of precipitation on the mirror. Extending his index finger, he traced a large backwards "F" in the fog. Aaron watched as Matt added a backwards "U", (which looks very much like a frontwards "U") then a backwards "C". Matt began to draw a fourth letter, but before he could finish, the lights flickered and died.

Aaron looked around the darkness. From behind him came a loud *whoosh* and a cool breeze blew his hair into his face.

"Did you feel that?" he asked. As the words escaped his lips, emergency lights kicked into action, casting the entire room in an eerie, red glow. Aaron turned his head to find that the entry hatch was open. He looked back at Matt to find him staring at the hatch, eyes wide.

"I guess it's time."

Matt nodded his agreement. Placing his back against the wall, he inched his way toward the exit. Aaron looked at Matt questioningly as he placed his hands on the table and pushed himself to his feet. He followed closely behind Matt and together they made their way toward the exit.

As they crept through the threshold, an overhead speaker squawked to life.

"ATTENTION! ATTENTION! WE HAVE AN ESCAPE ATTEMPT! ALL HANDS REPORT TO ROOM TWELVE ON THE DETENTION LEVEL!"

Matt looked at Aaron, indicating a plaque bolted next to the door. Embossed on the small metallic rectangle was a black '12.'

"Told ya she'd lampoon us."

Aaron felt his heart drop but kept it to himself. He didn't want to believe that Matt was right. Didn't want to think that Twilana had betrayed them. He searched for a justification for this duplicity but he found none that could excuse her. She lied, plain and simple.

Ignoring the breach of trust, Aaron returned his attention to escaping. Staring down the stark, metallic hallway, he surveyed their surroundings. Large bulbs cast red light throughout the hallway while small color coded LEDs ran the length of the floor, illuminating paths around the detention level. To the right, the walls were lined with thick glass windows, creating portals to the bleak, lifeless desert outside. The left side held doorways, creating portals to who knows what. A low buzzing noise dominated the atmosphere of the room.

Aaron traced the line of lights on the floor with his eyes, noticing that they stopped just before a wall.

"Dead end that way," he said, pointing toward the end of the hallway. Turning, Aaron followed a second set of lights as they disappeared around a corner. "Looks like we go this way."

They sprinted toward the end of the hall, hoping to keep ahead of the phalanx of guards that would eventually flood the level. As they rounded the corner, Matt noticed a strange, dark shape lying in the center of the corridor. He motioned for Aaron to stop as he crept closer to it. Though Matt stepped as softly as he could, each footfall was like a small explosion in the quiet, enclosed space.

Stopping about a foot from the shape, Matt realized that what he saw were the bodies of two Janian soldiers sprawled out on the floor.

Matt raised his hand, signaling an OK to Aaron. Crouching down, he placed his fingers on the necks of one of the soldiers, spotting their guns lying on the floor a few feet from their bodies.

"Looks like Twilana kept good on her promise of weapons," he said.

Aaron looked down at the soldiers. "You think she did this to her own people?"

Matt nodded. "They're both alive. If they were attacked by an enemy, they'd be dead and their weapons would be gone. She was being nice." Matt reached over and picked up a long-barreled rifle, looking it over carefully.

Though made of metal, the gun was much lighter than Matt expected. It looked like every other shotgun he had ever seen in all of the gangster/bank-heist/Scorsese movies he watched, with a long metal barrel and black stock. However, the weapon had no pump action or any sort of reloading mechanism. Matt turned it over and examined its side. On the stock were two small dials, about an inch in diameter, with a small red button just below them. He pushed the button and the gun began to hum. It was slightly disconcerting at first as he had never held a gun that hummed before. Then again, he had never held a gun that didn't hum, either.

He handed the shotgun to Aaron and reached for the second weapon. A handgun, one half of a pair. Solid silver, at least in color. A black rubber grip encircled the butt. It had more heft than the shotgun, despite being less than half its size. The barrel was taller, the trigger thicker. He handled the gun, depressing the trigger slightly. A green laser line shone to the end of the hallway. *Cool*, he thought. He tucked the gun into the waist of his pants and pulled the other closer to his feet.

Matt noticed a pouch next to the holster attached to the soldier's belt. Opening the flap, he reached in and pulled out a handful of silver disks, decorated with a red button in the center. He eyed the disks, unsure of what they were, but slid them into the pocket of his pants anyway. If the soldiers were going to carry them around, he thought, they must do something good.

"What's that on his arm?" Aaron asked, pointing to the second soldier.

Matt duck-walked across the floor and examined the other soldier's arm. A thick, metallic bracelet enclosed a large section of his left forearm. A large screen was embedded in the top of the wristlet. Green and blue lines criss-crossed, intercut with smaller white dashes and red dots. A large brown spot flashed in the center of the screen.

"Looks like a mapping system," he said, looking up at Aaron. "Like a GPS."

"Take it."

Matt slid the wristlet from the soldier's arm and tossed it up to Aaron. Grabbing the second gun from the floor, he unlaced both sets of boots from the soldiers, dropping one of the pairs in front of Aaron. Matt slid his feet into the boots and tied them, pushing himself upright. "Which way?" he asked.

Now fully booted, Aaron examined the wristlet, unsure of how to decipher the map. Two blue lines emanated from the brown dot, rounded a set of white dashes, came to a stop at an elliptical red splotch. Looking around, he tried to translate the topography.

"I think this way leads to an elevator," he said, toward the far end of the hallway.

Wordlessly, Matt walked in the direction Aaron indicated. They came to a T-intersection in the hallway and Matt placed his back against the wall. He peeked around the corner cautiously. Satisfied that the hallway was empty, he bounded past, spying a door fifty yards from him. Above the door, a small, glowing white arrow pointed up, next to a display of green numbers. Matt observed the numbers steadily changing, increasing their value by one every few seconds.

Ting. The number changed to 5.

Ting. 6.

Matt turned to Aaron. "What floor are we on?"

Ting. 7.

Ting. 8.

Aaron glanced at the wristlet. In the upper left corner, he noticed the word 'DETENTION' displayed in large white letters, followed by the floor number.

"Nine."

CHAPTER 17

A shrill beep broke the silence as the elevator light ticked to '9'.

Aaron slammed his back against the wall, slapping a button behind him. To his right, a door slid upwards, revealing a dark room. He peeked into the open door, his eyes quickly darting to Matt. Grabbing Matt's arm, he tossed him into the room and followed closely behind. Aaron groped around in the dark for the button to close the door, watching as the elevator doors slid open. He spotted a trio of Janian officers, guns at the ready, when he felt a cold lump of plastic on the wall. He slapped it and the door dropped into place, cutting them off from the soldiers.

Matt blinked in the darkness, the pale glow from Aaron's wristlet the only light in the room. He put his hand out in front of him and carefully toed toward the wall. Feeling his way along the cold metal, he placed his ear against the door, listening to the guards outside. He followed their footsteps clanging against the floor, getting closer, retreating, sounding like they were going in circles. A voice rose above the sounds of the footfalls. Curt. Barking orders. It was muffled through the wall but he had no trouble recognizing it.

"She's out there," he whispered. "Leading the manhunt against us." Matt shot Aaron his best 'I-Told-You-So' face, not realizing it was completely wasted in the dark. "Think we can trust her now?"

Aaron pressed his ear against the wall and listened. Doors

whooshing up and down. Booted footfalls on the metal walkway. Twilana's voice booming throughout the cavernous hallway.

"Search every room," she shouted. "They couldn't have gotten far."

Aaron looked down at the wristlet and watched a group of blue dots sweep the length of the hallway. He ran his fingers through his hair as his heart thumped rapidly.

Matt pushed away from the door and paced the room. "So what do we do now?" he asked, his frustration seething from his words. "Sounds like your little buddy changed her mind. She wants our heads on a plate."

Aaron shushed him, flapping his hand up and down. Leaning against the wall again, he followed the sounds outside. He noticed a set of footsteps getting louder. Closer.

"Someone's coming," he whispered. Swiveling to the side of the door, he pressed his back firmly against the wall. He lifted the gun and steadied the barrel on the entrance, readying himself for the door to open. Matt imitated Aaron, shifting his body to the other side of the door, holding one of the pistols in both hands.

They heard a faint *bleep* as someone pushed the door button. The door slid upwards, and a body strolled through the opening into the darkness.

Matt reached one hand towards the figure and closed his fingers around its throat. He wrenched the body inwards, forcing it against the wall. Aaron quickly hit the button, closing the door. He slid the wristlet under the figures face, lighting up its features. Two violet eyes looked back at them.

Twilana held a pistol in one hand, Matt's arm in the other. She struggled to breathe, gasping and coughing as Matt held her windpipe. He looked into her face, his eyes narrowed in anger.

"Why are you coming after us?" he asked with a snarl. "You asked for our help."

Twilana's mouth formed the words but no sound escaped her lips. She tried to pull Matt's hand from her throat but her struggle only caused him to squeeze harder.

Aaron placed his hand on Matt's arm, gently squeezing his wrist. "Ease up. Let her speak."

Matt released his grip and dropped his arm to the side. Shaking his head, he turned away from her as she doubled over gasping for air. Rubbing her throat, she righted herself and steadied her weapon on Matt's back. "I should kill you for that," she said, raspy and breathless.

Matt spun on his heels and raised his pistol, pointing it at Twilana's face. "Do it, lady" Matt growled. "Just give me one reason." Aaron stared at them as they faced off like an Old West show-down.

Twilana looked at Aaron, back to Matt. Shaking her head, she slipped the gun into the brown leather holster on her right hip. "We haven't much time. You must hurry."

Matt cut her off. "Not until you tell us what's going on." Aaron could hear the illitation in his voice and, given their circumstance, couldn't blame him for feeling that way.

Twilana removed the cap from her head and wiped her brow with the back of her hand. Replacing the cap, she inhaled deeply. "I've told you most of the story already.

"For hundreds of years, my people, the Janians, have been at war with the Lacertidae, a vicious alien race that want our city. Our mining facilities. They want to rape us for our resources and enslave us." She strode over to Aaron, grabbed his hand, and examined the wristlet. She tapped the screen, bringing up a small keyboard.

Twilana continued. "However, it seems that our dignitaries just want to end the conflict, even if that means committing their people to slavery." Twilana tapped the keyboard quickly, the screen changing shape with each new command. Aaron tried to follow her, but wasn't able to keep up. She punched one final button and dropped Aaron's arm. She walked up to Matt, completely ignoring the gun aimed at her. She stared into his eyes without fear.

"The dignitaries made this decision without the public's approval and I suspect there are other reasons behind the treaty. I am not alone in my opinion, either." She reached up, placed her hand on Matt's arm, and slowly pushed the gun down. Matt looked back into her eyes and saw the deep purple irises. No gray. No blue. Just purple, showing neither fear nor anger at her current situation.

Twilana's eyes held Matt's. "I have not lied to you. I will help you. But I have a job to do as well." She turned to Aaron. "I have to keep up appearances that you are being hunted, but I am true to my word."

Removing her hand from Matt's arm, she walked back to

the door. Looking at Aaron, she said, "I've programmed your mapping unit to show you where the negotiations are being held. It will also detect other units around you. All of my soldiers wear one, including me." She held up her arm, displaying the wristlet. "You will know when we are close." With that, she pulled the gun from its holster, raised the door, and left.

Aaron looked at the wristlet. Bright blue dots now littered the screen. Most were moving back and forth, sweeping the detention level. A few were still, stationed at the far ends of the hallway. Aaron watched as a small purple dot approached the blue dots, stop, then lead all the dots down the hallway in which they arrived. Seconds later, they disappeared.

Aaron looked from the screen to Matt. "They're gone."

Matt nodded. He stood in silence for a moment, the pistol in his hand hanging limply at his side. He stepped toward the door and pressed the button. Snapping the gun up, he grasped it with both hands and skulked from the room. Aaron waited a few moments before following him. Matt looked down the length of the hallway. Finding no threats, he rushed toward the elevator.

He pressed the button on the wall and stepped back, raising his pistol and training it on the doors. Matt stood in a half-crouch, gun pointed at the elevator as Aaron crept down the hallway. The elevator *dinged* and the doors slid open, revealing an empty car. Matt allowed himself to breathe and lowered the pistol, stepping into the elevator.

"Which floor?" Matt asked, his finger raised and ready to push the button.

Aaron checked the wristlet. "Three."

The button beeped and the doors shut. Matt and Aaron stood in the center of the elevator in complete silence, the anxiety beginning to overtake them. Chills ran through Matt's body as beads of sweat rolled down his back, collecting at the waistband of his pants. Aaron clutched the gun with both hands, turning his arms to check the wristlet like a tardy commuter checking his watch. Though he was just as anxious as Matt, his body reacted differently. His muscles were taut, primed for action. His heart-rate was steady and his breathing even. Aaron was, as they say, 'in the zone'.

The elevator came to a stop. Matt and Aaron pressed their backs to the wall, guns ready. The doors slid open.

Matt peered around the corner and found the room empty. He cocked his head, motioning to Aaron that it was clear. Aaron nodded and slunk through the elevator door. Matt waited two seconds before following.

Aaron glanced down the hallway, down to his wristlet, and back down the hallway. He turned to Matt, held up four fingers and pointed to the left wall. Matt understood. Fourth door on the left.

They skulked along the wall, counting the doors as they made their way through the hall. Stopping at the fourth door, Aaron checked his weapon. It hummed loudly, and five of the eight circle wedges were glowing green. Aaron had no idea what that meant, but it didn't make much of a difference. He looked over at Matt with a smile.

"This is so exciting," he whispered.

Matt's brow furrowed questioningly. "What are you talking about? We're fighting in a battle we have no reason to be involved in for the off-chance of finding our way home. How's that 'exciting'?"

Aaron shook his head. "No. It's more than that. It's the…thrill of the fight. Rising up to the challenge of a rival."

Matt shook his head. "OK, *Eye of the Tiger*. Let's just get this over with."

Aaron's heart pounded in his chest. He felt as if he were in a real-life video game, stalking his enemies and looking for the next save point. But Matt had a point; this wasn't a game. He couldn't take a shot to the head and respawn in a different area looking for revenge. He had to take it easy.

Matt leaned over and bashed the button with his elbow. He raised his pistols and spun towards the doorway, his eyes going wide in fear.

What scared Matt the most wasn't the three Janian men dressed in tight, black bodysuits. It wasn't the Janian guards who stood in shackles against the side wall. It wasn't even the seven-foot tall, lizard-humanoid creatures holding really large guns and wearing body armor.

In reality, what scared Matt the most was that one of the lizard-humanoid creatures spotted him.

The Lacertus' tiny black eyes focused on Matt. Its long snout curled up into a snarl, revealing a row of dirty-yellow, razor-sharp teeth. A low, guttural growl rumbled from its throat, catching the attention of the two Lacertus soldiers standing behind him. They turned, their beady eyes glaring at Matt standing in the doorway. They raised their weapons, laser sights casting red dots on Matt's chest and face. Matt raised his arms and squeezed the triggers of his pistols. Glowing green orbs shot from the barrels as he pivoted on his feet behind the safety of the outer wall. Blue bolts shot past him through the doorway, leaving scorch marks on the far wall. Matt looked at Aaron.

"Appears Twilana forgot to mention that these Lacertidae she wants us to stop are giant alligator people."

Aaron's eyebrows shot upward. Crouching to his knees, he pointed his gun through the doorway and fired. A thick red beam shot from the end of the gun, hitting one of Lacertus soldiers square in the chest. The Lacertus fell backward, his weapon dropping to the floor. The Janian men ran toward the exit at the opposite end of the room, escaping the fracas. Aaron raised himself, flattening his back to the wall.

"I got one."

"Do I even need to say 'don't get cocky, kid'?"

For a moment, the remaining Lacertidae stopped shooting. They looked to their fallen comrade, anger welling up inside them. The Lacertidae rushed toward their attackers.

Peeking around the doorway, Matt spotted the Lacertidae heading straight toward them. Their weapons were raised, scaly brown fingers on the triggers, ready to avenge the death of their brother-in-arms. Matt pointed to the adjacent hallway. "Time to go," he told Aaron.

Matt and Aaron raced down the corridor, blue orbs whizzing past them. One orb shattered a bulb in the ceiling, sending a shower of glass tinkling to the floor. Matt was grateful for having taken the boots from the Janian soldiers as he trampled the broken glass in his haste to escape.

Aaron and Matt ducked to avoid shrapnel and debris from objects exploding all around them. Turning, Matt raised one of the handguns. He squeezed the trigger and a blast of green light rocketed down the hallway. One Lacertus leapt to the side, easily avoiding the assault, but leaving the solider behind him wide open. The blast hit the second Lacertus in the shoulder, knocking him backwards. He slapped wildly at his shoulder as a small patch of flesh burst into flame.

Rounded a corner, Aaron looked down at the wristlet, trying to find an escape route. The blue dots and green blobs, and brown splotches all converged on one point, blocking most of their options. Aaron tapped the screen, switching between modes. Matt leaned over his shoulder, shouting above the noise of gun fire.

"Where to, buddy boy?"

Aaron grew frantic as their options grew fewer and fewer. "I don't…I…I have no idea!"

"Meet me in the loading bay," Twilana's voice rang out from his wrist.

CHAPTER 18

Aaron looked down at the wristlet with a look of shock on his face as Twilana's voice broadcast from his arm. Examining the wristlet, he noticed a lighted ear-shaped icon on the screen, surmising that the wristlet has more uses than he originally thought. He wondered what else the device could do.

"The elevator at the end of this hallway will take you there," the disembodied voice continued. Aaron nodded, feeling like an idiot when he realized that she couldn't see him.

He rushed down the hallway, quickly closing the distance between him and the elevator. Flashes of blue energy exploding around him and the rain of sparks falling on his head told him that the Lacertidae were quickly gaining ground.

Matt spun on his heels, aiming the pistols down the hallway. He slowed his pace slightly, the oversized boots dulling his ability to run backward. He squeezed off a half dozen shots at the Lacertidae. The green energy spheres flew wildly, sending the lizard people ducking for cover. Content with the diversion, Matt pivoted toward the elevator, doubling his pace.

Aaron stretched his arm out in front of him, launching himself the final few feet. His palm collided with the elevator call button and with a *ding*, the doors split apart. Matt ran straight into the elevator car, pausing to catch his breath. Aaron turned and raising his rifle, firing at the incoming soldiers. A sonic pulse erupted from the barrel, slamming him back against the wall. The pulse knocked the Lacertidae to the ground, giving Aaron the chance to stumble into the elevator.

Wheezing, Matt punched the button marked "LB". He hunched over in the center of the elevator, trying to catch his breath. A blue orb winged past his face, narrowly missing his nose. Cocking his head to the side, he spotted a pair of Lacertidae lumbering down the hallway. He jabbed the button again and again, hoping that the machinery would recognize his authoritative and furious button-mashing, translate it into urgency, and close the doors immediately. Finding the elevator to be completely uncooperative, he reached into his pocket and removed one of the small silver disks. He pressed the red button in the center of it and it beeped. The button lit up and flashed rhythmically.

Matt crouched down and slid the disk along the floor. It came to a stop a few feet from the Lacertidae, beeping wildly before releasing a flash of blinding white light. The Lacertidae reared back, their hands rubbing their eyes as the elevator doors closed. Rising on his feet, Matt looked smugly at Aaron, proud of himself for having the foresight to take the disks from the Janian soldiers.

The sounds of groaning Lacertidae and sizzling electrically charged metal faded as the elevator car descended. Matt leaned against the wall, his chest heaving with exhaustion. He inhaled deeply through his nose, forcing the oxygen into his lungs. Opening his eyes, he spotted Aaron looking at him.

"You OK?" Aaron asked.

Matt nodded, unable to form words. So far he was holding up pretty well. Breathing deeply caused his chest to hurt, the kind of sensation one gets when they spend too long in a swimming pool. Which, given his near drowning experience a few hours ago, would make sense. As his breathing steadied, Matt slid one of the pistols into the waist band of his pants. He rested his head against the wall and closed his eyes. His body was tired, so tired, having little rest for well over twenty hours. His skin tingled as his nerves screamed out for a break. Matt struggled to open his eyes and stared at the dim light in the ceiling. His body shook and a roar of laughter erupted from his throat.

Aaron jumped at the sound of Matt's laughter. He tilted his head toward him, his brow furrowed. Matt rolled his head against the wall and met Aaron's gaze.

"We're gonna die here, aren't we?"

A smile spread across Aaron's face and a chuckle shook his chest. He gazed down at the gun in his hand, then to the wristlet. He nodded, looking back at Matt.

"Yeah. Yeah, probably."

Matt's laughter faded away as he contemplated Aaron's response. Pulling the pistol from his waistband, he held it in two hands, looking down the sight along the barrel.

"Well, if we're going down, let's take as many of them as we can with us."

The elevator *dinged* as the car came to a halt, a white 'LB' blinking cheerfully above the door. Matt dropped the pistol to his side and watched the doors split. The bright lights beyond the elevator blinded him as he stepped from the car. He lifted his hand to shield his eyes and squinted, looking around the spacious room, awestruck by its brilliance.

The massive room was constructed completely of highly polished metal, the walls glittering under the harsh, fluorescent lights. A thick glass window ran the length of the far wall, revealing the vastness of the desert outside. Stars littered the dark sky, twinkling a curious spectrum of colors, like rhinestones threaded to brown velvet. The moon floated high up, winking down at the world below.

Rows of large trucks lined the walls opposite the window, each parked facing a black, corrugated metal door. The doors gave the room and eerie feeling, making the side walls look like the toothy grin of a Jack-O-Lantern. The smell of ozone and motor oil wafted through the air.

In the center of the room sat two large computer stations, comprised of what looked like tracking monitors, radar controls, and a communications station. Pretty much everything a desert resource miner would need to accomplish their task. Twilana stood hunched over one of the computers, typing furiously on the console's keyboards. Her head bobbed up and down, looking between the keyboard and the large monitor over her.

Aaron stepped from the elevator, stopping next to Matt. He stared up at the ceiling, entranced by the vastness of the room. Feeling a slap on the arm, he looked down at Matt as he nodded his head at Twilana.

Twilana looked up from the computer console as the two men approached her. She stared at them, her eyes kinder than they had been earlier. She opened her mouth to speak but quickly closed it. Straightening her body, she turned to Aaron and Matt, clasped her hands together, and bowed.

"Thank you. You have done well." Twilana rose.

"So we did our part," Matt proclaimed, crossing his arms over his chest. "I hope you plan on doing yours."

Twilana cocked an eyebrow at him. "You have earned my respect and I am a woman of my word. I said I would help you get home. That's my intention."

Aaron rubbed the back of his head, unsure of how to interject his apprehension. "Yeah, about that. We're not really sure…"

Matt slapped Aaron on the arm. "Never mind him. We need a truck. Something to take us out into that desert. Where the guy with no teeth found us."

Twilana nodded, turned back to the computer. Aaron leaned closer to Matt. "Dude, he had teeth. They were black, but he still had them." He looked back to Twilana. "So, what about the pissed off dinosaur people? What's gonna happen there?"

Twilana tapped away on the keyboard, glancing up at the screen sporadically. "I have dispatched my men to control the carnage upstairs. They will detain the Lacertidae for a while." She slid behind the console, clacked away at another keyboard. Behind her, a truck sprung to life, its engine revving furiously. Red and yellow lights blinked in sequence as the vehicle ran through its start-up procedure.

"Take this truck," she continued. "I have programmed the coordinates to the center of the Wastelands. Hopefully, you will find the key to your return home." She pressed more buttons on the keyboard, bringing up a live satellite-feed of the Wastelands on a video monitor above her head.

"Well, let's go see if we can find that swirly blue thing and get our asses back home," Matt said, turning toward the truck.

Twilana watched Matt walk away. She looked at Aaron and said "I cannot thank you enough for the help you've given me. Maybe now, my city's leaders can start to rebuild and earn the trust of their citizens."

"I just hope we didn't make your situation worse," he said.

"Whatever happens, it will be up to us to handle it," she replied. "Now go. You have a journey to complete."

Aaron hesitated. As he stood watching Twilana, he noticed the irises of her eyes swirl. But there was something different about them. Instead of getting darker like they did in the interrogation room, the colors in her eyes became lighter, fluctuating between shades of pink, lilac, and fuchsia. His breath caught in his throat and he swallowed hard. He nodded and spun on his heels, following Matt to the truck.

Aaron took two steps and stopped. He tilted his head, watching Twilana over his shoulder as she typed her authorization code into the computer. His heart was beating furiously in his chest and he could feel his palms moisten with sweat. He inhaled deeply, calming his nerves before he turned back to her. His body cast a dark shadow over the console.

Twilana looked up at him, her eyes catching his.

"Why don't you come with us?" Aaron asked, his voice cracking like a nervous teenager.

Twilana rose from the console and stared at Aaron as he hovered beside her. She watched his face, a strangely familiar face, even though they had only known each other for a few short hours. She struggled with a feeling inside of herself; a feeling of longing. It had been a long time since she shared a deep, meaningful experience with a male. Her career as a Captain in the Janian Task Force was trying, and it affected her personal relationships.

Aaron stared into Twilana's eyes as she stepped closer to him. The swirls of pink and red were mesmerizing. Twilana rested her hands on his chest, his body tightening at her touch. Aaron wrapped his arms around her waist and pulled her closer, closing his eyes and enjoying the warmth of her body against his.

"Hey, we going or what?" Matt's voice rang through the loading bay.

The passion of the moment was completely erased by the sudden interruption. Twilana smiled at Aaron and gently pushed him back. She cleared her throat and ran her hands down the front of her uniform before returning to the computer console.

Aaron stared at her for a moment as she worked the keyboards. He turned and hurried across the loading bay toward the waiting truck, determined to punch Matt in the face. As he approached the truck, he found Matt hanging out of the open window of the passenger side door. A smile spread across his face, stretching from ear to ear.

"You're a dick," Aaron said. He reached for the door handle and swung it open forcefully. Aaron pulled himself up into the cab of the truck as Matt sat back in his seat, laughing hysterically. Aaron shook his head.

Twilana glanced over at the truck, a look of delight on her face. Though short-lived, the moment with Aaron had made her feel different, revitalizing a part of her that had been ignored for so long. But she shook the feelings from her mind, realizing the foolishness of her emotions. She was a soldier. She didn't have time for relationships like that. Turning her attention back to the console, she pressed a large green button to activate the loading bay doors.

Aaron jumped in surprise as the mechanical door wound up into the ceiling. Matt had been so engrossed in his fits of laughter that he noticed neither the opening door nor Aaron's sudden surprise. Composing himself, Aaron watched as the door rose, the unyielding desolateness of this world slowly coming into view.

"Just follow the coordinates on the vehicle's GPS." Twilana's voice emanated from the wristlet on Aaron's arm.

Shifting his eyes to the truck's side-view mirror, he watched as Twilana stood hunched over the computer console. He examined the shape of her body as she worked the keyboard. Though he had an unexplainable feeling of trust when he first met her, those feelings had suddenly changed into something else.

Stupid, he thought to himself. *I'm about to go home. I'll never see her again anyway.*

Aaron had been contemplating his emotions so deeply that he hadn't noticed the bay door close in front of him. He watched as Twilana's head snapped up, her eyes focused on the large doorway that lead into the loading bay. He saw her right hand drop to her hip and she pulled her gun from its holster.

Throwing the door open, Aaron jumped from the cab of the truck. Matt's fits of hysterics finally calming, he watched as Aaron dropped to the floor, out of sight.

"What's wrong?" Matt asked.

Receiving no answer, Matt leaned over the cab of the truck and stuck his head out through the open door.

"What's going on?" he called again.

"Twilana's in trouble," Aaron shouted over his shoulder, rushing toward the computer console. He watched as Twilana dodged laser blasts winging toward her, raising her arm to return fire. The onslaught quickly overpowered her, forcing her to take cover behind the computer banks. Balls of green energy collided with the computer screens and shattered them, causing a rain of glass and sparks to fall down around her

The hollow beat of Aaron's footfalls echoed in the vast room, competing with the electrical fizz of the flying energy blasts. Forcing his body to the ground, Aaron slid to Twilana's side. Flakes of ash fell into his hair as he covered her body with his own.

"Are you OK?" he asked, receiving a short nod as an answer. He poked his head over the console to assess the situation.

A group of four Lacertidae had descended the elevator. The farthest kept himself planted in front of the elevator, firing in their direction, laying ground cover while two others flanked their position. One lay sprawled out on the floor in front of the elevator, dead, a smoldering hole in its chest. He wasn't sure if Twilana was a really good shot or just lucky as hell but Aaron was relieved to have one less threat.

As Aaron eyed the advancing Lacertidae, the elevator doors slid open, revealing three more soldiers accompanied by a familiar, ginger-haired woman.

Just great, Aaron thought.

CHAPTER 19

Michael's voice rang in my head, breaking my concentration on the Oculus. The angels perfected the use of telepathic communication, using it to speak to each other over extremely long distances. Though they usually reserve telepathy for Inter-Angel discussions, they will sometimes use it to initiate conversations with others. I've had a number of telepathic dialogues in the past but it is always disconcerting when not expecting one to happen.

It was also disconcerting that Michael was requesting my presence. I really didn't have the time to spare for him at the moment but I knew ignoring him wasn't an option. I strolled from the Ocularium, in no rush to meet with him.

As I rounded the hallway, I spotted a figure leaning against the wall next to the elevator. Clad all in black, he looked more like the frontman for a heavy metal band than like the kind of man you'd see in an Angelic Government building. Torn black jeans, a well-worn black leather jacket and a black t-shirt that proclaimed his desire to "Reign In Blood." The man chewed on his thumbnail, staring at me as I approached.

It wasn't until I noticed the wings folded behind his back did I realize who the man was. Feathered wings as black as ash. Only one angel in New Eden had wings like that.

"Nathaniel!"

I spun on my heels and ran back down the hallway. I hadn't gotten two steps before Nathaniel's shadow swooped over me, blocking my path. I tried to stop but my foot slipped out from under me and I tumbled forward.

Nathaniel's hands shot out and grabbed me by the arms, breaking my fall.

"Easy there, Metatron," he said to me. "Don't want to hurt yourself."

I struggled to break free of his grip which only caused him to grasp me tighter. "Release me, traitor," I shouted, "or I'll summon the guards."

Nathaniel threw his head back and laughed, calling my bluff. He knew as well as I did that Angelic Telepathy can only be initiated by an angel. There would be no way I could call anyone.

"Just relax. Please. I only came here to talk."

Raising my head, I looked him in the eyes. Despite everything he's done in the past, for some reason, I believed him. Nathaniel released my arms and took a step backward. We looked at each other in silence for a moment.

"Well?" I asked. "You're the one that wanted to talk."

"It's about Lucifer. He…he's gone too far this time."

"Lucifer always goes too far. That's his M.O."

"Not like this," he said. He dropped his eyes to the floor and ran his fingers through his hair. "He's got everything planned out. Jehoel. Those two guys…"

"You know about the travelers?"

Nathaniel looked at me and nodded. "Yeah. That wasn't his doing, though. But he was more than willing to take advantage of it." He went back to biting the thumbnail.

"You need to tell Michael of this. About what you know."

"No!" Nathaniel shouted, his face going white. "I can't do that. He'll know."

I stood there watching the worry on Nathaniel's face. For years, he was one of Michael's most trusted confidants. A decorated warrior in the Angelic High Military, Nathaniel was crucial to winning countless battles. But that was before… Circumstances sent him to Lucifer. Caused a rift between him and the rest of the AHM. Michael most especially. I can't really say that he's wrong because I wasn't there. But based on what I've heard secondhand, he does have some valid points.

But I understood his fear when it came to Michael. After he joined Lucifer, Nathaniel quickly became one of Michael's most wanted. If the General caught wind that he was here, Nathaniel wouldn't get the chance to get a word out before he was bombarded by a legion of angels.

"What else can you tell me about his plans?" I asked. If he wouldn't go to Michael, maybe he would tell me. But Nathaniel shook his head furiously.

"No. No way. I can't. I've said too much as it is. I should go." And with that, he extended his wings and flew off down the hallway, rounding the corner almost before I could turn and watch him disappear. I stood in dumbstruck silence, trying to make sense of our conversation.

I turned back to the elevator, thumbing the button on the wall. As I rode the elevator to Michael's office, I ruminated on what Nathaniel told me. He said Lucifer was using the travelers but they weren't part of his plan. But if Lucifer didn't drop them through the dimensional fold, how did they get there?

I knocked on the heavy oak door and it swung in suddenly, revealing Michael seated behind his desk. Gabriel stood on my left, his hand on the door knob. Michael's second in command, Gabriel served Michael for years, earning the General's trust. The years of battle took their toll on him, his dark hair turning shades of white. Had he been human, born on Earth, Gabriel could have easily become a movie star in Hollywood, with his handsome, angular face. Though a long, thick scar, extending from his ear to his chin, marred his good looks, he wore it with pride, as it was a scar earned in the heat of battle.

Though Gabriel was Michael's Lieutenant General, for the life of me I couldn't figure out how. He was a very skilled fighter, but not all that bright. He had a difficult time piecing together military intel to decipher an enemy's plans. And you can forget about him devising an attack strategy. His idea of a "plan" is to barge through the front door, swords blazing. If anything, he's a thug. A foot soldier. Not what I imagine when I think of tactical strategies. But of course, no one asked my opinion when issuing promotions.

"What took you so long?" Michael asked, barely looking up from the paperwork on his desk.

"My apologies, sir. I was…" *Speaking with one of your most hated defectors?* "…preoccupied with a student."

"Yeah, well, you shouldn't have kept me waiting," he said,

pushing the papers away. He nodded to Gabriel, instructing him to close the door. Michael turned to me and waved his hand to the chair in front of his desk.

"Sit."

I lowered myself into the chair, my irritation returning. Gabriel brushed past me and stood next to Michael's desk. With two sets of eyes staring at me, studying me, I soon felt like I was being interrogated.

Michael placed his elbows on the desk and steepled his fingers. "Have you sent the travelers home yet?"

"No, not yet. Galgaliel went down to confront them, but that's when we ran into Lauren."

Michael moaned an acknowledgement. "Yes, Lauren. A definite indicator that Lucifer is behind this."

"Actually, I was thinking."

Michael chuckled, looked up at Gabriel. "Oh, have you?" he said mockingly. "Please tell me all about your assessment of the situation." Gabriel joined in his sarcastic laughter. I could feel my face flush, my cheeks growing hot. Breathing deeply, I steadied my nerves.

"Well, I was thinking, what if Lucifer didn't drop those two men into the other world? What if that was an accident?"

Michael went quiet. His eyes narrowed, focusing on me. "In the entirety of the multi-verse, all of the millennia that the Angelic High Military has been in existence, there has been only one documented case of someone falling in between the divide by complete accident." He leaned in closer to me. "What do you think the chances are of that happening again?"

"But we should also consider the other incident that occurred today. Jehoel's disappearance. What if they are more closely related than we thought?"

Michael froze, his jaw dropping ever so slightly. That got him.

He leaned back in his chair and looked up at Gabriel, all humor gone from his face. Gabriel, on the other hand, still wore the same blank expression that he had when I walked in. Michael pushed his chair back from the desk and rose to his feet. Folding his hands behind his back, he paced the room. Gabriel noticed his unease.

"How could they be related?" Gabriel asked. "Jehoel went

missing hours before we knew about these two humans."

Michael shot him a cold look. He turned back to me, his face belying his interest in my opinion. "Do you think Jehoel could have helped him? Could he have gone over to Lucifer's side?"

"No, no, no," I said, shaking my head. "I didn't mean to imply… My thought was that…" I stumbled over my words, unable to form my thought coherently. Inhaling deeply, I considered what I was trying to say. "Jehoel isn't an archangel; his powers are limited. But perhaps Lucifer doesn't need him for his *powers*, but for his *knowledge*."

Gabriel scoffed at my statement. "Please. Jehoel doesn't know anything. He's a low ranking officer and isn't cleared for privileged information."

Michael's glare was icy. Gabriel looked up to meet his gaze and instantly shrunk back, as if Michael had raised a hand to him. "No, you buffoon," Michael said. "There's a reason Jehoel isn't an officer. He serves a higher purpose." Michael turned back to me. "Do you think that is what Lucifer is after?"

Gabriel's forehead scrunched, unable to keep up with the conversation. "After what?"

I nodded to Michael. "Yes. It would make sense."

"What would make sense?" Gabriel asked, growing impatient.

Michael rolled his eyes and sighed loudly. "Idiot," he said under his breath. He turned to Gabriel.

"Lucifer wants the Leviathan."

CHAPTER 20

Lauren raised her hand over her head and motioned to the soldiers to hold their fire. She exchanged her sleek white dress for a set of pink army fatigues with a pink beret laying lopsided on her head. "You boys should have realized that this wasn't going to be easy," she said, a slight cackle in her voice. "You've only witnessed a small display of my power. Did you not think I couldn't do worse?"

"Can't blame us for trying," Aaron shouted from behind the bank of computers. A small gash in his cheek left a trickle of blood running down his face. He turned his rifle over in his hands and checked the amount of charge. Spinning the dial on the stock, he added a slice to the glowing pie chart. The rifle's hum raised an octave in pitch. Aaron wasn't sure what he had just done, but he hoped the changes made the gun more powerful.

"Friend of yours?" Twilana asked, pulling a small silver disk from the pouch affixed to her belt.

"Why?" Aaron asked, flattening his body on the floor. He angled the gun around the corner and squeezed the trigger, his arm convulsing from the weapon's recoil. "You jealous?"

Twilana chuckled as she pressed the button in the center of the light disk, activating it. She was impressed with Aaron's ability to remain lighthearted even when he was being shot at. It was another of his qualities she admired.

"She's the one who sent us here," Aaron said. He raised himself on his knees, taking aim over the computers and let off a couple more shots. Two bolts of bright, red energy exploded from the barrel and raced toward the waiting soldiers. Twilana arched her back around the console and tossed the disk in Lauren's direction.

Lauren flicked her wrist and redirected the blasts back toward Aaron, forcing him to duck behind the console. They shattered the machinery, sending shards of metal and sparks falling down onto Aaron and Twilana.

The disk landed on the floor a few feet to Lauren's side. Rolling her eyes, she raised her hand and pointed to it. Thick, black ooze flowed from her fingertips, engulfing the light grenade in a small, opaque dome. The grenade exploded, a muffled *pop* emanating from beneath the dome. Lauren twirled her wrist and the dome dissipated, releasing a wisp of smoke, revealing a charred section of metal where the grenade once lay.

"Now, now, children," Lauren cooed. "If you don't start playing nice, I'll have to take your toys away."

Lauren balled her fist and yanked her hand back. Aaron felt a stiff tug on his rifle. He clenched his fingers around the gun's barrel, holding it as tightly as he could. Lauren shook her head, irritated at Aaron's futility. She raised her other hand and waggled her fingers.

Aaron could feel her grip on the rifle intensify and it slipped easily from his hands. He watched in fear as it floated through the air towards Lauren. She snatched it and snapped it in half, tossing the pieces of torn metal to the floor.

Lauren giggled. "You turned me down when I gave you the chance to join me," she shouted. Lauren pointed at two Lacertus soldiers, motioning to them to circle around the computer banks and surround Aaron and Twilana.

"But I'm here to give you another chance," she continued. "Join me, and not only will I let you live, but I'll bring you home. Safe and sound. You know I can do it, too."

Matt leaped down from the cabin of the truck, peeking under the vehicle. He counted seven pairs of feet, one of which sported a pair of pink combat boots. He noticed one pair of feet slowly sneaking along the far end of the room. He aimed a pistol beneath the truck and fired. The energy bolt screamed across the room and struck the boots. They burst into flame and the solider attached to them fell to the ground, swatting at his feet to put out the fire. He roared in pain as the flames licked at his flesh. The other soldiers raised their weapons and opened fire at the truck. A flurry of energy bolts flew in Matt's direction, burning holes in the truck and trailer.

Lauren stomped her feet, shouting over the noise like a child denied a new toy. "Stop! Stop! Who told you to fire?"

The Lacertidae lowered their weapons and the sound of the gunfire slowly died away. Lauren looked toward the trailer, her face bright red with anger. She inhaled deeply, composing herself.

"I will assume that your response is the same as before," she said, brushing her fingers through her hair. She placed her hands on the beret and shifted it, ensuring that it was lopsided at exactly the right angle.

"You got that right, lady!" Matt shouted across the room. He skulked to the end of the trailer and aimed his pistol at Lauren. He slowly squeezed the trigger but before he could fire, something caught his attention. He turned his head and watched as a door swung open in the back corner of the room. Four Janian soldiers rushed in from the stairwell, their weapons raised, ready for battle.

Matt looked at Aaron and Twilana, pointing frantically as the soldiers came running in. "We got incoming," his voice boomed in the quiet, cavernous room.

"Praise Janus," Twilana sighed, spotting her men. "Backup is here."

Green lasers winged over their heads, colliding with what remained of their cover. Aaron peered around the corner of the bank of computers at the Janian soldiers and found himself staring down the barrels of their guns.

"I don't think they're our backup," he said. "They're firing at us."

"That's impossible," Twilana shouted, her voice drowned out by the gunfire. Looking toward the Janian soldiers, she watched as they advanced in the standard two-by-two formation, used to overtake a pinned-down hostile. She should recognize it. After all, she trained these soldiers to use it properly.

Twilana shook her head, her eyes gazing at Aaron. "This is not good." Aaron watched as her irises changed colors, morphing from deep purple to a bright green.

The assault stopped as suddenly as it began. A voice echoed throughout the room.

"Surrender now, Captain Salizar," the voice said. "Your punishment will be severe enough. There's no need to make matters worse."

Matt peeked under the truck again, staring at an entirely new set of feet. At the far end of the room stood a nice pair of black boots. The supple leather shined in the lights, beautifully polished, decorated with golden rivets. Matt kind of hoped he'd have the chance to take them for himself.

"I should have known," Twilana growled under her breath. "That back-stabbing son of a bitch."

"Who?" Aaron asked.

"Rek."

Aaron looked over the console, spotting a tall, Janian man dressed in a ceremonial bodysuit. The black suit was adorned with gold buttons that lined his shoulders like military pins. A long, gray swathe encircled his chest. The man's bald spot reflected the light from above, turning his head into a tiny spotlight. His eyes were pinched, making his face look too small for his head.

"That's the guy that was in the room with the Lacertidae," Aaron said. "He was one of the men negotiating—"

"Our surrender," Twilana interrupted. "Samuel Rek is a military magistrate. He is going to give control of the army of Janus to the Lacertidae in exchange for a big, fat payday. He will live like a king while his people are slaves."

Rek continued. "You should have accepted things, Captain. This is the only way to ensure the protection of our race."

Anger flashed in Twilana's eyes. Aaron watched as her irises swirled from green to gray to black.

"You are selling your people to these monsters!" she shouted. Her voice echoed off the walls of the loading bay. "We will not be safe. We will be slaves!"

Matt remained crouched behind the trailer of the truck, staying low and out of the Janian soldiers' sights. His mind raced, formulating a plan to use that to his advantage. He reached into his pocket and pulled out a light grenade disk, grateful at how handy they had become.

He waved at Aaron wildly, attracting his attention. As Aaron looked over at him, Matt held out his hand, showing him the light grenade. Aaron nodded, understanding the gamble Matt was about to take.

"Close your eyes," Aaron whispered to Twilana. "And get ready to run." He grabbed Twilana's hand and steadied himself on the balls of his feet. Reaching around her waist, he pulled the second pistol from the holster on her hip.

Matt pushed the button on the light grenade disk and stepped out from behind the trailer. He reached his arm back and snapped it forward, sending the disk flying across the room.

"Now!" Aaron shouted, springing to his feet. He pulled Twilana toward the truck and they sprinted across the room. Aaron fired the pistol at the soldiers, using the cover fire to confuse them long enough to get to the truck.

"Shoot them!" Rek shouted, his voice straining for dominance over the sound of Aaron's pistol. "Don't let them get away!" The soldiers obeyed, both Janian and Lacertian alike, shooting green and red bolts of energy in the direction of Aaron and Twilana. Aaron ducked his head, pulling Twilana lower. His shots flew wildly but a few were lucky enough to hit their mark. Two Lacertus soldiers dropped to the ground dead, their chestplates burned straight through. One Janian soldier took a shot to the leg and fell to the floor, howling in pain.

The disk hit the floor with a pop, engulfing the room in a powerful explosion of white light. The attack on Aaron and Twilana stopped but they continued to run as fast as they could.

As they reached the trailer, Matt jumped through the open door of the cab. Aaron followed closely behind as Twilana made for the loading bay door. She slapped a red button on the wall and the loading bay door began to rise. Twilana spun back toward the truck to find Lauren standing in her way.

"You could have avoided this," Lauren said. Her hand snapped up to Twilana's neck and her fingers wrapped around her throat, holding her like an iron vice.

Twilana burrowed her fingers under Lauren's hand and tried to pry it from her neck. Lauren laughed at Twilana's feeble attempts to break free, enjoying the sound of her gasps as she struggled to breathe. Lauren lifted her from the floor, slamming her against the hood of the truck. Twilana's feet kicked against the chassis and tried to find leverage against the floor, the tire, anything she could to push Lauren off her balance. She wrapped her fingers around Lauren's wrists and pulled herself up to take the pressure of her body weight off her neck.

Aaron leaned out of the open door of the truck and fired three shots at Lauren's back. Lauren's laughter stopped as her shirt burst into flames. She turned her head to Aaron, her eyes filled with anger.

"You ruined my favorite blouse," she shouted. Waving her hand, a cold breeze blew past her, extinguishing her shirt. "You like fire?" she asked. "Have some." Lauren extended a finger and lowered it at Aaron. Fire shot from her hand and encircled Aaron's arm. He dropped the gun and fell backwards, his sleeve bursting into flame. The fire licked his skin, leaving brown marks in his flesh.

Aaron fell backward into the seat of the truck. Matt slid next to him, slapping at his arm to extinguish the fire. He looked down at Lauren, hatred seething from his eyes as her mouth curved into a wicked smile.

"You're next," she said, extending an index finger to him. She turned back to Twilana. "It's too easy to kill you," Lauren said, the smile fading from her face. She raised her hand toward the desert outside and the air split, revealing the churning abyss that served as the passageway between worlds.

Seeing the nexus appear, Matt concocted a plan. He turned to Aaron, waving the smoke away from the charred sleeve of his shirt.

"Can you move?" he asked. Aaron nodded.

"Good. Follow my lead."

Matt jumped from the truck and slammed his shoulder into Lauren's back before throwing himself into the nexus. Lauren stumbled and her grip on Twilana's throat slipped. Twilana coughed as the air circulated into her lungs, relieving the tingle that began to spread through her body. Aaron rushed toward them, grabbing Twilana by the waist and pulled her from Lauren's grip. He carried her into the void behind Matt.

Lauren caught her balance in time to see Aaron and Twilana disappear in the nexus, her anger revealing itself in a throaty growl.

"Big brother is not going to like this," she said to no one before disappearing in a puff of smoke.

CHAPTER 21

The smoke lingered in the air for a moment. Lauren blinked and looked around the room. A second ago, she was in the middle of a colossal metal warehouse, surrounded by a platoon of enormous lizard-men, choking the life out of a woman with blue hair. Now, she was standing in an office decorated with mahogany wood paneling, an ornate Oriental rug, and the ugliest Jackson Pollock painting she had ever seen, which is saying something since she considered all of Jackson Pollock's paintings to be equally ugly.

In front of her sat a large oak office desk, the varnish so thick it shined in the light. A mesh pencil cup rested at the corner of the desk, overflowing with blue-capped Bic pens, a pair of scissors, and a letter opener shaped like a sword encircled by a serpent. Behind the desk sat a broad-shouldered man, hunching in his high-backed chair as he shuffled through a stack of papers. His slicked-back hair shimmered in the light cast by a green-shaded bankers lamp, giving his head the impression that he was accosted by a bucket of glitter.

Though she couldn't see his face, Lauren recognized the man immediately. She stared at the top of his head for longer than she should have, transfixed by the blinking blue light on the wireless cellphone headset wrapped around his ear.

Lauren turned toward the door, hoping to leave before the man realized she was there. But of course the man was well aware of her presence in the room. After all, he was the one who brought her there.

As Lauren's hand fell upon the doorknob, Lucifer spoke. "How?"

She froze at the word, her feet wired to the floor. Lauren slowly turned and found a pair of blazing eyes boring into her, the red irises pulsating with anger. She opened her mouth to speak, but he raised his hand, silencing her. He motioned to the chair in front of his desk. Lauren dragged her feet toward the chair and gently lowered herself into it, her fingernails scratching at the wooden arms.

Lucifer leaned back and folded his hands on his chest. His eyes widened slightly, making him seem vaguely less threatening, but his face maintained its intensity. He studied Lauren closely, weighing his approach with her. Lucifer was well aware that she was a temperamental girl. Though he was angry with her actions of the day, he knew that he had to be careful dealing with her. He didn't want to upset his baby sister.

To be clear, they weren't blood related. After all, Lucifer was an angel, the ruling race in New Eden. When he was cast out of the Angelic High Military and found himself scraping by on the streets, he came across a runaway girl, a Succubus by nature. She had been reduced to cheating, stealing and even selling herself to stay alive. But Lucifer took a liking to her from the moment they crossed paths.

Lucifer's rise to power in this seedy world was quick as he was the only one intelligent enough to organize the city's lower echelon. His business acumen and shrewd way with words led him to become a successful businessman, turning one, small convenience store into a worldwide chain; it's become so popular that "Satan's" is almost synonymous with running out to grab a gallon of milk or a pack of cigarettes.

Lauren was right around 150 years old, barely out of puberty for a Succubus, when she walked into Satan's. She stuffed her pockets full of Twinkies, potato chips, and candy bars. Anything that she could smuggle out in her clothes. When the clerk stopped her on her way out, questioning why every crevice of her body bulged to almost bursting, she pulled a knife from her sleeve and buried it in his ribs. His noisy thrashing drew Lucifer's attention. When Lauren saw him, she tried to run, but he detained her, questioned her, and finally decided that he liked her style.

Lucifer took her under his wing, grooming her to become

a cog in his machinations. He allowed her to tap into the Hellfire, giving her power she never could have imagined. She became part of his Inner Circle, had a seat at the big kids' table, and the better Lucifer got to know her, the more he cared for her. And she him. She became an integral part of his plan to take back the power of New Eden, a goal he was so very close to achieving.

So close that he couldn't tolerate Lauren's failing. When he discovered the existence of the two travelers from another world, he thought Lauren was the perfect fit to lead them into his plans. After all, who better than a woman who held a certain power over men? Whom men found irresistible? So he sent her to bring them to New Eden. But, that did not go as she had planned.

"How did you allow them to escape?" Lucifer's voice was flat. Steady. He was angry but didn't show it in his voice.

Lauren paused before answering to consider her response. She knew that he knew what happened. He had the resources to keep an eye on her no matter where she went. He even pulled her from that world once everything went sour.

Lauren inhaled deeply. "They got the drop on me," she said. "Took me by surprise."

"Don't give me that," Lucifer replied. "You got sloppy. Tried to have fun with them. Why wouldn't you charm them? That's what you're good at."

"I'm trying a new angle."

"Goddammit, stick with what works!" He slammed his hands on the desktop and the wall sconces behind him burst into flames, sending pillars of fire into the air. Lucifer's eyes glowed red, their ominous light spreading throughout his face. Lauren leaned backward, retreating from her brother's fury as far as the hard, wooden chair would allow.

The glowing, orange eye-light faded and the flaming torches settled. Lucifer lifted himself from his chair and slid the suit jacket down his back, hanging it carefully over the back of his chair. He flexed his broad shoulders, rolling them around to relieve the building tension in his neck. He unbuttoned the sleeves on his dark red shirt and rolled them up to his elbows. He walked around the front of the desk and exhaled, shoving his hands into his pants pockets. He stared at Lauren for a long minute, studying her as she kept her eyes focused on the floor.

"What am I going to do with you?" She looked up at him

and he extended his arms to her. She stood, wrapping her arms around his waist. He hugged her consolingly, as only a big brother could. "I'm sorry I got angry at you," he said, stroking her hair gently. "It's just that I've been planning this for a long time, and I don't want anything to screw it up."

"I know," she said, the tears leaving moist streaks on her cheeks. "I'm sorry."

"I know you are. But if you fail me again, I will tear your throat out."

She nodded, believing the promise of a man with the will to keep it. A knock at the door interrupted their touching moment. Lucifer pushed her away, fixing the beret on her head. "Come in," he bellowed.

The door swung open to reveal Nathaniel. He held his heavy, leather jacket over his shoulder by two fingers, his other hand thrust into him pants pocket. He strolled through the door and glanced at Lauren with a nod. She returned his greeting with a flirtatious look. Since the day Nathaniel joined Lucifer's team, Lauren had a school-girl crush on him. It was the "good boy" quality that she found attractive which, oddly, was the only quality that Nathaniel worked to shed.

Lucifer greeted him with a hearty smile. "How did your meeting go?"

Nathaniel slid the jacket from his shoulder and draped it over the back of the leather couch next to the door. He plopped himself down on the cushion, crinkling the supple leather. "Like a charm. He fell for every word."

"I knew he would. Metatron is such a bleeding heart that there was no way he couldn't."

"All it took was a little quavering in my voice and pleading for help. He actually told me I should talk to Michael!"

Lucifer broke out into laughter. Knowing the history between Nathaniel and Michael, he knew Nathaniel would never consider going to Michael for anything.

Lauren shuffled over to the couch, rested herself in the seat next to Nathaniel. She eyed him closely, watching his mouth as he laughed. His body stiffened as he realized her gaze was glued to him.

Lucifer slid his hands into his pockets and rested on the edge of the desk, extending his legs before him. "Good. Let

Metatron chase shadows, thinking he has an ally."

"I do have to say, Lou, that this makes me uncomfortable."

Lucifer tilted his head, eyes closed, and gently raised his hand to Nathaniel. "I get it. I do. And I appreciate the effort you're giving me. But this will be different from last time."

Nathaniel's eyes focused on Lucifer's. He nodded, feeling the apprehension subside. He still wasn't completely comfortable with the plan but Lucifer's words helped put him at ease.

"I don't get something," Lauren said, turning to Lucifer. Her mouth was twisted to the side, a habit she had when forming a question. "Why would you let them know what you're up to? What if they figure it out?"

"It makes no difference if they know what I'm doing," he said, pushing himself to his feet. He walked around the desk and spun his chair. "The way my plan works, I can tell them exactly what I'm doing and they can't stop it." He sat in the chair, leaning back into the big, cushioned headrest.

Lauren scratched his head. "But why do you need the two guys from Earth?"

"I don't *need* them. They're my plan B." He leaned forward, placed his elbow on the desk and pointed a finger at Nathaniel. "Provided you get me the information I need."

Nathaniel nodded and rose from the seat. He leaned over the couch and grabbed his jacket, brushing his hand against Lauren's shoulder.

Sliding his arms into the sleeves he said "Looks like I'm off to torture an angel."

CHAPTER 22

The rain had been falling for days, gushing rivers of muddy water down the sides of the mountain. The plants had become so waterlogged, the soil so wet that the roots barely held to the ground such that a stiff breeze was enough to uproot them and send them sailing.

Matt landed flat on his back, sending up a splash of mud in all directions. The cold rain pounded against him, stinging his skin. He felt as if he was being attacked by thousands of frozen needles. He rolled on his side and tried to push himself up on his arms but the mud was so loose his hand went out from under him and he fell on his face. He felt his body shift and realized he was sliding. He grabbed out for a tree branch but it slipped through his grasp, leaving a gash in his palm. His body picked up momentum as the mountain grew steeper. Mud and wet leaves kicked up in his wake as he tumbled down the mountain. Matt's heart pounded in his chest and his arms flailed around for anything to slow his fall. He could feel himself sinking in the mud like it was quicksand, the water's current sweeping him closer to the edge.

Aaron appeared in the sky seconds later, his arms still wrapped around Twilana's waist. They struck the ground together, Aaron's shoulder breaking their fall. A crack sent a wave of pain through his chest and his arm seized. Twilana rolled out of his grasp, falling into the muddy trench left in Matt's wake. She reached out for Aaron's hand, thrashing to grab for his wrist but he tumbled just out of reach. The slick ground swept her away, taking her along the same path Matt's body dug in the mud.

Aaron watched as Twilana disappeared over the side of the mountain and out of his sight. He pushed himself to his knees but, like Matt and Twilana, couldn't find purchase in the mud. His knees sank. He tried to pull himself out but fell to his back. Aaron lost his bearings and tumbled end over end in the muck, all the way to the bottom.

*   *   *   *   *

Twilana landed at the foot of the mountain, a gash opened in her forehead. Blood oozed down her eyes and cheek. She wiped her face with the back of her hand, mixing blood with mud but doing nothing to enhance her vision. She leaned over a large puddle and splashed water on her face. The muddy blood (bloody mud?) washed down her cheeks and her vision cleared.

Spitting out a clod of mud, she surveyed the area. Through the haze of the rain, Twilana saw a mostly open plains land. The tall grasses bent under the weight of the rain and large bushy trees dotted the landscape. Twilana had never seen real trees before, the vegetation on her world having died long before she was born. She watched as the raindrops splashed on the leaves, their weight causing the braches to droop and sway. She reached up and pulled a leaf from the tree above her head. Flipping it over, she examined the veins running through it. She was fascinated by the leaf, hypnotized by the magnificence of its construction. So engrossed that she barely noticed the noise in the distance. She lifted herself to her feet, feeling a wave of aches flooding her muscles. She rolled her neck, working out the kinks, and stretched her arms behind her back, loosening her joints. The aches dulled and she walked off toward the ruckus.

Twilana rounded a large boulder and found Matt standing in front of a group of soldiers, his hands raised in the air. He clutched a thick, brown tree branch spattered with blood. At his feet lay a gangly, unconscious man next to a large bronze shield.

The soldiers pointed long-barreled rifles with fixed bayonets at his chest and shouted at him in Japanese. Matt's lack of fluency in their language frustrated them, causing them to shout louder and more rapidly. They wore armor similar to that of Japanese samurai, with large wooden plates covering their chests and backs. Helmets fit snugly upon their heads, hanging so low as to nearly cover their eyes. A few wore sheathed swords from their belts. One carried a long bamboo handle, the Japanese flag flapping limply in the rain. Baggy black pants, thick fabric gloves, and heavy boots completed their ensemble.

Twilana skulked around a tree, staying out of their line of sight. Dropping her hand to her hip, she reached for her pistol, finding her holster empty. She cursed, remembering that Aaron had taken it from her. Sliding her hand to the pouch next to the holster, she grabbed a light grenade. Pressing the button, she tossed the disk at the soldiers.

Matt watched as the disk hit the ground. Seeing the familiar blinking red light, he turned his head and squeezed his eyes shut. The soldiers shouted at him, demanding his attention. A sudden blast of white light blinded them, cutting their shouts short.

Twilana moved toward the closest soldier and wrapped her arms around his neck. Tightening her grip, she cut off the supply of air to his brain. He pulled at her arm, trying to free himself, but he quickly grew weak from the lack of oxygen. As his trashing lessened, she lowered him to the ground, releasing him when he lost consciousness.

Opening his eyes, Matt saw the soldiers staggering, blinking wildly as they tried to recover their vision. He noticed Twilana standing over a man and smiled, raising the tree branch high above his head. He rushed the soldier with the most gold in his uniform, assuming him to be the leader. A loud clang reverberated from the soldier's helmet as Matt brought the branch crashing down on his head. The soldier dropped to the ground and his rifle fell in the mud.

Twilana rushed in, scooped up the rifle and aimed it. Pulling the trigger, a silver ball exploded from the barrel, hitting a second soldier in the chest. The remaining two soldiers turned their attention to her.

Twilana aimed the gun at them and squeezed the trigger again. Nothing happened.

She squeezed a third time, with similarly disappointing results.

Matt ran toward the soldiers, his tree branch at the ready. He swiped at the soldier holding the flag, but the branch glanced off his backplate. The soldier turned and raised his elbow, striking Matt in the face. He stumbled backward, a gush of blood flowing from his nose. He reached up for his face and the soldier swung his flagpole, knocking Matt in the side of his head and sending him reeling. He fell to his knees, the world spinning around him. The soldier dropped the flagpole and pulled a pistol from his belt. Matt watched as the soldier steadied the gun on his head, staring at the decorative pistol, an intricately carved dragon staring back at him. His eyes flicked up to the soldier's face and he flopped backwards just as the soldier pulled the trigger. The pellet grazed Matt's arm and he screamed in pain. The soldier pulled the pistol up, dropping a wedge of black powder into the barrel but before he could load the pellet, Matt swung his legs, kicking the soldier in the knee. His leg buckled and he dropped to the ground. Matt rolled to his side and, with his good arm, punched the soldier in the face. The soldier fought back, swinging for Matt's chest but Matt dropped to the ground, the punch sailing over his head. Matt brought his knees up, hitting the soldier in the face. The soldier fell backwards and Matt rolled away.

The pain in his arm was staggering but Matt managed to get to his feet. He searched for Twilana and found two soldiers rushing toward her. She tossed the rifle to the side and balled up her fists. The first soldier lunged at her. Twilana side-stepped his attack and grabbed his arm. She pulled on him, spun her body around and sent him headfirst into a tree.

As she pivoted to face the second soldier, his fist slammed into her face. She stumbled backwards as he punched at her again. She ducked beneath his fist and spun on her left foot. She kicked the soldier in the chest, his wooden chestplate *thumped*. The force of the kick sent him backward but he remained upright.

The soldier swung at her again. Twilana put her hands up to block the attack and the punch landed on her wrist, breaking the clasp on her wristlet. The device slid from her arm, landing in the underbrush. Ignoring it, she raised her fist in an uppercut, catching the soldier just below his armpit. He exhaled a loud *oof* and stepped back a few feet.

Regaining her balance, Twilana stared at the soldier. She advanced toward him, not allowing him a moment to recover, completely unaware that the gold-plated soldier was regaining consciousness behind her. Through bleary eyes he turned to the battle, slowly rising to his feet. He picked up the matchlock and padded softly toward her.

Matt watched as the squad leader crept up behind her. He

opened his mouth to shout a warning, but all he could muster was 'Look' before a boot connected with his stomach, knocking the wind out of him.

Twilana turned in time for the butt of the rifle to crash down on her forehead. The blow knocked her dizzy, stars dancing behind her eyes. The gash in her forehead tore open further and blood darkened her sky-blue hair. She tried to remain on her feet, but her eyelids grew heavy and refused to obey her. Her legs wobbled before they gave out on her completely. She dropped to her knees. The butt of the rifle crashed down on her face again, knocking her out cold.

The three conscious soldiers converged on Matt. He lay in a mud puddle, listening to them argue about what to do with him. Though he couldn't understand a word they said, Matt caught the gist of their conversation. Judging by the pantomime one soldier performed on holding the gun to his head while another nodded furiously, he could tell that the vote to kill him had been two to one. Luckily the only hold out had been the one trimmed in gold, and as the leader, his opinion was the only one that mattered. The leader grunted to the soldier holding the gun on Matt, and was contented to merely stab his bayonet through the palm of Matt's hand.

A scream escaped Matt's lungs as the sharp metal pierced his flesh, leaving behind a throbbing pain. He balled his fist and drew it to his chest. The blood flowed from his hand, mixing with a stream of muddy rainwater beneath him. Clenching his eyes and gritting his teeth, Matt rolled on his side, wishing the pain would stop. It eventually did, but not until one of the soldiers brought his boot down on his temple, kicking the consciousness out of him.

CHAPTER 23

Aaron fell down the mountainside like an Olympic gymnast practicing his somersaults after a night of heavy drinking. As he reached the bottom of the hill, his head slammed against a rock and blood trickled from his temple. The resulting blackout became a relief from the view of the world spinning circles before him.

Hours passed as Aaron lay unconscious at the bottom of the mountain. He awoke as twilight broke, the setting sun casting the lush fields around him in an orange-red sheen. The rain stopped, the grass and trees shimmering in the dwindling light.

Aaron observed his surroundings. The grassy land spread out for miles in all directions, a small stream cutting through the center of it. Save for a few squirrels and birds, there was not another living creature within view.

Anxiety gripped Aaron's chest as he realized that for the first time since he had gone fishing with his friend, what seemed like weeks ago, he was entirely alone.

"All right, calm down, Aaron," he said aloud. Being all alone in an open field, he wasn't worried about looking crazy. He *was* worried about looking crazy if he ever had to explain this ordeal to anyone. "They have to be here somewhere. After all, we all came through the portal together."

His consoling words relaxed his anxiety. He inhaled deeply and rose to his feet. His shoulder screamed as he moved, reminding him of the fall from earlier. He raised his arm above his head slowly, testing the limits of his flexibility, satisfied that the shoulder will at least hold up under normal circumstances.

Aaron looked down at his body and limped to the stream. He stooped over and examined his reflection in the water. His clothes and hair were covered in dried mud, the obvious explanation for the crackling noise he heard as he moved. A large red and purple welt decorated his left temple. Instinctively, he touched it, sending a swirl of pain through his head, causing him to cringe. He made a mental note to stop following stupid instincts.

He crouched to the ground and scooped water over his face and hair, washing off the mud. The daylight grew scarcer, the darkness now overtaking the sky. Thoughts of wolves, bears, and rattlesnakes tearing his body to pieces and feasting on his intestines under the cover of night danced in his mind. He needed to find some kind of shelter and look for Matt and Twilana in the morning. Looking up, he saw burning torches far off in the distance. Deciding he had no other course of action, he lifted himself to his feet and limped downstream toward the flickering lights.

As he followed the twisting stream he noticed movement ahead. Squinting his eyes to see better, Aaron realized that two men had situated themselves by the stream, dragging a net through the water. Judging by the state of their tattered pants, stained shirts, and misshapen straw hats, Aaron pegged them as peasant fisherman, and decided they were safe to approach.

"Excuse me," he shouted, hoping that his evaluation of the situation was correct. "Can you tell me where I am, please?"

Both men turned to Aaron. They mumbled something to each other, their eyes never leaving his face. Their faces were blank, belying neither fear nor confusion. They didn't seem hostile, but they weren't exactly coming off as friendly either. Aaron strained to hear them, trying to understand what they said, but both the distance and his inability to comprehend their words prevented that from happening.

The older of the men barked at Aaron, a strange command of a question. Aaron shrugged. "I…I need to find my friends. I was with them, up there." He raised his arm and pointed to the mountaintop, gritting his teeth through the pain in his shoulder. "But we got separated."

The barking man looked at the mountain, his eyes growing

wide. He stared at Aaron as a thin smile spread across his face. "Ohhhhhhhh," he said before turning to his companion. He rattled off a few more words, nodding his head. The younger man smiled, nodding back to him. They turned back to Aaron and approached him, their stoic faces replaced with over-joyous looks.

The older man grabbed Aaron's wrist and tugged him, urging him to follow them. His words came out slower, more pronounced, like he was speaking to an infant. But the joke was on him since an infant would be able to understand him better than Aaron could. Aaron just nodded along, hoping he had answered correctly to a series of Yes/No questions.

The younger man shook his head, realizing the futility of the language barrier. He stepped closer to Aaron.

"You do speak English, right?"

This time it was Aaron's eyes that went wide. "Yes! Yes, I do. I'm so glad you do, too."

The younger man smiled. "Yes, I've been speaking English since I was a child." He dipped his head to the older man. "I told him you were speaking English, but he seemed to think it was some kind of Holy tongue that only a god could understand."

Aaron's eyebrows formed a V. "Wait. What do you mean 'a god'?"

The old man tugged on Aaron's wrist, urging him more strongly in the unknown language. The younger man brushed Aaron's question aside. "He says we must hurry. With the sun almost gone we will have to move fast."

The old man pulled on Aaron's arm, practically pulling him as they strode down the riverside, followed closely by the younger man. "Wait. Where are you taking me?"

The younger man answered from behind them. "Hsai will want to see you."

CHAPTER 24

It didn't take long for the news of the world-hoppers to spread throughout the Angelic High Military building. Little by little, the Ocularium filled with uninvited guests that heard about the exploits and wanted to see the travelers for themselves. I admit, this was a pretty exciting experience so I really can't blame anyone for wanting to be here. But as the events unfolded, the room filled to near capacity with Cherubim, Archangels, and Grigori alike.

As I returned from my visit with Michael, I found it close to impossible to make my way back to the Oculus. I pushed my way through the crowd like an overzealous fan at a rock concert. A few unruly folks chose to push back as I tried to get by but luckily Galgaliel spotted me in the fracas. She pulled out her official AHM credentials, ordering the crowd to disperse (they didn't need to know that her task within the AHM was filing paperwork and categorizing evidence). They backed away from us and she escorted me back to the Oculus.

"They disappeared again," she said. "Lauren showed up and they jumped into a portal. Then Lauren just vanished."

Shaking my head, I gave her a confused look. "They jumped into the portal? Why"

She shrugged.

I placed my hands on the Oculus and concentrated my power to locate them, but my focus kept slipping as I was knocked around from the swaying of the crowd. It got to the point that Galgaliel had to order everyone to step back, creating a perimeter around the sphere. Nodding my thanks, I turned back to the Oculus.

It only took a few moments to find them as their movements have become easier to follow. As I tuned into the new world, I discovered the one named Matt and a woman being led away by a group of soldiers.

"This isn't right," I said. "Where's the other one?"

"What do you mean?" Galgaliel asked, leaning over my shoulder. "No, all three of them jumped through the rift. Why are we only seeing these two?"

I widened my focus on the world and worked my way backwards. Following the residual energy left behind by the travelers I was led up the side of a large mountain where the energy signature was the strongest. Searching the area, I found a second path that led down the other side of the mountain, ending near a small stream.

"They got separated," I said, my eyes fluttering as I followed the second path.

"That's not good."

Galgaliel's words were the height of understatement. The damage to the universal bonds was bad enough having these people in a dimension they had no role in but to have them trampling across a wider area would increase the chaos exponentially.

"We need to get them back together," Galgaliel said, her voice cracking with fear. "We need to get them home."

"I understand that, but there's nothing I can do."

"Maybe I can…"

I waved my hand at her, cutting her off. I could see the fatigue in her face. She still wasn't back to strength after her last jaunt planetside. And by the way she didn't argue with me told me that she felt as bad as she looked.

A low, booming voice rose up from the clamor behind us. "Let me help."

Turning to the crowd, I saw a pair of crystal blue eyes looking up at me. His kind face was warm, a soft smile on his lips. Dirty blonde hair framed his face, giving him an aura of youth. Sauriel was only with the Angelic High Military for a short time but his reputation already preceded him. He had a knack for making friends as he was easy to trust. "Metatron," he said with a tight nod.

"What brings you here, Sarge?" I asked. I realized it was a silly question as soon as it passed my lips.

"Michael sent me here. To keep an eye on you." Well, at least he was honest.

"He doesn't trust me."

Sauriel shook his head, slowly and deliberately. "You know he doesn't believe in the Grigorian oath. But I do. Let me help."

I considered his request for a moment. After being rebuffed by Michael earlier, I was growing a distaste for AHM officers. I carefully weighed my options. If Michael sent him to intervene on his behalf, it would be a show of will, proving that the Angelic High Military has total control over the Grigorian Watchers. I could maintain my bureaucratic pissing match with the General, but at the end of it, we're likely to both come up as losers.

Sighing, I placed one hand on the Oculus and stretched the other out to Sauriel. Closing my eyes, I pulled his mind into mine. Using my abilities as a Watcher, I tapped into the world below, allowing Sauriel to sweep across the cosmos. The room filled with the smell of strawberries and brimstone, a crackle of electricity flowed through my body. When I opened my eyes, Sauriel was gone from the Ocularium. I looked down at the Oculus and found him standing at the foot of the mountain.

Galgaliel stepped beside me and placed her hand on my arm.

"Do you think we can trust him?" she asked.

"We have no other choice."

CHAPTER 25

A breathy groan escaped Matt's throat as he regained consciousness. His face hurt all over and he struggled to open his eyes, the dry, crusted blood having sealed his eyelids shut. Forcing them apart, he quickly snapped them shut again as the light assaulted his corneas. He squinted through slits, allowing his eyes to adjust to the light. Spotting two barely burning torches on the far wall, he realized he must have been unconscious for a long time.

The world around him was blurry. Turning his head to the left, he felt a wave of nausea rise from the pit of his stomach. His gag reflex reacted, contracting his throat violently. Leaning to his side, his stomach emptied itself, adding bad breath and a burning throat to his list of woes.

He wiped the vomit from the corner of his mouth and noticed that his hand had been wrapped in a familiar plaid cloth. A chill went through his body as he realized that his shirt was gone, used to staunch his bleeding hand. The dressing was stained with dried blood and by the throbbing he felt in his palm, did nothing to alleviate the pain. He opened and closed his fingers, testing their flexibility. Each movement sent pain shooting up his arm, where it collided with a dull throb in his shoulder. He looked down and saw his shoulder was wrapped as well. At least someone had taken the time to tend to his wounds.

The fuzziness began to fade and he saw the definition in the objects around him. What he saw, however, were not the most uplifting things in the world.

Matt sat in a small cage, in a small room, guarded by a large man. The man sat on a small wooden stool next to the door, his legs splayed out in front of him. His clothing was dark and unkempt, and he looked as if he hadn't shaved in a week. He had thin black hair that hung down over his eyes. Not that it mattered since his eyes were closed anyway. He crossed his arms over his chest and snored loudly.

A small groan rose from his right. He turned his head slowly as to not repeat his vomiting incident, and found Twilana lying in a cage next to his. She had a large red welt on her forehead and all of her equipment was gone, including her belt and holster. But at least she still had her shirt. She pushed herself up onto her elbow and rubbed her head, noticing Matt staring at her.

"What happened?" she asked.

Matt shrugged, causing his shoulder to ache again. "We're prisoners," he said, rubbing his shoulder gently.

Twilana rolled her eyes and the pounding in her head intensified. She fought to remember what had happened when they arrived. She noticed the bandages on Matt's arm and hand. "Are you OK?"

Matt nodded, pushing himself to his feet. The room spun as a dizzy spell overtook him. He placed his good hand on one of the bars of the cage to hold him up and waited for the spinning to subside. He was proud that he had won at least one battle today. Grabbing another bar, Matt pulled at them, testing their strength. Though made of wood, the cage was stronger than it looked.

"Yeah, I'm fine," he responded. "How about you? You took a nasty hit."

Twilana sat up. She felt the lump on her forehead and examined the flecks of dried blood that decorated her fingertips. She turned her head, inspecting their prison. The small room held little. No chairs. No tables. No furniture of any kind. Each wall was roughly the same size. Three of the walls were lined with prison cells, identical to their own.

Matt turned to the guard and whistled to get his attention but only succeed in producing a spray of spittle.

"Hey, buddy," he shouted. The guard's eyes lifted slowly. His face was wide, his cheeks sagging on both sides. His dark eyes squinted at Matt, like a gardener spotting vermin.

"What do you say we get some grub in here?" he asked, rubbing his stomach. "I'm starving."

The guard showed no expression, his face completely stoic. He reached down to his belt and pulled a small, silver dagger from its sheathe. Flicking his wrist, he flung it at Matt. It spun end over end in the air before catching in the bar of the cage, less than an inch above where Matt's hand gripped the wood.

Matt swallowed hard and backed away from the bar. He held his hands before him, surrendering to the guard "It's cool, man," he said. "I'm really not that hungry."

The guard rose from his stool and tottered to the cage. He snatched the dagger from the bar and slid it back into his belt.

Twilana looked at Matt. "I don't think we should be making jokes."

Matt's eyes remained glued to the guard. "Yeah, I think you're right."

A sudden knock at the door broke the tension, startling the guard. He jumped from the stool and pulled a large, brass key from his belt. He inserted the key into the door and turned it, pulling it open. A tall man dressed in a long, red kimono glided through the doorway. The man's hair was slicked back, ending in a long ponytail. He sauntered into the prison room, hands folded behind his back. He squinted at the guard and waved, dismissing him. The guard hurried from the room, pulling the door closed behind him.

The man's eyes slid between Twilana and Matt, raising one eyebrow in contempt. He placed a hand on Matt's cage. Matt noticed that the hand was well maintained, the nails perfectly manicured. Clearly this man hadn't seen a day of hard work in his life. "So you're the pair who almost took down my best squad of soldiers."

"Who are you?" Twilana asked.

The man's eyes snapped to her, a look of disgust spread across his face. "Did I give you permission to speak, wench?"

Hisaki Kaito was a man who ruled by fear. Descended from a long line of despots, Hisaki has known little else. His father raised him with an iron fist, demanding nothing short of perfection. He wasn't the kind of man to show compassion, and when you're ruling a country, small things like being kind and having manners tend to go out the window.

Needless to say, Hisaki's father's bad habits rubbed off on Junior. But Hisaki became more than just a tough leader; he became cruel and heartless. He would often take slaves as a result of a battle, forcing them to work in the kitchens or stables. Those that were too feeble for manual labor were executed in the town square, in front of a gathering of people. His nation had grown so accustomed to these public executions that they became celebrated, like a county fair.

But Matt didn't know anything about the man. He was cold, he was hungry, and his hand hurt like hell. If he had known of the ruthlessness of the man who stood before him, he probably would have tried harder to keep his cool.

"Hey!" Matt shouted. "We've been here for God only knows how long with absolutely no explanation of why we're being treated like this. You take all of our gear and toss us in a cage like some damn canaries and we can't even get some food."

Completely unfazed by Matt's tirade, Hisaki turned to him. His dark eyes stared at Matt, eyes so dark they seemed almost black. Despite the intimidation Hisaki held, Matt stood his ground, feeling empowered by his anger.

"We are in the midst of a great war," Hisaki began. "Our eternal enemies plot our destruction. They wish to take our land and kill our families. We have no time to treat you with kindness and respect like some household pets." Hisaki spat on the floor at Matt's feet to punctuate his words. He turned and strode toward the door.

"At least tell us why we are here," Twilana said, pleading for information.

Looking over his shoulder, Hisaki replied "All spies are taken prisoner before they are executed."

Hisaki opened the door and disappeared into the darkness of the hallway. The guard returned, settling himself onto his stool.

Twilana watched as Matt lowered himself to the floor, his eyes fixated on the door. He pulled his legs close to his chest, folding himself into a fetal position. He turned his head to her and for the first time since they had met, she saw the fear in his eyes.

CHAPTER 26

Aaron stared up at the palace in disbelief. He glanced at the two fishermen, his mouth agape, before returning to the castle. It was made of a dark stone, becoming it almost invisible in the dark of the night. The windows shined with the light of flickering torches, their flames dancing in the night breeze. As they approached, a massive wooden drawbridge lowered, allowing them passage across a large moat that encircled the entire castle. As they walked across the bridge, Aaron looked down into the chasm, expecting to find it filled with dirty brown water. Instead the moat was lined with hundreds of sharpened spears packed closely together.

At the end of the drawbridge stood a short, stocky man in poorly fitting clothes. The man had a thin mustache that curled around his mouth and hung to his chest. The fishermen introduced the man as "Hsai" and took their leave, but not before hugging Aaron tightly in turn.

"Your highness," Hsai said, bowing deeply. Aaron felt his face flush with embarrassment, unsure of how to respond. Hsai straightened and looked Aaron up and down, examining the filth that covered his body.

"You must be in want of a cleaning."

"I could use some asprin and a nap, too."

Hsai cocked his head to the side and squinted at him.

"Nevermind," Aaron said. Hsai smiled. Raising his hands, he gave two quick claps. A pair of serving girls dressed in matching red and white robes appeared behind him.

"Please allow these girls to attend to your needs. I will meet with you shortly."

The girls flanked Aaron, each grabbing him by the arm. Aaron smiled, nodding to Hsai, and allowed the girls to lead him down a hallway. Hsai watched as they left, his warm smile slowly fading from his face. He lingered a moment before turning and walking across the courtyard.

Reaching the end of the hallway, the girls rounded a bend and stopped in front of a large, wooden door. The girl to Aaron's left pushed the door open, revealing a spacious room. Aaron stepped through the threshold and stared down at the pool of water sprawling before him, its size rivaling the pool at his local YMCA. He turned to find the girls loosening the sashes around their waists. Dropping their robes to the floor, they stood before Aaron in all of their naked glory.

"Whoa, whoa," he said, his face turning bright red. "What's going on here?"

One of the girls stepped next to him, speaking rapidly in Chinese. She pulled at his clothes, removing his mud-caked shirt.

"I'm sorry but I don't understand you."

The second girl approached him and pulled the shirt from his arm. "Hsai said we are to attened to your needs. You need to bathe." She reached down to unbutton his pants. Aaron jumped, pushing her hands away.

"I...I can do this part."

Fully undressed, the girls lead Aaron down a set of steps into the pool. He stood in the warm water as the girls scrubbed the dirt from him. He felt self-conscious, never having had the experience of being bathed by a pair of women before. But that's not to say he didn't enjoy it.

The girls dried Aaron with a fluffy, blue towel and wrapped him in a long, golden robe. The silk was soft against his freshly cleaned skin, almost making him forget about the throbbing in his head. He followed the girls from the bathing room and through the winding hallways, up flights of long, stone staircases.

The steps came to an end and the girls turned. Aaron spotted Hsai at the end of the long hallway. The girls released him and bowed, retreating down the steps. Aaron walked the length of the hall.

"Master," Hsai said, bowing. "I almost didn't recognize you.

"Yeah, it's a nice feeling being clean."

They lingered in silence for a moment. Hsai looked down at his hand and spotted the small, golden cup he held. He handed it to Aaron.

"What is this?"

"For your pain," Hsai replied, motioning to his forehead. Shrugging, Aaron lifted the cup to his lips and swallowed the liquid. He gagged as the bitter taste flooded his mouth. The back of his throat burned as the warm elixir drained into his stomach. His body shook. Hsai took the cup from him.

"I am sure you would like to rest now." Without waiting for a response, Hsai pushed the door open, wishing Aaron a good night before turning and disappearing down the hallway.

Aaron looked into the bedroom and marveled at its opulence. The room was trimmed with gold, the mantle, moulding, and even the four dragons that hung in each corner of the room were made of solid gold. The dragons' jade eyes kept watch over the room's occupant. The entirety of the far wall was glass, looking out upon the city below. In the distance Aaron spotted the mountain range and wondered which peak he had fallen down earlier. He turned to the massive four-post bed to his right, and was enraptured by the silken bedsheets as they glistened in the light from the wall sconces. Across from the bed was a bookshelf that ran along the wall. The shelves were stacked full of books of various sizes and colors. He walked to it and browsed the titles on the spines. *The History of the Japeo/China War. The Industrialization of Britain. The Fall of the American Colonies.* Aaron pulled one titled *Science and Alchemy* from the shelf and flipped through the pages as he sauntered toward the bed. Sliding under the sheets, he laid his head on the mountain of pillows behind him and was asleep within seconds.

* * * * *

Aaron awoke to the sound of the curtains being drawn. He opened his eyes and was blinded by the sunlight flooding his room.

"Time to awaken, your highness," he heard Hsai announce. "We have much to do today."

Aaron grabbed one of the pillows and held it over his head. Hsai leaned over the bed, pulled the pillow from Aaron's face and tossed it to the side.

Groaning, Aaron sat up and watched Hsai as he stood in the center of the room. "What do you want with me?"

"We'll get to that in time," he said. "But first, you must be hungry." He clapped his hands and two women strolled into the room. The women, the same ones who washed him the night before, carried silver, covered trays. They placed the trays on the bed and lifted the covers, revealing a buffet of foods; a mountain of hard-boiled eggs, roasted duck, baked potatoes, hot brown bread, and slices of fruit. The smell of the food hit Aaron like a punch in the face and his mouth began to water. He grabbed a drumstick of roasted duck and took a huge bite of it, chewing noisily as grease dribbled from the corner of his mouth. The women bowed to Hsai, then to Aaron, and quickly shuffled from the room. Aaron bit a second mouthful of duck meat as he watched them leave.

Hsai paced the room as Aaron enjoyed his breakfast. He swallowed hard, reaching for a pitcher that sat next to the tray. He gulped the juice down and refilled the cup, taking reasonable sips from it the second time around. Wiping his face with the back of his hand, he tore off a piece of bread and shoved it into his mouth. He looked at Hsai and spoke but all that came out were unintelligible mumblings.

Hsai stopped and smiled, bowing his head. "Your Highness, today you are to meet your army. They have long been awaiting your arrival."

Crumbs flew from Aaron's mouth as he chewed. "What are you talking about?"

"Your arrival is a portent of our inevitable victory, my lord," Hsai responded. He walked to the bookshelves and traced his fingers along the spines. He pulled a book from the shelf and flipped through the pages, stopping on a painting that spanned two pages. The scene illustrated a large nude man, skin pale as a ghost, flames shooting up from behind him. He faced a platoon of soldiers in ceremonial Chinese armor. Their weapons dripped blood and their feet were littered with the bodies of fallen enemies.

Hsai paused a moment, staring at the painting. He looked up at Aaron and continued "The ancients told of a great rift that would open in the sky on the day our master would lead us to victory over our sworn enemy." Hsai walked to Aaron's side and placed the book in his lap. He wrapped his arms behind his back, clasping his hands together. Turning from his exalted leader, Hsai paced the room contently.

Looking down at the book, Aaron noticed a familiar scene. A large mountain loomed in the center of the image, a swirling purple hole in the sky above it. At the base of the mountain stood a white-skinned man covered in war paint that oddly resembled himself caked in mud when he met the two fishermen. It seemed that Hsai was translating this picture too literally. Aaron shook his head in disbelief, watched as Hsai walked across the floor, his padded shoes shuffling silently against the ornate Persian rug. Or maybe it was an Oriental rug. Aaron couldn't tell the difference.

Aaron sighed loudly. "No, something's wrong here. I'm not your master. I can't help you win a war." He leaned back against the pillows, running his fingers through his hair. He paused a moment and reconsidered the idea before shaking his head again. "No, I can barely take care of myself."

"You came to us from the sky." Hsai spoke without breaking his stride. "You appeared at your throne. This is what the ancients predicted."

Aaron dropped his gaze to the book in his lap, absorbing the image. He turned the pages absentmindedly, letting his eyes wash over the prints of the white figure in different scenes. Standing before a sea of fire. Being revered by an army. Flying to the top of the mountain on long, white wings.

"That portent can be no coincidence," Hsai said

Aaron snapped the book shut and the loud thump startled Hsai. "My throne," Aaron asked, swinging his hand toward the window. He pointed past the rolling hills full of trees blossoming with tiny pink and white puffs. Past the rows of houses along the country side. He pointed directly to the smoking volcano in the far distance. "You mean the mountain?"

Hsai pinched his eyes and nodded. "Yes, my liege. The ancients built a temple at the peak of that volcano many years ago. It was your final request before leaving this world, to act as a doorway between your world and ours."

Aaron decided to play along with the deity façade. "What's in my shrine? Is there anything of importance in there?"

Hsai was taken aback by the question. He answered carefully, afraid that he may offend the exalted one before him. "I would not know, sire. I have never been inside your shrine. In fact, no one has. It is forbidden. We would not take the chance of angering you by trespassing within your domain."

"Well, yes, of course," Aaron said. "I would expect no less of you." He started to wonder about the shrine, thinking that it may be worth checking out. But he would need to find Matt and Twilana first.

Hsai strode to Aaron, grabbing the book from the bed. He turned to walk toward the bookcase. "But that is of little importance now. All that matters is the great battle that is brewing."

Hsai placed the book on the shelf, pushing it silently into place with two fingers. "It is destiny, my lord," he said, his gaze never leaving the book. "You have risen to aid us." He clapped his hands again and the door swung open. A trio of boys no older than eleven walked into the room carrying the components to a suit of armor. The first boy dropped to his knee and held up the helm for Aaron's inspection. Aaron took the helmet from the boy, examining the detail. It was crafted into the shape of a dragon's head, its open mouth surrounding the visor. The eyes were large spheres of obsidian, the blackness of the gems so deep they reflected Aaron's image. The helm gave Aaron chills just looking at it. He looked down at the boy, still on his knees, eyes not deviating from the floor.

"You can stand now," Aaron said. The boy hopped to his feet and rushed to the door. His eyes washed over the other pieces of armor, all intricately detailed in the same dragon theme. He looked up at Hsai and found the man staring at him. The disbelief engulfed Aaron's face. His eyes creased and his mouth fell into a frown. The strangeness of the situation froze Aaron in place, the weight of the task adding a droop to his shoulders. He considered his options for a moment. There was no way Hsai would allow him to run up the side of the mountain without helping him first. Besides, maybe he could convince Hsai to help him find Matt and Twilana.

"All right," he conceded. "Who do I have to smite?"

CHAPTER 27

Pieces of tinder fluttered from the torches as the flames devoured the pitch. The guard rose from his stool and took the torch from the wall. He unlocked the door and left the room. Matt heard the keys rattle as he locked it from the other side.

He lost track of how long they had been held captive, having no access to a watch or the sun. Growing bored, he kept himself occupied by whistling, which also helped to console his nerves. Being threatened with execution also seemed to set him on edge. He didn't devise any kind of playlist or anything; he just whistled whatever popped into his head, which, for some reason, happened to be mostly showtunes. *Don't Cry For Me Argentina.* The theme from *Phantom of the Opera.* That kind of thing. Once he got to the title song from *Rocky Horror Picture Show,* Twilana lost it. She groped around the dirt floor, searching for a rock or a piece of wood or basically anything heavy to throw. Having found something, she heaved it in Matt's direction. Luckily for him, though, it was too dark for her to aim properly. The dirt clod struck the bar of his cage and shattered, sprinkling him with a shower of dirt.

"What the hell did you do that for?" he shouted, shaking the dirt from his hair.

"Would you please stop that annoying noise," Twilana said. "It's bad enough we've been imprisoned. We don't need to be tortured as well."

"Sorry," he said, brushing the dirt from his chest. "When I

get nervous, I tend to be annoying." He lay down on his side, placing his head on a pile of dirty straw.

Twilana looked at Matt, feeling bad for having accosted him. She hadn't considered that his irritating nature was tied to his fear. She just thought he was an annoying person.

"I'm sorry I threw dirt at you," she said.

The silence hung in the air as they sat in their cages, contemplating their situation. Twilana had been taken prisoner before; this type of thing was a risk one takes when joining the military. But Matt grew up in a relatively safe neighborhood in the suburbs of New Jersey. He wasn't used to being in the middle of a war, being thrown in a cage with no food, water, or light. Twilana watched Matt as he scratched at the mortar between the bricks in the floor.

"Try not to think about it too much," she said consolingly. "It helps to think of capture as just a really bad vacation."

The advice made Matt smile. Though she was terrible at being comforting, he appreciated her attempt to calm him. "I just never considered this happening." He pushed himself up on his butt and crossed his legs. He placed his elbows on his knees and cupped his chin in his hands, wincing as a bolt of pain shot through his injured hand up his arm. Shifting his body, he laid his hand on the floor next to him. "All I wanted to do today was go fishing. Just my luck that I would wind up in some kind of alternate reality."

Twilana nodded in the dark. Being one of the few people to actually share the experience, she could relate. "There's still hope," she said. "Aaron's out there somewhere. He'll be looking for you." She wanted to say 'us', but she wasn't sure Aaron's loyalty to her was as strong as it was to Matt. She doubted he would even give her a second thought.

Matt heard something peculiar in her voice but failed to pick up on her choice of words. He nodded and moaned in agreement. They allowed a few minutes to pass in silence.

Twilana inched closer to the bars. "Can I ask you a question?"

"Mmm hmmm."

"What's the deal with you and Aaron? You two don't seem like you come from the same ilk."

The question made Matt chuckle, only because it wasn't

the first time he'd heard it. "We've known each other since elementary school. He was the quiet kid that kept to himself. I was the obnoxious kid that no one wanted to deal with." Matt stretched his legs out in front of him and leaned his back against the wall.

"One day during recess, some kids were picking on him, making fun of him because he'd rather read a book instead of playing dodgeball with everyone else. I stepped up. Stuck up for him. We've been friends ever since."

Twilana enjoyed the sentimentality of his story. She could tell from the tone of his voice how much Aaron meant to him. Twilana didn't have many friends back home. No family besides her parents. She wished she could know what it was like to have someone care for her as much as she cared for them. Unfortunately, if Aaron didn't find them, she might not get that chance.

"I'm sorry you got dragged into this," Matt continued. She was surprised by his unnecessary apology.

"Don't be," she said. "If you and Aaron hadn't taken me, rescued me from that woman, I'd be dead."

Matt knew this was true, but hearing Twilana say it made him feel better. Not because it made him feel more heroic that he helped to save her life, but that he didn't feel like a kidnapper by taking her against her will.

The door to the prison room swung inward, slamming against the wall. Matt and Twilana's heads snapped in its direction, finding Hisaki standing in the doorway. He entered, followed closely by two armed guards. Without a word, he raised his arm and pointed to Twilana's cell. The first guard marched to the cell, slid a key into the lock, and opened the door. He grabbed Twilana's arm, pulling her from the cage. She twisted, trying to free herself. The guard grabbed her throat and squeezed, strangling her. She grasped at his hand, digging her fingernails into the vice around her neck. The guard squeezed harder and Twilana let her body go limp.

Anger spread through Matt. He felt the blood rush to his face, the heat rising from his chest. "Leave her alone, asshole," he shouted as he sprang to his feet. He stretched his injured hand through the wooden bars, grasping at the guard's armor. The second guard grabbed his arm and shoved it sideways against the bars. Matt yelped in pain as his arm bent awkwardly. Hisaki reached into the cage, grabbed Matt by the hair and pulled his face against the bars. Matt clutched the bar with his other hand, to push himself away, but Hisaki pulled again, smashing his face even harder into the bars. Matt's cheek burned where it struck the wood, splinters dug into his nose and face. His eyes watered as the pain spread.

Hisaki lowered his head, leveling his eyes with Matt's. Matt blinked, causing tears to roll down his cheeks. Hisaki's breath felt hot on his face. He watched as his jailer's lips curled into a devious smile. Matt struggled to break free, but he had no vantage to push himself away.

"What do you want from us?" Matt asked through clenched teeth.

Hisaki's smile grew wider. "That, you are about to discover."

CHAPTER 28

Hsai led Aaron down a long brick hallway. Aaron was dressed in his gilded armor, the gold shimmering in the light from Hsai's torch. The armor was lighter than he imagined it would be, and he had a wider range of motion than he expected. The final piece presented to him was a longsword, intricately smithed with an edge so sharp he could practically see through it. The blade hung on his belt, the scabbard clanking against his leg as he walked. Aaron placed his hand on the hilt, feeling the grooves in the leather that wrapped the handle. The pommel was fashioned in the same dragon motif as his armor, right down to the obsidian eyes.

As he walked, Aaron examined the tapestries adorning the walls. Each depicted the same white figure he saw earlier in Hsai's book. But these images were far more detailed than the prints in the book. They seemed so alive. In a few of them, Aaron could see the resemblance in the figure's face to his own. It was a little unsettling to be revered as a god, but Aaron was starting to like it.

The air in the room was cold and Aaron's breath escaped in puffs of condensation. He could feel the cold metal of the armor through the boiled leather jerkin he wore. A chill ran up his spine, prickling his skin with goosebumps. His anxiety reached a fever pitch, even after everything he'd already been through. He wondered how he would be able to fake his way through this, find his friends and get home.

Aaron turned to the guard escorting him. He was an intimidating creature; his armor was polished and well presented, despite a number of dents and gashes in the metal. His visor was bent at the corner, allowing Aaron a glimpse at the side of his eye. The black circle of his iris remained focused ahead, his determination never wavering. He exuded a sense of confidence that Aaron admired. To become a royal guard, he must have shown great bravery and skill on the battlefield, both also qualities that he admired in the man. Aaron wished he could be brave at that moment.

Aaron looked at Hsai. Though he could only see the back of his head, he imagined Hsai's expression to be similar to the guard's. Impassive. Cold. Stoic. Hsai's life had been fostered for this very moment, for the return of China's salvation. And the man took his job seriously. But there was something under the surface, something that made Aaron uncomfortable. He hoped that he was just being paranoid after everything he's been through but he wasn't about to stand by and let someone take advantage of him.

The three men walked in silence and the quiet began to wear on Aaron's nerves.

"So earlier," Aaron began, "when you were talking about your 'greatest enemies.' Who exactly were you talking about?"

Hsai answered without breaking his grim determination. "The Japanese."

Aaron waited a moment, expecting Hsai to elaborate on his answer. When he realized that was not going to happen, he delved deeper. "And how did the Japanese become your greatest enemies?"

Upon hearing the question, Hsai stopped in his tracks. He released a deep sigh, wishing to avoid going into details. Now that the savior had arrived, the war was going to move quickly, events would begin to escalate. They needed to be ready. They didn't have time to discuss the past. He resumed walking. "It is a long and boring tale, my liege," he said dismissively.

Though Hsai's tone was calm, Aaron was shocked by his answer. Hsai had given in to everything he asked for since he arrived. He didn't expect to be denied an answer to a simple question. Aaron was irritated by the rebuff and felt his face growing hotter. "You're the one that said I was going to lead you to victory, didn't you? If you don't tell me why I'm fighting, then maybe I'll just choose not to fight."

A chuckle escaped Hsai's lips. "I'm afraid that is not

possible, your grace. As it is told in the scriptures, you must choose a side." Hsai shuffled his step and his face scrunched up in a grimace. He realized his mistake as soon as the words escaped his lips. His only hope was that Aaron would not pick up on it.

Peering over his shoulder, Hsai spotted the smile on Aaron's face.

"So, what you're saying is, I can choose to help you defeat the Japanese, or help the Japanese defeat you?"

Hsai felt his stomach flip, a wave of fear spreading through his body. He knew that if the savior sided with the Japanese, the Chinese would have no chance of winning the war. He shivered at the thought of his people's eradication and decided the best course of action was to placate his master's curiosity.

"Very well." Licking his lips, Hsai spoke, retelling a story that he disliked knowing, a story that he wished was a work of fiction. "Many years ago, our people lived in peace. The Japanese had a thriving fishing economy while we had a quickly maturing produce economy. Our two countries had developed a relationship, becoming interdependent on each other to barter for goods. And everything was well. The Chinese government even gave our most profitable port city, Hong Kong, to the Japanese as a sign of our friendship."

They reached a large wooden door, trimmed with a golden doorknob. Hsai slid his hand into a pocket of his robe and pulled out a long silver key. He unlocked the door and gave it a hard push. The door's hinges made a harsh, screeching noise as it swung open. The sound pierced Aaron's skull as it reverberated off the closely contained corridor. When the noise died down, Hsai continued his story.

"One day, the English sailed into our ports. They heard of our bounty and wished to skim a portion of it for themselves. They inhabited our country and arrested anyone who opposed them."

"Hold on," Aaron interrupted. "How did the English overpower both the Chinese and the Japanese? You had the home field advantage."

Hsai shook his head. He stopped walking and faced Aaron. "The English had an advanced military, with firearms that we had never seen before. Our cultures had no military at that time. We never had any use for them, having lived in peace for so long. We did what we could. But our efforts were fruitless.

"What followed was a slaughter. The English wiped out nearly all who volunteered to face them.

"But then the English called a conference with our leaders. This was surprising, considering they had defeated us so easily. Regardless, the King of Japan and the Prime Minister of China both agreed to meet with the Queen of England. The discussion got heated as the King and the Prime Minister believed the Queen's terms to be unfavorable. However, given time, the King wavered to the Queen's way of thinking. Much to the Prime Minister's embarrassment, the King struck an accord with the Queen."

"What sort of things was Japan given?"

"England promised Japan the faith of its Navy in exchange for free use of the ports in Hong Kong. Japan would receive weapons and training from the British military for a portion of Japan's fishing industry."

Aaron smiled. "Well, the Brits do love their fish 'n chips."

Hsai looked at him, his brow furrowed.

"Stupid joke. But anyway, it sounds like the English are your enemies, not the Japanese."

Hsai shook his head. "You may be a great leader, but you are quite naïve. Despite the way the English invaded our country and took control by force, it is nothing compared to the embarrassment and insult we faced at the hands of the Japanese. We are a people that cherish honor, and the way our *friends*," he spat the word with derision, "turned their backs on us when we needed them the most... That was a huge dishonor, one that cannot be forgiven."

Hsai hurried down the corridor, veering to the left as the hallway split.

Aaron watched as he disappeared around the corner. He looked to the guard next to him, shrugged, and sprinted after Hsai, spotting him standing on a large stone balcony. Down below, the courtyard twinkled like bright sunlight reflecting off the ocean. As Aaron got closer to the balcony, the shapes of the soldiers below became more defined. He could see the light shining off of the soldiers' helmets, armor and swords.

Aaron stood at the edge of the balcony, looking over the army. Upon the grass stood thousands of armored soldiers. As he leaned over the stone banister, the soldiers raised their weapons, a sea of swords, spears and axes waved at him frantically. They chanted in unison, the courtyard vibrating from the *boom* of a thousand voices shouting out at once. Despite the sun warming the metal of his armor, Aaron's goosebumps returned.

Hsai bowed his head and the soldiers lowered their weapons, the chanting faded in the afternoon breeze. He turned to Aaron and waved his arm across the courtyard.

"My lord, I present to you your army."

CHAPTER 29

Hundreds of people piled into the center of Puyoa City, the city once referred to as Hong Kong. Some had painted faces and were dressed in outlandish costumes, celebrating the fairy tales of the past by representing them in the present. Other people pushed carts full of wooden statues and silk robes and all different types of food. They hawked their wares to the spectators just to scrape together a little money to support their families. Times were hard in Puyoa City, its citizens doing whatever they had to do to survive. Music rode the winds, caressing the ears of all those in attendance.

Twilana sniffed at the air, the sweet smell of candy and savory aromas making her mouth water. She knelt on a large, wooden stage in the center of the square, her hands tied behind her back. They placed her head on a wooden platform and tied her neck down to prevent her from moving. She watched the citizens shuffle through the square, heard the shouts of delight as children chased each other, slipping through the throngs of people. They munched on rice balls, throwing pieces of food at each other. Any other time, the scene would make Twilana smile.

But not now. Twilana's eyes shifted to the adults, to the people who were aware of the reasons for the gathering. Their eyes looked at her with disgust. With revulsion. They condemned her for what they've been told she'd done. *They don't know the truth*, she told herself. *They've been fed lies.* But then again, she wasn't innocent of believing preconceived notions.

During her time with the Janian Task Force, Twilana took part in many interrogations of accused criminals. While a few easily admitted their crimes, most of them proclaimed their innocence. To Twilana, it did not matter. Her job was to uncover the criminals, and she was good at her job. She looked upon all of the accused in the same way. She saw them as disgusting creatures, delinquents unfit to mingle with the good people of Janus. She viewed herself and her team as being superior to them.

And in that moment she hated herself for it.

Finding herself in a similar position, Twilana wondered if those she interrogated deserved her derision. She had done nothing wrong, and she was in the same predicament as they had been. Could her position have gone to her head and clouded her judgment? Had her superiors lied to her about the so-called crimes they had committed, like their jailor had lied to his citizens?

Twilana angled her head to look at Matt. He knelt next to her, bound in the same way she was. She noticed the way he sat, his eyes closed, arms relaxed, his face obscured by streaks of dried mud. Beads of sweat formed on his forehead and rolled down the side of his face. From her vantage, she could see the injury in his arm, the plaid wrapping fully crusted with blood and pus. Judging by his sweating, the gash was most likely in need of medical attention. She wanted to tell him that everything would be okay. To let him know that she had a plan to free them so they can find Aaron and disappear from this planet.

But she could not. And she hated herself for that, too.

A gong sounded in the square. Twilana turned her head to the noise but the sisal rope cut into her neck, preventing her from moving. She didn't know where the sound came from, but she assumed that it was not a good sign.

Hisaki appeared from a long hallway and sauntered to the stage. As he carefully climbed the wooden steps, the crowd erupted into a wave of cheers and applause. The sound echoed in the small courtyard, amplifying the fanfare. Following Hisaki was a large man, clad completely in black, carrying a long-handled, ornamental axe. He walked across the stage, taking a place next to Matt, resting the blade of the axe on the floor. Matt's eyes looked down at the blood-splattered axe and he swallowed hard.

Hisaki reached the center of the stage and looked over the crowd. He raised his arm and waved the crowd to silence. They obeyed his command, keeping their eyes fixed on him, awaiting his next word.

Scanning the courtyard, he looked at the hundreds of pairs of admiring eyes staring up at him. He glanced over his shoulder, glaring at Matt and Twilana as they knelt upon the stage. Matt raised his head to look at him. As he did so, a balled, black fist connected with his cheek, sending a wave of pain through his face. The tears welled in his eyes and Matt heard a voice chastise him. "Do not dishonor Lord Hisaki."

Matt shifted his eyes to the man in black. His eyelids narrowed into slits. A small cut opened on his cheek and blood trickled down his face. His eyes floated back to Hisaki and found him glaring at him. His lips curled into a devious smile as he turned back to the crowd, raising his hands above his head

"My people."

The flourish returned as Hisaki spoke. The sounds of clapping and cheering filled the air, creating a deafening atmosphere in the walled courtyard. Hisaki reveled in the adoration, his smile growing wider and wider. He clasped his hands behind his back and waited patiently for the noise to subside. When it did, he continued his speech.

"Long have we lived together and long have we thrived. In the past, we felt we needed help in order to prosper. First, it was the help of the Chinese. Later, the English. But when the English broke the pact we had agreed upon all those years ago, we decided it was time for us as a society to be self-sufficient. And we succeeded!"

Hisaki raised his hands to emphasize his final words, causing another commotion to erupt from the crowd. He smiled again, knowing that his people loved his leadership and would do anything for him.

"But now our enemies engage us once again," Hisaki continued. "Though we have lived our lives in peace and solitude, and choose to stay away from the battle, they send us spies to infiltrate our way of life. To topple the empire we have built. Our privacy is in peril and has been for who knows how long. We must defend our great country from all interlopers, even those that appear from the sky as if by magic."

Hisaki turned and looked at the prisoners. His face pinched with repugnance at the sight of the two who had the audacity to enter his kingdom. Only the thought of their imminent fate was able to forgive the insult of having to be in the presence of such creatures.

"Now the time has come to make an example of these...these people."

Hisaki looked back to the crowd one final time before walking toward the edge of the stage.

Twilana watched Hisaki's movements carefully. She studied the man as he folded his arms behind his back. She examined his movements, searching for that one weakness. She had seen many men like this in her days with the Janian military. They were the men who committed the most heinous of crimes. The men who everyone knew were capable of almost anything. These men were smart enough to cover their tracks and charismatic enough to lead everyone to believe they were incapable of such actions. But these men always had a weakness, a part of them that, given the opportunity, someone bold enough can play off of, allowing them the leverage to bring down such sycophants.

Hisaki tilted his head to the executioner, signaling him to begin. Grasping the axe with both hands, the black hooded man grunted as he lifted the heavy blade from the floor.

A strange feeling of relaxation spread throughout Matt's body. He shut his eyes tightly, hoping that the blade of the axe was recently sharpened. He saw no way out of his situation and decided that if he was going to die, he just wanted it to be quick. And as relatively painless as possible. Death he could handle. But pain... he really didn't want the pain.

The executioner raised the axe above his head. Twilana watched his muscles tense as he steadied the blade in line with Matt's neck. In those last minutes, her brain kicked into gear, figuring out a plan to save her new friend. She couldn't let him die like this, not after he had helped her before, helped to save her people from the Lacertidae. She needed to help him now.

That's when she realized Hisaki's weakness. Though she didn't know the man, she knew his type. And now, watching as Matt readied himself for his death, she knew how to react.

"Wait!"

Hisaki raised his hand to the executioner. The executioner rested the handle of the axe on his shoulder. Hisaki turned to Twilana, his eyes slits, patience waning. His lips parted and with a derisive frown asked "What have you to say, cow?"

Twilana ignored the insult, allowing it to roll off her back. After all, given the position she was in, she couldn't really argue the ideals of respect with Hisaki, despite the retort that formed in the back of her mind. Clearing her throat, she looked up at Hisaki.

"What if I could give you a weapon that could help you defeat your enemies once and for all?"

Hisaki stared at her blankly as he considered her proposal. His eyebrows rose, intrigued by the idea. As she suspected, Hisaki's vanity would be her opportunity. He wanted power, by any means necessary. Even if it meant making a deal with a stranger, one that he accused of being a spy.

"Tell me more."

CHAPTER 30

The forest had settled into tranquility, all life seemingly at rest. Occasionally, a stiff breeze would blow through the trees, gently bending the branches, swirling the leaves into tiny tornados. This forest had not changed for nearly four hundred years, and has offered a number of beautiful sights within that time. Spring brought a fresh palette of color, when the flowers bloomed and the buds on the trees began to sprout. When summer rolled in, the colors changed again, painting the leaves in earthly tones that lingered until the end of autumn. The arrival of winter brought with it the monochrome white, lasting until the cycle began again the next spring.

The Chinese landscape has been the source of inspiration for many artists over the years. Painters came to capture the changing colors and the essence of the land. Stories of loves won and loves lost have been written here, along with countless poems and sonnets. If the blades of grass could speak, they would recite any of the hundreds of plays, in the voices of the thousands of characters that sprang to life from the vistas of the hills.

But all of that changed on that afternoon. Though the forests had been a cherished area to the Chinese, they also held the shortest distance between their village and Hong Kong. They tried their hardest to disturb the land as little as possible, but an army of 10,000 fully armored men is bound to make an impact.

Aaron rode at the rear of the army, atop a well-groomed, white destrier. His golden armor clanked as the horse trotted across the fields. Aaron had never ridden a horse before and his gloves clutched the reigns tightly, his fingers turning white in the scalloped gauntlets.

But despite his fear of riding, Aaron was completely fascinated by the land around him. The view from all sides was amazing; he watched as a light wind flicked a leaf from the branch of a tree, laying it gently on the ground. He looked down at Hsai walking beside him, keeping pace with the stallion. He considered asking Hsai about the area, inquiring about the plant life that he himself was unfamiliar with, but quickly decided against it. Hsai had seemed somehow different since their last conversation, acting colder to Aaron. So he opted to ride in silence.

The army reached the edge of the forest when Aaron saw it beyond the hills. The crest of a long, white-stoned wall came into view. As they walked up the hillside, more of the wall revealed itself. Aaron estimated its height to be nearly 25 feet, but having been built on the top of a hill created an illusion that forced Aaron to recalculate his estimate each time they got closer.

As they reached the edge of the wall, Hsai placed his hand on the reins of Aaron's horse. With a sharp tug, the horse stopped. He looked up at Aaron and pointed to the wall.

"We have reached the Great Wall of Japan," Hsai said. "On the other side lies Hong Kong, the last remaining Japanese settlement on the Chinese mainland." Though it had been centuries since the Chinese inhabited the city of Hong Kong, they refused to refer to it by the new Japanese name of "Puyoa City". "This is where our enemies live. This is also where they will die."

Aaron turned from Hsai back to the wall. The sunlight reflected off the massive structure, burning Aaron's eyes but he was unable to blink. He shook his head and looked back at Hsai.

"So, what do we do now?"

Hsai chuckled and turned to him. "We await your orders, my liege."

As the sound of his words dissipated among the wind, something caught his attention. Lifting his head to the sky, Aaron spotted a tiny white speck and watched as it fell through the clouds, trying to discern exactly what it was. Two long, white appendages, wing-like in appearance, projected from each side, flapping wildly from the wind resistance. As the object got closer to the ground, Aaron swore that he could make out the shapes of arms and legs.

Aaron turned back to the wall, his interest in the strange man-bird falling through the sky waning. Far off in the distance, the object collided with the side of the volcano, kicking up a cloud of dust.

CHAPTER 31

Lucifer's shoes clacked against the concrete floor as he strolled through the dank hallway. The cold air of the basement formed a sparkling sheen of condensation on the walls. The blinking light of Lucifer's Bluetooth headset reflected off the walls, illuminating the tight room in continuous blue flashes. A drip of water fell on Lucifer's shoulder. He stopped in his tracks and turned his head toward the wet spot. He looked at it with disdain and tugged on his pocket square and wiped the drip off his suit jacket. Carefully folding the moist fabric, he slid it into his pocket and resumed his walk.

Approaching the door, Lucifer heard the painful shouts from the other side. He turned the knob and gave it a shove, the hinges squealing as the door swung inward. Hearing the noise, Nathaniel hopped up from his stool, a thin, silver chain swinging from his neck.

"Lou," he said, his eyes wide, surprise in his voice. "What are you doing here?"

Lucifer studied the angel chained to the wall. His face was a mess of bruises and contusions, making him nearly unrecognizable. One of his wings hung limply from his back. The other wing was torn from his back and lay on the floor in a puddle of blood and feathers.

Lucifer turned to the Demon. His hands were swollen, his knuckles raw from a night of punching. Blood splattered his face and body. Lucifer reached into his pocket and handed him the handkerchief. "Would you excuse us please?" The Demon nodded, wiping the blood from his face. He walked to the door, closing it as he left.

Folding his hands behind his back, Lucifer walked up to Jehoel. He grabbed the angel's chin and lifted his face. He turned it left, then right, examining the damage the Demon had done. He dropped Jehoel's face and turned to Nathaniel, staring at him for a full minute.

"Has he broken yet?" Lucifer's voice was flat and even, his emotions held in check.

Nathaniel's wing twitched and he reached up to scratch the back of his head. "No, not yet."

Lucifer's eyes flared, red flames engulfing his eyelids. He balled his fist and turned, punching Jehoel in the face with such force that a loud *BOOM* enveloped the room. Jehoel's head snapped to the side, flopped back the other way, before his chin settled to his chest. Lucifer looked down at the splattered blood on his hand and regretted giving the Demon his pocket square. He walked over to Nathaniel and grabbed the corner of his t-shirt. As Lucifer wiped the blood from his hand, Jehoel spoke.

"You'll never win." His words were gurgled as he fought through the blood and saliva pooling in his throat. He opened his mouth and forced himself to cough, a thick wad of phlegm splashed at his feet.

Lucifer rushed back to Jehoel, shoving his face right up to his, careful not to dip his Bruno Maglis in the puddle of bodily fluids. "What was that? Have you even seen the state you're in?"

Jehoel smiled, a stream of blood dribbled down his chin. "What happens to me is irrelevant. Even if I gave you..." He broke into a cough mid-sentence, his body began to convulse. Lucifer took a large step backwards, hoping to avoid getting any other fluids on himself.

The coughing fit subsided and Jehoel continued. "Even if I gave it to you, you'll never be able to control it."

Lucifer returned his smile. He turned to look at Nathaniel, pointed to Jehoel and chuckled. "You hear this guy? He thinks I can't control it." He looked back at Jehoel and stepped closer to him. "And what makes you say that?"

"It was my burden...from its inception. I carry the weight of the Leviathan. Through me, the beast remains docile. I'm the only thing that can keep it tame. If anything should happen to me, it would become a mindless brute, devouring anything in its way."

"Ah, yes. That's all true," Lucifer said, his tone sarcastic. "But you're forgetting one thing. There is something else in the universe that can control the Leviathan. Something more powerful than the Angelic bond you share with it."

Jehoel nodded as well as he could without being able to control his neck. "I haven't forgotten. But the Blade has been lost for millennia. When Belial was exiled, the High Military never recovered his sword. For all we know, it could be anywhere."

"Yes, it could be anywhere." Lucifer extended his arm. Energy crackled around his hand, licking at his fingertips. Flames shot from his palm, wisps of smoke filling the room, Jehoel titled his eyes to the side, watched as the shape of a sword emerged from Lucifer's hand. When the fire and smoke subsided, Lucifer clutched a long sword, black as coal, speckled with tiny white flecks. Jehoel's eyes filled with fear, the remaining blood draining from his face. He didn't have to ask about the appearance of the Blade; he knew it as soon as he saw it.

Before Lucifer came into power, before he was banished from the Angelic High Military, before the AHM even came into existence, Belial held control of the galaxy. He ruled the worlds beneath him, and he did so with the Blade. A weapon crafted from the Universe itself. Completely unbreakable and indestructible, Belial held his power for years, before a crafty upstart soldier named Lucifer tricked him into giving up the sword. The temporary distraction allowed Michael and the AHM to gain the upper hand and overpower Belial, usurping the power from him. But Lucifer, in all his cleverness, hid the blade away, claiming that it was lost when Belial was defeated. Waiting for the moment when it would be useful.

"You're not so impertinent now, are you?" Lucifer asked with a grin as he waved the Blade in front of Jehoel. "You may as well just tell me where I can find the Leviathan so you can save me some time and you tremendous amounts of pain."

The sword flashed and disappeared in a puff of flame. Lucifer straightened his suit jacket and turned to face Nathaniel. Nathaniel crossed his arms, shifting his weight to one leg.

"It's only a matter of time now," Lucifer whispered. "We'll have the Leviathan soon."

"What makes you so sure?"

"He knows he's beaten. He can only hope for a quick death." Lucifer turned back to Jehoel to see his body drooping in the chains. "Finish up here and get everything ready. We're going to the AHM headquarters."

"So soon? We don't have its location yet. What if he…"

Lucifer's eyes flared again. "I said he will." The flames subsided as Lucifer brought his anger under control. "We need to be ready."

CHAPTER 32

"It's a mapping system," Twilana said. "It's small. Portable, but it can scan an area and create a topographic map in real time."

Twilana remained calm as she explained the functions of the wristlet to Hisaki. She knew that if she came off as too eager or too flippant, he would think she was lying. She needed to keep her emotions stable and accentuate the benefits of the weapon to him so that he'd decide the gamble was worth the risk. But ultimately, Matt's and her lives were in his hands.

"A map," he said with disgust. "What good will a map serve? We have maps. We do not need more." Hisaki was displeased with the interruption. He had listened to her explain the "weapon" she promised him, but he seemed skeptical. It is only natural that a criminal sentenced to death would sing her final swan song in the hopes of being freed. He had allowed her bleating to go on for too long, growing impatient with her.

Twilana shook her head. "No, it's more than a map," she said. "It will also show you the locations of your enemy's troops. Imagine knowing where every soldier on the field of battle is."

Rubbing his chin, Hisaki considered the probability. A device that showed him the location of enemy soldiers would be quite powerful. It would mean his army would never be the victim of a surprise attack. And he would be able to plan attacks against enemy camps based on knowledge of their defensive positioning. The idea of owning such a device excited Hisaki, but he remained cautious of his prisoner's proposition.

"And where can I find this 'mapping system'?" he asked.

Twilana tried to lift her head but the ropes kept her from moving. The rash on her neck started to burn. She shifted on her knees to get a better vantage, a wave of painful tingling shot through her legs. "It's in the woods," she said, lifting her eyes to Hisaki. "By the mountain. Where we first met your soldiers." The back of her throat felt dry. She swallowed, but as her mouth had quit producing saliva hours ago, the motion made her break out into a coughing fit.

Hisaki's anger swelled. He stomped toward Twilana and his arm flew across his chest, slapping her across the face. Her head snapped to the side, a large, red handprint quickly developing on her cheek. The force of the slap would have knocked her down had the ropes not held her in place. Hisaki leaned over her. "How do I know you aren't lying to me?" he questioned. "That you aren't just trying to save yourselves?"

"You're going to kill us either way," she replied, her chin resting on the tree stump in front of her. "After we're dead, what do we care if you have the weapon? But if you kill us now, you'll never figure out how to use it"

Hisaki straightened his back and turned to the executioner, giving him a sly smile. She was right; he would kill them no matter the outcome. But could the weapon really be as difficult to control as she claimed? It was possible. He weighed his options for a moment, thinking about the number of casualties his army could suffer at the hands of the Chinese. Having a secret weapon would prevent any needless loss of life. Well, Japanese lives, anyway. If the weapon was as powerful as the woman claimed it to be, the Japanese could easily crush the Chinese.

"Very well then," Hisaki said. He raised a finger to Matt. "He will stay here while you accompany me and a group of soldiers to this weapon. If at any time you attempt to double-cross me, I will kill your friend."

Twilana nodded, her chin scraping against the rough wood.

"When we return," Hisaki continued, "and after you demonstrate the use of this weapon, we will continue here."

Twilana nodded again. It didn't surprise her that he intended to kill them, but at least she bought them some time. She would have to come up with a plan quickly if she wanted to keep them alive.

Hisaki turned to the executioner. "Take the dark one back to the holding cells." He turned and pointed to three armored soldiers. "You will come with us."

One of the soldiers climbed the steps to the stage, pulling a knife from his belt. He cut Twilana's bonds and yanked her to her feet. A second guard grabbed her arm and they dragged her to the front of the stage next to Hisaki. Turning her head, she watched as the axeman cut Matt's ropes and wrenched his arm behind his back. The axeman led Matt down a partially hidden corridor behind the stage and into the castle. She watched him until he was fully engulfed by the darkness before turning back to the crowd and flinching as a tomato smashed against her chest.

Hisaki chuckled as the guts of the tomato dripped down Twilana's shirt. Raising his arms, he called for the crowd to be silent.

"My people! I know I promised you a show. I know I told you that you will bear witness to the deaths of Chinese spies. But that will have to wait."

The crowd erupted into a wave of disapproval, booing and hissing at Hisaki's broken promise. The noise resonated through the courtyard, causing the flimsy wooden platform to vibrate. Hisaki folded his hands behind his back, allowing them a few brief moments to express their concerns, understanding their disappointment. He raised his arm, and the crowd fell into silence.

"These two have information that will allow us to defeat the Chinese with the swiftest of actions. Once we have what we need, what we deserve, then I promise you, the show will commence."

The disapproval of the crowd quickly turned to excitement. Hisaki lowered his arms and placed his palms together. He closed his eyes, bathing in the adoration of the crowd. A smile spread across his lips as he imagined his victory. He turned and walked down a set of rickety wooden steps, heading down the corridor toward the castle.

CHAPTER 33

Aaron gave a short, shrill whistle, startling Hsai. The plump man covered his ears as Aaron chuckled beside him on his horse. Aaron looked up at General Po as he trotted closer.

Shortly after arriving at the wall, Hsai told Aaron that General Po would be his right-hand man for the coming battle. The oldest, highest-ranking man in the Chinese army, Po had been in the military since his youth. He spent years as a footsoldier in the army before proving himself as a competent strategist. Hearing this, Aaron expected a chiseled, hard-ass soldier, like a mix between R. Lee Ermy and Chow Yun Fat. But Po was nothing like he imagined. He had a genial demeanor and was very relatable. He was a man of few words, but he managed to make those words count. From the moment Aaron met him, he had liked the man. Po very much reminded Aaron of his own grandfather. That is, he would have, if Aaron's grandfather were Chinese.

Aaron gave Po a warm smile. "Before we can do anything, we need to get inside the wall," Po said. "Chow should be returning soon with news of what we can expect to find." They sent a soldier out to recon the area surrounding the wall, hoping to compose a viable attack plan. He had been gone for hours and Po was secretly beginning to worry. He considered sending out a second wave, perhaps a group of soldiers this time, but he didn't want to alarm His Majesty.

"Good," Aaron said with a tight nod. He felt his stomach do a back-flip, nervous at the thought of invading a town. Though he felt confident, emboldened by his previous battle experience, this was certainly different. For starters, he had the burden of being in charge, leading an army that would probably be better off without him. Wait…probably? No, they were definitely better off without him.

But Aaron was also feeling lost without Matt. The pair had been together since second grade. Granted not every single, solitary moment but just about. By the time they got into high school, they already earned the nicknames "Batman and Robin", though the argument stood about who was who. So now that Matt wasn't with him in what was about to be his most nerve-wracking experience left him feeling…empty. He still held hope that Matt was alive but as time went on, those hopes became smaller and smaller.

Aaron swallowed his hesitance. "Good," he repeated. "Once we know where we can enter, we will send in three men." Aaron hopped down from his horse, dug around in a pile of tall grass, pulling out a long, gnarled stick. He shook the dirt from the stick and traced a rectangle in the dirt. He then added three lines within the rectangle, two of which arched to the sides while the third extended straight out. "These men will survey the city, and look for any weaknesses in the wall."

Aaron drew a circle on the opposite side of the rectangle. "On the other side, here, we will have a group of men dig a hole beneath the wall. When that hole is large enough, we will send three more men inside, and discover where the soldiers are stationed."

Hsai and Po looked at the shapes Aaron drew in the dirt. They turned to each other, faces canvases of confusion. Though they remained silent, their eyes spoke volumes about the validity of Aaron's plans. Above Hsai's shoulder, something caught Po's attention. He spotted a lone soldier stumbling down a hill, rushing toward them.

"Chow returns," he announced.

Pushing himself the last couple of feet, Chow stopped among the circle of men, panting heavily. His chest shook with each breath. He placed his hands on his knees and drew in deep, steady breaths. After a few moments of this, he turned to General Po and delivered his intel. "I have found the gate, about two miles over that hill," he said, pointing to the east. "A small group of soldiers just exited Hong Kong, heading into the forest." He turned his waist, pointed off into the direction of the forest. "They were accompanied by The Lord Hisaki and a female."

Aaron's heart fluttered at the news. Could it be that Chow saw Twilana? Could Twilana still be alive? If she had made it through the portal OK, then that means Matt could have too. Realizing his thoughts had turned hysterical, Aaron forced himself to look at this situation rationally; the woman Chow mentioned may not even be Twilana, but a concubine that these soldiers are taking out into the forest to have a good time. Aaron imagined this was the kind of thing people did before cable television was invented.

Aaron stepped up to Chow, his eyes focused on the scout's face. "What did the woman look like?"

Chow stared at Aaron, his face turning from exhaustive fatigue to horrific embarrassment. He dropped to his knees and bowed his head. "Please forgive me, Lord, for disrespecting you so. I should be flogged a thousand times with the tentacle of a squid. I am truly sor-…"

Aaron waved his hand, interrupting him. "I don't care about that. What did she look like?"

Without looking up, Chow answered. "Very strange. She had long blue hair, unlike anything I have ever seen on a woman."

Aaron's stomach did another flip, but this time in a good way. It was Twilana. She's alive and out there in the forest. Overpowering a few soldiers in the cover of the trees was going to be much easier than taking an entire city. Then when Twilana was back, she could help them find and rescue Matt. He would also appreciate having her combat experience handy if Hsai forced him to follow through with attacking the Japanese.

"OK, listen up" Aaron said, much more aggressively than he had intended. He didn't care if he offended anyone. He wanted his friend back. And besides, he was a god to them. Gods were supposed to be jerks, or at least that's what the Greeks led him to believe. "I want a group to follow this Hisaki guy and the woman. Chow, you show them where they were headed and stick with them."

Chow lifted his eyes to Aaron and nodded, quickly dropping his gaze to the ground again.

"But I want you to stay out of sight. The rest of us will station ourselves on the edge of the forest. When they come out into the field, that's when we will make our move. Everyone understand?"

A roar of agreement erupted from the soldiers. Aaron smiled, both surprised and appreciative of the support he was receiving from the army he had known for less than a day.

"All right, everyone. Let's roll out."

The soldiers' excitement settled. They looked around at each other, their faces a sea of befuddlement. Aaron looked out at them, wondering why they weren't moving. Hsai cleared his throat, leaned in closer to Aaron. "I'm sorry, sire," he said. "Would you like them to advance now?"

"Yes, yes," Aaron said, flicking his wrist as if he were shooing a fly. "Get moving."

Hsai relayed the order in Chinese and the soldiers dispersed. A small group led by Chow broke off and headed toward the hills. The remainder of the army followed Aaron and Po to the edge of the treeline, fanning out to cover the forest.

Aaron had a feasible plan in place. Now all he had to do was figure out how to hide an army of 10,000 men on the outskirts of a giant field. He looked up at the sun and watched as it dipped below the horizon, hoping the coming darkness would help to keep them out of sight.

CHAPTER 34

The soldiers led Twilana around the foot of the mountain, retracing her footsteps from the moment she landed on this world. Hisaki had taken a number of precautions with her to ensure she didn't try to overpower them. They bound her wrists with thick, hempen rope, which was secured to a rope tied around her waist. One of the soldiers held the other end of the rope, leading her around like a dog on a leash.

Despite her bonds, her mind never stopped developing a plan to escape. She led them around the area, searching for signs of the battle that ensued just after her arrival. Many of the landmarks were familiar; a pine tree, a boulder, a large ditch. She knew they were close, but she couldn't seem to find the location. The rain had been so strong that it washed away almost all trace of the battle.

Turning her head, she caught a faint glint of light in the distance. She bolted toward the object but was quickly jerked back by the soldier. She dropped to the ground on her butt, her breath cut short by the impact. She pushed herself up on her hands. The soldier grabbed her arm and yanked her back to her feet. She looked at him from the corner of her eye, determined to cause the man pain. He escorted her to the object on the ground.

Twilana picked up the cracked, silver helmet, recognizing it immediately. It belonged to the soldier that she threw into the tree. She turned her head quickly, replaying the fight in her mind. The sun was setting and only a few rays of light cast themselves on the ground. Shadows already began to cover the area, making it difficult to see. She knew that her time to locate the wristlet was short so she needed to hurry.

"I need some light," she shouted.

Hisaki looked at the soldier carrying their only torch and nodded. The soldier rushed to Twilana, holding the sputtering flame high above his head. She looked from side to side, frantically searching the ground, trying to remember every detail of the incident. Though she maintained her sense of urgency about the situation, the soldier holding the rope did not. Each time she tried to rush over to a place the wristlet might be, he would pull her back, forcing her to move slower. The soldiers all thought this was hilarious; even Hisaki chuckled the first few times. But Twilana failed to see the humor, growing more and more impatient with his actions. She looked over her shoulder, shooting the soldier a nasty look, when a second glimmer at the base of a large bush caught her attention.

"There," she said, pointing at the glimmer. "There it is."

The guard looked in the direction she pointed and turned back to her. He cocked his head, indicating that she should retrieve the object. Twilana hesitated, knowing his intentions. She walked toward the bush, slowly wrapping the rope around her hands until the rope grew taut. As she neared the object, she gave the rope a hard yank, dragging the soldier. He fell into a deep puddle, splashing mud as he landed. The other soldiers broke out into fits of laughter as he tried to pull himself up from the ground.

Hisaki, on the other hand, was less amused. Gliding up to Twilana, he backhanded her across the face. She doubled over as her cheek tingled. Hisaki grabbed a fistful of her hair and pulled her backward.

"Do you not grasp the danger you are in, woman?" A stream of spittle formed at the corner of his mouth. "I suggest you quit toying with me and produce the weapon that you promised."

Twilana nodded as best she could with her head being impeded. He released her with a shove, pushing her backward. She reached up to rub the back of her head but the ropes prevented her from moving. She looked back at Hisaki before walking toward the bush.

She dropped to her knees and fumbled around on the ground. He fingers landed on a sharp, cold object. She pulled it closer to get a better look and saw that it was a long, jagged rock, about the length of her index finger. Glancing back she saw Hisaki and the torch bearer padding closer to her. She slipped the rock into the sleeve of her shirt and went back to digging in the dirt and nettles.

Her fingernail *tinked* on something hard. Wrapping her fingers around it, she pulled it closer. The torch bearer was right behind her, casting the area in full torchlight. She brushed the dirt from the object and breathed an audible sigh of relief when she recognized the familiar display screen.

It's still here, she thought to herself. *Thank Janus, it's still here.*

Hisaki looked down at her as she hugged the object to her chest. He stepped backward, cautious that she had not lured him into a trap. He waved his hands and pointed to the woman. The two soldiers came from behind him and grabbed Twilana's arms. They pulled her to her feet and spun her around to face Hisaki. One of the soldiers pulled his katana from its scabbard and placed the blade against her neck.

"If you make a move," he said, his voice a higher pitch than Twilana expected, "your blood with be spilt upon this ground."

Twilana nodded, careful of the blade near her neck. Hisaki moved slowly, his eyes never leaving the metal object in her hand. His arm shot out before him and snatched the wristlet from her grasp. He turned it over in his hands, examining the alien technology. He ran his fingers over the smooth, silver casing, felt the buttons scratch his fingertips. Even with all of the things he had received from the English over the years, gifts bestowed upon him for his faithful service, he had never seen a device like this.

He motioned for the torchman to examine the device in better light. As the torchman approached, the light from the flame rolled across the dull, black screen. Hisaki stared at his muted reflection, unsure of what to do next.

Hisaki looked up at Twilana. "How does it work?"

"Press the big, red button to turn it on," she said calmly.

Hisaki chuckled. "And I suppose that this button ignites the powder inside, causing the device to explode."

"No," Twilana said, shaking her head. "It doesn't use powder."

Hisaki stared at her blankly. "Either way, I will not take my chances." He handed the wristlet to the torchman and instructed him to press the button.

Hesitating, the torchman took the wristlet from his master. His hands shook as he steadied his thumb over the button. He squeezed his eyes tightly and pressed. It clicked and a soft humming noise filled the air. Satisfied that all of his appendages were still intact, he opened his eyes and looked at the device. The screen blinked to life, casting a blue light across his face. On the screen, the word "PROCESSING" shone proudly. Hisaki grabbed the device from the torchman and stared down at it.

"What's next?" he demanded.

"Just wait," she replied. "It's scanning the topography of the area and building a real-time map."

As if on cue, the wristlet beeped. Hisaki looked down at the screen and saw the different colors that denoted his surroundings. Bunches of green coalesced on a black plain, which faded through shades of grey. Five small, yellow dots congregated in the center of the screen.

"So this must be us," Hisaki said, pointing to the dots. "And these the trees behind us."

"Yes," Twilana said. "If you slide your finger across the screen, it will show you everything else around you."

Intrigued, Hisaki swiped the screen with his finger and the image shifted, the yellow dots disappearing and more green bunches coming into view. Hisaki smiled as he moved the terrain, tossing it from side to side. He stopped as he noticed a line of reds dots floating back and forth next to a row of green bunches.

"What is this?" he asked, tilting the wristlet toward Twilana.

Twilana looked at the screen and shrugged. "Other people, apparently. It looks like they're lined up on the edge of the woods."

His soldiers would never move without his orders, so this formation couldn't be friendly. Hisaki surmised that it must be the Chinese waiting to attack. Ordinarily, their position would be a sound and tactical move. But the Chinese could not have realized that Hisaki would come across a device that would invalidate all of their strategies.

A greasy smile spread across Hisaki's face. He turned back to Twilana and gave her a mocking bow. "You have done the Empire of Japan a great service," he said, looking to the guards. He held the wristlet out before him. "With this, we will be unstoppable."

The guards looked at each other and smiled. One of them looked back at Hisaki.

"Should we kill the woman now, my lord?" he asked.

Hisaki considered the guard's proposal for a second. "Not yet," he replied, shaking his head. "All the way out here in the dark, her death will have little celebration. We shall execute her and her friend in the morning."

*   *   *   *   *

Matt lay on the floor of his cell, the dirt from the ground sticking to his sweaty body. His temperature had risen well above normal, the effects of the infection now swimming through his bloodstream. He hadn't eaten a full meal in almost two days. Sleep deprivation clouded his judgment and wrecked hell on his imagination. Staring at the far wall of the prison, he watched the torches' light dance like ballerinas on stage. He hummed the theme to the *Nutcracker Suite,* though he was still lucid enough to wonder to himself how he knew the theme to the *Nutcracker Suite.*

The guard stood next to the door and watched as Matt rocked back and forth mumbling softly to himself. Not being a native English speaker, the guard did not understand the words his prisoner spoke. Little did he realize, not even someone who spoke English fluently would understand the gibberish Matt muttered. The guard felt sorry for his prisoner, an emotion he had never shown in his career before. Granted, he still despised him based on the fact that he was a spy for the Chinese, but even a dying dog on the side of the road draws pity from an onlooker, despite the dog's reputation as a savage beast.

Pushing the feelings from his mind, the guard relaxed himself knowing that it didn't matter. In a couple of hours, this pathetic man would be out of his misery.

CHAPTER 35

The sun was beginning to set over New Eden, the tall buildings casting long shadows across the street. Though rush hour traffic had thinned over an hour ago, there was still a steady stream of cars on the road. Throngs of people crowded the sidewalks, a few of them heading home from a hard day's work, others looking to drown the night away at a local bar. The heat of the city began to dissipate, leaving behind the sweet smell of summer. Of course, this being New Eden, the air always smelled wonderful.

Lauren wove her way through a crowd of pedestrians. Having traded her pink camouflage for a pair of form fitting blue jeans and a red tanktop, her long red hair pulled back into a ponytail, she blended in with the crowd. No one paid her any mind, until she elbowed her way past a group of business-suited professionals. A few of them hurled insults, saying accusatory things about her mother as she brushed stiffly past them, but she ignored them. She didn't have time for pleasantries, which was a good thing for the yuppies; Lauren's idea of "manners" is to minimize the pain when she obliterated someone.

She looked down at the paper in her hand, her lips moving as she read the address. Looking up, she spotted the street sign on the corner. *A couple more blocks*, she thought to herself. She darted into the street, narrowly missed an oncoming taxi. The cab driver blasted the horn, shouted something to Lauren behind the safety of the vehicle. She turned to the driver and placed her hand of the hood of the car. A moment later, black smoke billowed from the hood as it began to melt around the engine block. The driver's eyes went wide as he watched the outline of his car's innards begin to form in the yellow metal. Lauren smiled at the man, tipped her head and hurried off.

Rounding a corner, Lauren looked up at the building. Framed in gold, the glass structure was the tallest in New Eden. The sun's rays reflected off the golden trimming, the street around the building shined in a bright, orange hue. Golden letters hung high up on the building, twenty five feet tall if they were an inch. "AHM" they announced. Angelic High Military. Lauren wasn't one for anxiety, but her stomach began to do cartwheels. She took a deep breath to calm her nerves.

Lauren casually strolled up to the entrance, trying to avoid looking suspicious. Placing her hand on the revolving door, she gave it a gentle push and entered the lobby. Black and white checked titles spread out along the floor, the lobby's walls featured beautifully painted Renaissance-style frescoes. Each painting featured the image of an angel. A few were portraits, commissioned to showcase some of New Eden's most influential angels. Others depicted famous historical battles, the kinds of scenes found in a standard cherubic school book.

In the center of the lobby stood an enormous marble fountain, two figures entwined in a loving embrace. The lovers had a spray of water erupting from all sides, cascading down their bodies into the pool below. Lauren eyed the fountain as she walked past it.

Looking up, Lauren glanced at the sun through the skylight. Her eyes traced the top floors, a long, silver banister encircling each level. The open layout of the building gave each floor a breathtaking view down into the lobby, making the building one of the most visited office buildings in New Eden.

"Can I help you, miss?" A voice called out from the back end of the lobby, startling Lauren. She looked up to find a stout man dressed in a blue button down shirt. A tiny gold shield was pinned above his left breast, an even tinier nametag on the right. He sat in a circular enclosure, surrounded by computer monitors. Lauren's face changed from bewildered to confused as she shuffled toward the man.

"I'm sorry, sir," she said, allowing her voice to crack. "I think I'm lost." She breathed quickly, letting her hands tremble slightly.

The man grinned at her, warm and fatherly. He could sense her nervousness. "It's OK, sweetie. Just take a deep breath and calm down." He raised and lowered his hands a few times, pantomiming his advice. He pushed a tall, wheeled chair around the desk and indicated that she sit. Lauren complied and inhaled deeply releasing her breath slowly. Her face changed to a placid calmness and the security guard's smile grew.

"Good, good. Now, what can I help you with?"

"Well, see, I'm looking for my brother, but I don't know his phone number. There's been a… It's our mother. She's sick and I can't call him while he's at work. But I really need to talk to him because he…"

"Whoa whoa whoa," the guard said. "Slow down a little. You're getting excited." Lauren inhaled deeply again. "Now, what's your brother's name?"

"Mendrion. He works in the records room."

"OK. Mendrion," he repeated. He waddled around the side of the computer and hunched over the keyboard. He hunted-and-pecked the name into the computer, searching the buildings staff records for a match. A list of names blinked onto the screen and he scrolled through them. Lauren rose from the chair and leaned over the desk to watch the screen as the names flew by. The guard stopped at the Ms, using his finger to study each name individually.

"Hmmm… No, I don't see any 'Mendrion' here. You sure he doesn't work in the downtown branch?"

"No," Lauren replied, reapplying the flustered façade. "It's definitely here."

"OK, let me look again." The guard retyped the name, sorted through the list of results again. Lauren watched as his finger slid down the screen, spotting the name she was looking for.

Metatron……Grigorian Administration……..Floor 28.

The guard shook his head and looked back at Lauren. "I'm sorry, honey, but I don't see any 'Mendrion' on the list." He watched as Lauren's nervous smile turned to a grimace. His eyes flicked to her hand as a small sphere of fire formed in her palm.

"What are you…" His words were cut off as she waved her wrist, sending the ball of fire straight to him. His hands shot to his face, patting at the flames, struggling to put out the fire. But the

Hellfire quickly spread through the rest of his body, his poly-cotton blend uniform catching like dried straw. He dropped to the ground and flopped around feebly. The flames quickly burned throughout his body, leaving a pile of blackened bones and smoldering ash.

Lauren pulled a cell phone from her pocket and tapped the screen a few times. Holding the phone to her ear, she walked around the desk and clacked the keyboard with her free hand. The computer screen changed, the words "Security Protocol" scrolling across the top. She reached down and pulled a breath mint from a half-empty bag next to the computer and pushed it through the plastic wrap as a voice erupted from the phone.

"Do you have it?"

She slid the breath mint under her tongue. "Yep."

"Good," Lucifer replied. "It's time to let them in."

Lauren clicked off the phone and placed it on the desk beside her. With both hands she worked at the keyboard, changing the buildings security settings to OFF. Around her, the faint clicking sound indicated the electronic locks on the doors all releasing. She rolled the breath mint around in her mouth as she shut down the entire building's security measures.

*　*　*　*　*

Nathaniel circled the old, white box truck around the parking lot of the Angelic High Military building for nearly twenty minutes before his cell phone chirped from the center console. "About friggin' time," he muttered to himself before cutting the wheel, turning the truck to the roadway marked "Deliveries". Making a quick K-turn, he backed the truck up to the loading bay door. Normally, this area was reserved for deliveries of office supplies, bottled water, and battle weapons. Never before had it been used for a delivery like this one. As the truck bumped into the building, he threw the gear shift into "Park" and hopped down from the cab.

He walked up the steps to the side of the loading bay and turned the knob on the steel door. A sign hung on the door that read "PLEASE USE BELL". Nathaniel paid it no mind. Well, actually, he did pay it mind by tearing it down, but he wasn't about to follow their directions. As he passed through the doorway into the warehouse, he was immediately spotted by two cherubs unpacking a large, wooden crate.

"Hey, you can't be back here," one of the cherubs

shouted. They walked toward Nathaniel, trying to act tougher than they actually were. In truth, cherubs weren't the strongest of angels and were usually reduced to manual labor like moving boxes, cleaning toilets, and testing new brands of toothpaste. The stuff the other angels wouldn't do.

Nathaniel held his hand out to them and they paused, unsure of what the black-winged angel was doing. A pillar of fire flew from his hand, forming a sword. Quick as a shot, Nathaniel spun the sword around them, hacking at them with the flaming blade. Their eyes grew wide and they turned to escape but Nathaniel was in the air in a blink and swooped down, blocking their path. He thrust the sword at one of them, catching him just above the pelvis. The cherub stopped short. Nathaniel spun to his left, opening a huge gash in the cherub's stomach. He fell to the floor, his tiny wings twitching.

He reached out and grabbed the second cherub by the throat as he stunned stood over his co-worker. Nathaniel gripped his throat and lifted him off the ground. The cherub's hands clawed at Nathaniel, his feet kicked frailly. He tossed the cherub across the warehouse and he crashed against a metal rolling door.

Nathaniel walked back to the loading bay doors, counting them until he found the one that held the truck. He raised the sword and brought it down on the padlock securing the loading bay door. The metal dropped to the ground with a hard *thunk*. Nathaniel rolled the door upward, revealing the box truck. He opened the truck's door and was greeted by a hundred pairs of glowing eyes looking out at him from the dark.

"OK, boys," he said to the waiting Demons. "It's time to play."

CHAPTER 36

The sun dipped below the horizon, casting the countryside in near complete darkness. Only a thin veil of purple sky remained of the long, stressful day. Minute by minute, the darkness crept across the land, making Twilana uneasy. Having grown up in a world of man-made light, she was not used to this level of blackness. She watched the shadows from the torchman's light play among the trees, her mind recalling a few of the horrors of the wars she had led. She remembered the friends she lost as well as the lives she's taken.

Forcing these thoughts from her brain, she formulated a plan to escape. Now that Hisaki had the wristlet, she and Matt would be executed. She managed to buy them a few extra hours, but now she had to find a way to eliminate the inevitable.

One of the guards held her by the elbow and led her through the forest. She flexed her arm, testing his strength, trying to determine his weak point so she could figure out a way to overtake him. If she dropped her body to the ground fast enough, she would be able to slip free of his grip and use the surprise to her advantage. A kick to the back of his knee would knock him down, giving her the chance to attack the second guard, who walked a mere two yards from her. She could close that distance quickly, slipping the stone from her sleeve and burying it into his neck before the torchman even noticed what was happening. Taking care of him would be simple. From his countenance, she could tell that he had very little combat training, making him a simple target.

She could do that with both hands tied behind her back, so having them tied in front of her would make that task even easier.

But she was hesitant to attack. Though she could gauge the skills of the soldiers, Hisaki was much harder to read. He carried himself like a pompous, spoon-fed dictator, but his body structure told a different story. He was a tall man with broad shoulders, quite unlike the leaders and diplomats on Janus, which led Twilana to believe that he was accustomed to staying in shape. His knuckles were scarred and calloused, the markings of a man that has been in a few fights. Without being certain of his abilities, attacking Hisaki was far too risky. And he was too far away from her. If he was as well trained as she believed, Hisaki could easily over take her with a rock to the skull while she was busy with the soldiers. The risk, at this point, far exceeded the gain.

Twilana was also concerned for Matt's safety. He was still held prisoner in the well-guarded Japanese city. Even if she did manage to defeat the four men here, how would she be able to get back into the city and get to him? She knew nothing of the layout of the stronghold, and if one of these guards, or Hisaki himself, got back to the prison before her, then the citizens would again be deprived of a public execution because he would be killed on the spot.

Twilana couldn't let that happen. Matt risked his life to help her when she needed it. If she wasn't willing to help him at the risk of her own life... She wasn't about to fail him in his time of need.

She squinted against the darkness, spotting the edge of the forest and the wall surrounding Puyoa City far beyond that. Knowing they were close to the city, her mind again drifted to the idea of escape. *It's now or never*, she said to herself. If she were going to make her move, she was running out of time.

Hisaki raised his hand, ordering the party to stop. Looking down at the wristlet, he tracked the tiny red dots as they moved on the screen. Tilting his head up, he looked off ahead of him, peering through the darkness. It took a minute but he caught a glimmer of light, the reflection of moonlight off the metal of a soldier's uniform. He looked down at the wristlet and just as he figured, matched the location or the red dot to the location of the glimmer.

"Your device works well," he said to Twilana, a sinister smile on his face. Hisaki pointed to the two guards and motioned to the edge of the forest.

"Prepare yourselves for an attack."

The guards nodded. The one holding Twilana pulled her back, tying the loose end of the rope around a tree. He tugged on the rope to make sure it was secure, joining the other guard and rushed off.

As he disappeared among the trees, Twilana slipped the stone from her sleeve and sawed at the rope.

CHAPTER 37

Aaron watched the light as it flickered playfully between the trees. Since it first appeared, the flame remained in the same spot, swaying back and forth. It didn't move backward or forward. Just basically circled in one area. Aaron became transfixed by the flame, watching as it twinkled in the distance, the soft breeze flicking burnt embers from its crest.

"This is taking too long," Po said. "They should have arrived by now." His patience had been wearing thin since the moment they took their positions. Though he would never admit it, he felt that Aaron's attack plan was foolish. His plans to send soldiers into the fray proved that he had little idea of formulating an attack plan, utilizing men to maximize enemy losses while minimizing casualties. Aaron may have been the savior of China, but he needed to leave the strategizing to the professionals.

Hsai placed his hand on Po's shoulder, a small gesture to comfort the general. "Have faith, friend." He turned to Hsai, his eyes belying his impatience. Shaking his head, he looked back toward the flame in the forest.

Aaron spun his horse around, eyeing the walled city on the other side of the plain. He saw movement along the top of the wall, sentries keeping guard over Hong Kong. The large, wooden gate loomed in the center, the lone passage across the trench encircling the camp. He wondered what other defenses they had on the other side of the wall. Was it possible for this platoon, armed only with their swords, arrows, and spears to get past a fortress like that, fighting back flaming boulders, boiling oil, and maybe even trained alligators? And what about Matt? Could he be beyond that wall? Could the Japanese have found him like they found Twilana?

One thing at a time, he thought to himself.

"They are approaching," Po announced.

Turning back to the forest, Aaron saw the ball of light bouncing toward them. From its size, he could tell that it wasn't moving very fast but it definitely was heading their way. Aaron placed his hand on the hilt of the sword at his waist.

All eyes remained focused on the flame, eagerly waiting for the moment to strike. A few of them shuffled uneasily, anxious for the battle to begin. No one said a word, the only noise the chirping of crickets and the crinkling of leaves in the breeze.

The braying of a horse startled Aaron. He looked to his left and watched as the horse bucked wildly. The soldier atop the horse wrapped the reins tightly around his hands, struggling to keep from being thrown from the mount. However, the horse wasn't the only challenge the soldier faced; he also had to deal with a large battleaxe embedded in his chest.

Aaron's head snapped toward the woods, a quick movement in the bushes catching his attention. From the corner of his eye, he noticed Po nock an arrow to his bow and take aim at the area. A metallic clang rang out near Po, his arrow flying harmlessly up into the air. Po fell from his horse, a cloud of dust rising as he landed on the hard ground. Beside him lay an oblong helmet, a large dent in one side.

Po picked himself up and grabbed his bow. He notched a second arrow and turned toward the woods, ready to face the invading force. His eyes moved all along the treeline, widening as they noticed how the flame engulfed a number of trees and bushes and burned out of control.

"My Lord," cried Po. "I believe we have a problem."

Aaron watched the fire as it spread from tree to tree, fueled by the dried leaves and twigs that littered the forest floor. He felt the heat on his face, the smoke burning his eyes. His horse bucked angrily, frightened by the spreading conflagration. Aaron pulled at the reins, forcing the animal under his control. The destrier turned to the right, moving back a few steps. Aaron reached down and pulled on its bridle, patting its snout gently. Looking up, he spotted four dark silhouettes standing in front of the flames. Aaron sat up in the saddle, pulling his sword from its sheathe.

"Over here," he shouted, the tip of his blade pointing at the figures.

Po pivoted on his heels, ready to unleash his arrow. He paused a moment, steadying his bow on the nearest target. As he aimed, a loud *POP* erupted from the darkness. Po's hand went limp and the arrow flew harmlessly into the treetops. Reaching down, he placed his hand on his stomach. His fingertips came away bloody. He dropped the bow and fell to his knees, collapsing in the dirt.

A Japanese soldier burst through the bushes in front of Aaron, a small, silver dagger clutched in his hand. Dressed in only his underclothes, the soldier moved quickly, unencumbered by the weight of excess armor. His body was covered in dirt, making him nearly invisible in the darkness.

Seeing the half-naked soldier, Aaron thought he would have the upper hand. Not wearing armor made the man quick, but it also made him vulnerable. Aaron swung his sword but the soldier ducked, easily rolling under the attack. Rising swiftly from the ground, he thrust his arm toward Aaron's horse, burying the dagger in its neck. A stream of blood sprayed from the animal, its cries of pain echoing in the night. He dragged the dagger through the horse's flesh, opening a gaping wound in its throat. The horse dropped, sending Aaron tumbling to the ground. The soldier broke into a run across the plain, heading for the castle.

A second figure erupted from the woods, taller and leaner than the first, garbed in underclothes and dirt like his predecessor. The soldier spotted Aaron on the ground, noticing his sword lying a few feet away. He leaned down and scooped up the blade, aiming the point at Aaron's face.

A third figure closely followed the second. With an impressive leap, it landed on the soldier's back, and they tumbled together in the dirt. Pulling off his dragon helm, Aaron watched as the two rolled around on the ground, spotting the long, blue hair whipping back and forth during the tussle. His heart pounded in his chest, joy filling his body to see Twilana again.

The soldier swung his fist at Twilana, cracking her cheek. She ignored the blow and thrust her palm upward into the soldier's nose. Blood exploded from his face as his nose shattered, his eyes instantly swelling shut. Twilana intertwined her fingers and brought her fists crashing down on the man's chest. A breath of air escaped him and he wheezed maniacally. She pulled the sword from the soldier's grasp and dragged the blade across his neck. Blood gushed down his chest as a wet gurgling poured from his wound. He twitched a few times before his body went still.

Twilana straddled the man for a moment, her breath coming in short bursts. Placing a hand on her knee, she pushed herself to her feet, turning to find Aaron on the ground.

"Are you OK?" he asked, looking up at her with a mixture of concern and delight. He glanced at the bruises on her cheek, his eyes darting to the gash on her forehead. Twilana laughed as she extended her hand to him. He grabbed it and pulled himself up.

"I was going to ask you the same thing."

He stared into her bright, purple eyes. "I'm fine," he said through ragged breath. "I'm just glad to see that you're all right."

She smiled and wrapped her free arm around his neck, hugging him tightly.

Aaron placed his arms around her waist and pulled her to him. His breath caught in the back of his throat as they embraced, his heart jumping with relief. It had only been a day since he last saw her but it felt as if it had been years.

Twilana placed her hand on his chest and let it linger there for a moment before she pushed him away gently. "Come on," she said, slipping her hand into his. "We need to get to Matt."

They turned toward the castle, ignoring the raging blaze behind them. The fire cast the plains in an eerie orange light, making the sight before them all the more frightening. The Chinese army had charged against the castle, turning their assault on the Japanese. The sentries atop the wall spotted the attack and alerted the city guard. They lowered the drawbridge, releasing a phalanx of Japanese soldiers to meet the Chinese in battle. Swords *clanged* in the far distance. Large boulders flew over the wall, exploding in showers of dirt as they crashed to the ground. An ear-piercing screech sounded through the night sky as a barrage of missiles rocketed through the air and exploded on the wall around the city, tearing huge holes in it like wet tissue paper. A massive battle sparked as the two slides clashed in the moonlight.

"If we hurry," Twilana said, "we can use the confusion to our advantage and sneak into the city."

Aaron nodded and they began the long sprint across the

plain. They ran a few feet before a flash of white light exploded behind Aaron's eyes. When the light dispersed he found himself lying on the ground again.

Looking up, he saw Twilana being restrained by a large, well-dressed man. His fingers wrapped around her wrist, his fingertips leaving white halos as they dug into her flesh. In his other hand he held a small pistol, its barrel pressed to her temple.

The man spoke to her but the spinning in Aaron's head made it impossible for him to concentrate on the words. He fumbled around on the ground, searching for a rock or a tree branch or anything he could use as a weapon. His hand fell upon Po's lifeless body beside him, his fingers finding the bowstring lying next to his unmoving hand. Aaron wrapped his fingers around the string and pulled the bow closer. With his other hand, he reached for an arrow from the quiver still slung across Po's back.

Rising to his feet, Aaron nocked the arrow and raised it toward the man. Shaking the stars from his eyes, he said, "Drop it, sir, or I will drop you."

Hisaki turned to find Aaron staring at him, an arrow pointed directly at his chest. He watched the man, a stranger to him, feeling not an ounce of fear. He straightened his back, looked Aaron in the eyes and said, "You refer to me as 'sir,' but I do not believe you truly feel me worthy of the respect."

Aaron shook his head, embarrassed by Hisaki's words. He glanced at Twilana and asked, "Does no one know about *sarcasm* on this world?"

Twilana shrugged, unsure of the concept of sarcasm herself. Hisaki took a step to his right, dragging Twilana with him. Aaron lifted his arms, leveling the bow on Hisaki's head.

"That would not be wise," Aaron said, pulling the arrow back farther. He motioned to the weapon and said, "Drop it now."

"You do realize that I have a gun, right?" Hisaki asked. He was rather calm for a man with an arrow aimed at him. "Do you really think you can harm me before I kill her?"

"No, I don't," Aaron replied. "But what I do know is that your pistol needs to be reloaded after every shot. So, you can shoot her, but then my arrow *will* kill you. Or, you can use your shot and take me out. However, once the gun goes off, she will overpower you, slicing your head off at the neck. Either way, you die."

Hisaki considered the proposal, disliking both outcomes. He extended his arm and dropped the pistol. Twilana jerked her arm backwards, burying her elbow just under Hisaki's ribcage. He doubled over and she spun from his grip.

Aaron stepped up to Hisaki and placed the tip of the arrow against his neck, seething as he stood over the man. All of the fear and anger and anxiety of the last couple of days bubbled up inside of him, pushing him to do something outside of his nature. He wanted to hurt this man, to see him bleed. He dug the arrow deeper into his neck, feeling a tingle of joy as the man flinched in pain.

Twilana placed her hand on his arm. Aaron looked down at her fingers.

"Don't," she said, her voice flat and gentle. "We need him. He can bring us to Matt."

Aaron felt his body calming, the tremors in his hands subsiding. Stepping back, he jammed the arrow into the ground. Staring at Hisaki's hunched form, he watched as the man struggled to catch his breath. He lifted his knee, slamming his patella into his nose, crushing it. A loud *crunch* echoed in the darkness and a stream of blood flowed from his nostrils. Hisaki's hands shot to his face as he crumpled to the ground, howling in pain.

Twilana smiled.

CHAPTER 38

The prison guard sat on the stool, legs splayed, chin resting on his chest. The sound of his snoring echoed off the walls of the tiny room. Once Matt fell asleep, or more accurately, "passed out", the guard felt it safe to catch a little rest himself (though being on duty never stopped him from sleeping on the job before). After forty minutes of watching Matt lay unconscious on a pile of dirty straw, he nodded off

Despite his deep sleep, the guard was roused by the ruckus from out in the courtyard. Startled by the noise, the stool tipped over, spilling the guard out onto the floor. Looking around in confusion, he realized where he was and pushed himself to his feet. He brushed the dirt and hay from his uniform and cast an uneasy glance at his prisoner.

Matt lay in the center of the cage, his arms and legs sprawled out in a large X. The bandage wrapping his hand had turned almost completely brown with dried blood and his shoulder looked no better. Small snores emanated from his nose.

The guard tugged on the door of the cage, making sure it was fastened. Satisfied with the security of the prison, as well as the unlikelihood of the prisoner waking up any time soon, he unsheathed his sword and headed for the door. Disappearing down the hall, he made his way to the courtyard to join the battle.

The prison door swung closed, the loud slam snapping Matt from his sleep. His eyes scanned the room, the memories of his imprisonment returning to him. A chill raced throughout his body. He felt better than he had before. Less achy, at least. Placing his good hand on his forehead, he checked his temperature. His fever dropped slightly. The sleep allowed his immune system to kick in and stave off the infection for a while.

Matt rose to his knees and steadied himself against the bars. No dizziness. That was also a good sign. He got to his feet and looked down at the muddy imprint his body left in the floor. His chest was covered in sweat and mud, but at least he was feeling better.

Matt heard the clamor of the battle even in the recesses of the dungeon. He trudged over to the bars of the cage and rattled the door, holding onto the slim hope that the guard left it unlocked. But no, he was caged like a turkey the day before Thanksgiving. He tried prying the bars apart again; perhaps his strength had amplified from the rest he had just gotten. But the strong wood and the wound in his palm made separating the bars impossible.

Sighing, he closed his eyes and placed his head against the cage. He listened to the noises of the conflict coming from outside. *At least it will all be over soon,* he thought to himself. *One way or another.*

CHAPTER 39

Lucifer found himself winding through the basement hallway for the second time that day. He hated coming down here, with the risk of having his suits get dirty from some menial task. But he couldn't deny that what he had to do next was important. His plan was fully set into motion and running at top gear. There was still one final piece of information that he needed though and he wasn't about to let some stubborn angel keep that from him.

He threw open the door to the dungeon, slamming it against the side wall. The Demon shot out of the stool in the corner, his eyes wide as he spotted the boss. Lucifer paid him no mind; Jehoel had been effectively beaten to shit so he was willing to excuse his employees taking a short breather. Reaching his hand into his pocket, Lucifer pulled out a keyring and flipped it at the Demon, causing him to stumble backwards to catch it.

"Do me a favor guy and get the stuff from the trunk of my car," Lucifer said. The Demon nodded and headed to the door. As he passed the threshold, Lucifer called back to him "And be quick about it." The Demon broke out into a trot down the hallway.

Lucifer turned to Jehoel and flashed him a smile. Jehoel struggled to raise his head and meet his gaze.

"Well, here we are again," Lucifer said. He strolled over to the stool and brushed the seat with his palm. He lifted it and carried it closer to Jehoel, placing it a few feet from him. Brushing off the seat again, he settled into it.

Lucifer stared at Jehoel for a moment, the smile never

wavering. "He's a good kid, that one," he said, motioning toward the door. "I hired him for one of my nightclubs. Works security. But you probably could have guessed that." He chuckled at the joke. "He doesn't talk much though. You probably guessed that, too. Know why? I turned his tongue into a snake. The funniest damn thing I'd done in a while. Kid's name is Claude, did you know that? Yeah, Claude. Kind of an interesting name for…"

"What do you want from me, Lucifer?" Jehoel had enough of Lucifer's babbling.

"You know what I want, Joe. You seem to think that you'll be able to hold out on me. But you won't. I promise you that."

"You couldn't be more wrong. It doesn't matter what you do to me. The Leviathan is too important for you to have."

Lucifer's grin grew. "That's why I brought you a present," he said, sing-song. Behind him, Claude the Demon shuffled his way back into the dungeon, a large, black duffel bag slung across his shoulder. Lucifer rose from the stool and faced him. Claude lifted the strap of the duffel over his head and, at Lucifer's direction, placed it on the stool. Lucifer stepped closer to it and rubbed his hands in mock anticipation.

"What do we have in here?" he said aloud. Lucifer unzipped the bag, adding flair to each movement of his hands. He tossed the flap open and stuck his hands into the bag. He slowly pulled them out to reveal a thin, black laptop. He shoved the empty bag aside, letting it fall to the floor. He placed the computer on the stool, slid the latch and lifted the screen. He pivoted the stool toward Jehoel, giving him a clear view.

"So you say that no matter what I do to you, you won't reveal the location of the Leviathan?" Lucifer pressed a button and the laptop jumped to life. Images flashed across the screen, four different views from within the Angelic High Military building. The angles of each view were static, shot from a high, out-of-the-way vantage point, but Jehoel recognized them instantly.

The top left of the screen displayed the warehouse camera. Three of Lucifer's Demons were destroying the area, tossing crates across the room. They shattered them against the walls, showering the floors in splinters and packing peanuts. They had broken the locks to the Angelic armory and were raiding its contents, filling their arms with broadswords, golden shields and battle axes and were handing them out to other Demons like candy on Halloween.

The top right portion showed the main lobby. A crew of Demons, at least six by Jehoel's count, had destroyed the fountain, a mainstay of the AHM building. One of the military's most well-known landmarks had been reduced to rubble in a matter of minutes. That job completed, they fanned out among the rest of the building. One Demon jumped up to the second floor and was dangling by the banister. Three Demons stood by the elevator, waiting for the car to come, and two others heading for the stairwell.

The bottom left side of the screen showed the hallway of the Angelic Administrative floor. Jehoel knew this location well as this was the floor he worked out of. He watched as Demons tore the doors off the hinges, tossing them to the side like unwanted playing cards. His coworkers ran from their offices, their mouths agape in screams of terror. Jehoel was thankful that the laptop had no speakers as he wasn't sure he could handle the sounds of their fear. He watched in horror as one of the Demons, a large beast of a man dressed in a red, sleeveless shirt and faded blue jeans, caught Omael by the neck and lifted him off the ground. Omael was a close friend of Jehoel. They shared a cubicle wall and would spend their coffee breaks together when work wasn't overflowing. But Jehoel watched in horror as Omael struggled against the Demon, a hopeless battle based on their size difference alone. The Demon crushed Omael's throat and flung his lifeless form over the railing to the lobby below.

Jehoel squeezed his eyes shut, turning his face into his shoulder. Lucifer launched to his side, grabbing him by the chin and turning his face back to the screen. He placed his other hand on Jehoel's head, lifting his eye lids with his fingers. Lucifer leaned in closely to him.

"No, Jehoel. You're going to watch this." Spittle flew from his mouth, splattering against Jehoel's cheek. He could feel the anger in Lucifer's words. "This is your fault. Each and every one of your friends and coworkers that gets hurt is on you. You could have prevented this, Jehoel, but you didn't. When the survivors write about this in the history books, they will blame you."

A tear rolled down Jehoel's cheek, the salty fluid stinging the gashes in his face. His eyes burned as they filled with tears. He tried to blink them away but Lucifer's fingers kept his eyelids immobilized, forcing him to watch the carnage being inflicted on people he cared about.

"Oh, but look at this one," Lucifer said. He leaned toward the screen, pointing at the lower left box. The picture was a stark contrast to the others. It was a serene scene, lacking death and destruction. This box showed Michael seated at his desk, his second-in-command Gabriel sitting in a plush chair in front of him. Michael's hands were folded in his lap, his body still and Gabriel's hands flapped around, his mouth moving.

"Does Michael not know about what's happening just a few floors below him," Lucifer asked, "or does he just not care? It's a tough question, isn't it? Which sounds like the Michael you know? Because the Michael *I* know would have no problem leaving his friends to die. 'Sacrifices for the greater good' he would call them. You think you know Michael, but trust me. You don't. And you don't want to. Because there's no worse injury than to have someone you trust turn their back on you."

Lucifer's words sounded like a low, steady buzz in the back of Jehoel's mind. He watched that quadrant, the peaceful scene it displayed, and for a moment, he wondered if Lucifer had a point.

As Jehoel stared at the screen, the door to Michael's office exploded, sending a shower of splinters and shards of wood toward Gabriel and Michael. The force of the blast sent Gabriel flying forward, cracking his head on the edge of Michael's desk. Michael was knocked backward, his arms flailing and they searched fruitlessly for something to grab.

Lucifer's smile returned, his attention resting on the screen. "Ahhh. Looks like things are about to get good."

CHAPTER 40

Lauren stood outside of Michael's office, waiting for the smoke to clear. She worked her way through the Angelic High Military building, avoiding as much of the chaos the Demons wrought as she could so as not to ruin her clothes. The grin cut her face ear to ear and her heart pounded with excitement. She couldn't remember the last time she had so much fun.

Flames shot from her hands as the smoke dissipated, allowing her a view of Gabriel lying on the floor. He clutched at his head, blood pouring down his face and into his eyes. He looked up at her and struggled to his feet but Lauren shot a blast of Hellfire directly into his chest. He flew across the room, smashed into Michael's bookcase and dropped to the floor. Lauren giggled as hundreds of books clattered all around him, burying him.

Nathaniel touched down on the floor next to her, his large black wings settling him gently. "You should have waited for me," he said, his voice more concerned than angry. Lauren turned to him, looked into his big brown eyes and placed a hand on his chest.

"Ohhh," she replied flirtatiously. "You really do care ab—"

Her words were cut off by a pillar of blue energy crashing into her face. She soared backwards, her spine slamming into the silver railing with a sickening *CRACK*. Nathaniel rushed to her side and kneeled down beside her, rolling her to her back. He put his ear next to her mouth to listen for her breath.

"...about me," Lauren whispered. She sat up and pushed

herself to her feet. He looked up at her and the bright smile on her face. The flames engulfing her hands grew angrier and brighter as she stormed Michael's office.

Crashing through the threshold of the room, she found Michael standing before a large cabinet. He rifled through a collection of weapons, knocking the smaller, less effective ones to the side. Michael was looking for something large and sharp, that he could do the most damage with. He reached for the weapon he had the most experience with, the tool that hadn't let him down in all the years he'd been with the AHM.

Michael grabbed the longsword with two hands, held it out in front of him and pivoted to face Lauren. His wrist twitched and the blade burst into flame. Lauren looked at the angel, spotting the crazed look in his eye. She just shook her head and laughed.

"Do you think a flaming sword is going to scare me?" Lauren flicked her wrist and a wave of flame engulfed her arm.

Michael lunged at Lauren. He swung at her head but she ducked, rolling under the sword. She sprang to her feet, spinning her body to strike Michael but he reached back and blocked the attack. Lauren raised her leg and kicked him in the ribs. He doubled over, his breath escaping his lungs. She grabbed the back of his head and kneed him in the face. He tumbled backward to the floor.

Nathaniel leaned against the doorframe, arms crossing his chest, watching as Lauren swung at Michael with her flaming arm. Michael raised his sword and deflected it, grabbing her ankle with his other hand. He pulled her leg out from under her and she fell on her back. He jumped to his feet and brought the sword down on her but she rolled out of the way. The blade stuck in the wooden floor, leaving behind a flaming pockmark as Michael struggled to pull it free. He jerked the sword from the floor, stumbling backward from the momentum. Regaining his footing, he noticed Nathaniel.

"You!" he shouted, eyes narrowed, his mouth twisting into a grimace. Ignoring Lauren, he dove at Nathaniel, sword ablaze. Nathaniel grabbed Michael's wrists, spun him around and sent him headlong into the cabinet door. Dazed, he staggered backward. Lauren jumped, kicking him in the back, sending him into the door again. It wobbled as Michael's face struck the wood.

Gabriel struggled to his feet, lifting himself up by the edge of the desk. He watched as Lauren kicked Michael in the back, laughing as she turned to Nathaniel. Gabriel looked the beating Michael was taking evidenced on his boss's face.

Gabriel clenched his fists and leaped toward Lauren, his punch connecting with her cheek. She stumbled and fell to her knees. Nathaniel leaned down to pull her up but Gabriel raised his foot and delivered a spinning kick to his head. He struck the ground, landing in a pile of splintered wood. His wing slapped loudly against the wall. Gabriel turned and grabbed Michael's wrist, yanking him to his feet. Jumping over Nathaniel's legs, he led the general from his office.

"Where are you taking me?" Michael's words were slurred and he struggled to break free from Gabriel's grip. Gabriel tightened his grasp, hoping not to lose control of him.

"To the only place that can get us out of here quickly. I just hope Metatron is still around."

Inside the office, Nathaniel struggled to his feet. He brushed the splintered wood from his pants, leaned over and grabbed Lauren's hand, helping her up. His cell phone chirped in his pocket. He pulled it out and tapped the 'Answer' button. He didn't look at the screen. He didn't need to.

As he placed the phone to his ear, he was greeted with a huffy "How could you let them get away?"

"I'm fine, boss," Nathaniel replied sarcastically. "How are you?"

Nathaniel heard the deep breath Lucifer took, calming his anger. A moment passed before he spoke again. "Get Phase Two ready. I got what we needed."

Nathaniel held the phone to his ear long after Lucifer had disconnected, slightly surprise to learn that this was what Lucifer had planned all along.

CHAPTER 41

Aaron wrenched Hisaki's arm behind his back, digging the barrel of the pistol into his spine. Hisaki shook in pain as he led them along the open field back to Puyoa City, the battle fuming all around them.

Once word reached Hsai that General Po had fallen and Aaron was nowhere to be found, he ordered the Chinese army to charge headlong into Japanese territory. He feared that their savior had abandoned them and needed to begin the battle while his presence still blessed them. But he overestimated Aaron's magical abilities and were pinned down by heavy fire from the Japanese. Flying boulders and scorpion bolts rained down all around them, halting their advance. They fell back and reorganized, flanking the drawbridge and attacking the Japanese as they ran into the field of battle. The Chinese horns blared, calling reinforcements from a nearby campsite. They quickly rushed in, causing the appearance of more Japanese soldiers to engage the battle. Which then forced the Chinese to call in more reinforcements... This went on for quite a while.

Aaron and Twilana managed to stay out of the battle, travelling along the edge of the forest and using the thick foliage as cover. They pushed Hisaki through the leaves and the brush, staying low to avoid the keen eyes of the Japanese sentries perched at the top of the wall. With the Japanese military occupied by the Chinese, they had the opportunity to save Matt, but that wouldn't work out so well if one of them took a stray arrow to the face.

After a few minutes of "persuasion" by Twilana, Hisaki told them about a hidden passageway in the west side of the wall. Small and out of the way, he claimed that it would be lightly guarded, if it was guarded at all. He told them that it would be the most direct route to get to the castle, bypassing the need to travel through the heart of the city. Twilana questioned why he would build an entrance with such easy access to his home. He soon admitted that he would use it to smuggle concubines in and out of the city. Aaron shrugged, unconcerned with Hisaki's lasciviousness, just happy that things could possibly work out in their favor for once.

They walked for nearly an hour. The sounds of the battle dimmed as they got further away, replaced with the chirps of crickets and braying of frogs. Only occasionally did they hear the sound of a wounded soldier's cry on the night air. The battle drifted out of sight, making them feel slightly safer. They rushed across the grassy plain toward the wall surrounding Puyoa City, spotting the tiny wooden door.

Aaron jabbed the pistol deeper into Hisaki's back, shoving him against the wall. "Open it," he ordered, grabbing him by the scruff of the neck. Hisaki's face slammed into the wall, the rough bricks scrapping his cheek. He tilted his head toward Aaron, anger flaring in his eyes but Aaron ignored it and shoved him again.

Hisaki knelt down and faced the door. The small entrance rose about four feet from the ground, enough room for a young child to walk through comfortably. But three grown adults would have to crawl across the threshold. Hisaki raised his hand and rapped his fingers against the warped wood.

Aaron looked at Twilana. "I don't know if I like this," he said under his breath. "We should just leave him out here. Or hand him over to the Chinese. You can lead us to Matt."

"Not yet," she replied. "Having him may prevent us from getting into trouble."

The door swung open abruptly, revealing the outline of two guards, both very large and very armed. Twilana tightened her grip on the sword in her hand, swiveling her body to hide it from their view. She braced her back foot against the ground and bent the knee in her front leg, ready to pounce if necessary.

The guards looked at Hisaki, their faces scrunched in confusion. "My lord," the soldier pronounced, bowing low. "How are you outdoors? You should be tucked away in your sleeping quarters."

Hisaki dismissed them with a wave of his hand. "Get out of the way, you fools, and let me in." The guards rose and stepped back from the door, allowing Hisaki to enter. One guard extended his arm to him, offering his assistance. Hisaki grabbed it and duck-walked through the threshold. Reaching the other side, he straightened his back and brushed the dirt from his kimono. He made a flapping motion with his hand, gesturing to the door.

"Kill them," he said as Twilana poked her head through the door. The guards turned to her, hands on the hilts of their swords. Twilana's arm burst through the doorway, burying the point of her sword in the guard's chest. He dropped to the ground, his sword still in its scabbard.

The second guard pulled his sword and swung at Twilana. She ducked to avoid the attack and the sword clanged against the wall next to her. He drew his arm back, ready for a second strike when Twilana lunged at him, grabbing him by the waist. They fell to the ground and his sword tumbled away in the dirt. Hisaki watched as she punched the guard in the face. He turned to run off but Aaron emerged through the door and grabbed the back of his collar. He jabbed the pistol into Hisaki's side. "That wasn't very smart," he muttered, his face pushed close to Hisaki's ear. Wrapping an arm around Hisaki's neck, Aaron spun him around to face Twilana. She leapt to her feet and punched him in the stomach, forcing the air out of his lungs. He doubled over to catch his breath.

"Try that again," she said, "and the sword will be in *your* chest." She leaned over and pulled the blade from the dead soldier, wiping it on Hisaki's back. Aaron grabbed his collar again and pulled him up.

The three walked through the back roads of Puyoa City unnoticed. All of the soldiers had been called out to the field of battle and the citizens were safely locked away in their homes, leaving the way clear from prying eyes. Aaron relaxed slightly as they wandered the silent streets, happier still in the knowledge that, if they did encounter anyone, they had Hisaki to use as leverage.

Hisaki thought of all the places in the city that should be guarded. He formed a plan to lead them across the path of his guards, to have them overpowered and captured, relishing the thought of putting them to death. But he was slightly frightened of the woman. He'd never seen a female act so deftly in the face of danger and she impressed him. She was unlike any woman he had ever met; always poised for battle and possessing the skills to back up her words. He considered making her a part of his harem, imagining how powerful their offspring would be but thought better of it, knowing she had the nerve to bury a dagger between his ribs as he slept.

Hisaki led them toward the castle, turning down a small corridor hidden from the view of the street. The hallway was dark and musty, home to hundreds of bugs and vermin. Cracking bricks showered stone dust as they passed, the only light coming from the glowing streetlamps leaking in through tiny, barred windows. Hisaki stopped and motioned to a door to his left.

"This is where your friend is being held," he said to Aaron.

Aaron nodded. Twilana padded her way behind Hisaki and lifted the sword, bringing the hilt down on his temple. He fell to the ground with a resounding *thud*.

She stepped over his unconscious body and raised her foot. Putting all of her strength into the kick, she struck the prison door, shattering the wood. As the two halves of the door clattered to the floor, Aaron tucked the tiny pistol into the waistband of his pants and entered the room.

Matt leaned against the bars of the cage, the lock securing the door cradled in his hand. He had spent the last hour trying the pry the lock apart despite the heavy metal casing. His fingers were torn and blood trickled down his arms. Matt looked up as Aaron walked to him, his eyes wide with shock.

"You guys are alive," Matt said, more a question than a statement. He dropped the lock, withdrawing his arms through the bars. He examined his blood-soaked fingertips, wiping them clean on his pants.

Aaron stared at Matt, horrified by what he saw. Matt had multiple wounds on his body, each of them carelessly tended to. His body was caked in mud, made through a mixture of dirt and sweat. The white's of Matt's eyes had turned a pale yellow and his body was severely jaundiced. He cradled his injured hand against his chest. The bandage had crusted over, creating a gruesome collage of blood and pus.

"Move back from the door," Aaron said, stepping to the

side. Twilana strolled up to the cage and stomped the metal lock, shattering the wooden loops it secured. The door swung open offering Matt his freedom. He stumbled through the cage and was hit by a wave of dizziness, falling onto the dirt floor.

Aaron reached down, laced his arm around Matt's chest and lifted him to his feet.

"You don't look so good," Aaron said, steadying Matt's weight on himself.

"No shit," Matt replied, barely able to keep his head steady. He turned toward Twilana, his eyelids drooping. "Now what?"

Aaron shot Twilana a quizzical glance, his look similar to Matt's. The extent of his plan had been to rescue Matt; beyond that, Aaron had no idea what to do. He hoped that Twilana had the foresight to plan a little further in advance.

Twilana rolled her eyes and turned to the door. She had taken two steps when a pair of Japanese guards appeared outside of the prison. The guards rushed the room, moving so fast that Twilana barely had time to lift her sword. She managed to block the first soldier's attack, delivering an uppercut to his chin. He reeled backwards, losing his balance. She sliced at the second soldier, opening a gash in his cheek. He dropped back and raised his battleaxe. Twilana pressed on, hacking away at the air between them. Her sword caught the guard's arm, severing his hand and his axe clattered to the ground. He dropped to his knees, blood gushing from the stump. Twilana jumped over the bodies of the fallen soldiers, shouting to Aaron over her shoulder. "We can hide in the forest, figure things out there."

Matt pushed himself free from Aaron's grip and grabbed the fallen axe. He pried the hand from the handle, letting it fall to the floor with a wet *thump*. The axe was heavier than he expected, causing him to drift to the side as he walked. He stumbled through the doorway behind Twilana, barely able to stay on his feet. Though he was weak with fatigue and pain, Matt's rescue had energized him, filling him with enough vigor to keep moving.

Aaron reached up and grabbed a lighted torch from the wall. He carefully stepped over the bodies of the guards and followed Matt into the hallway. The torch light did little to illuminate the cramped room but provided enough light for him to see a second wave of guards converging on Twilana.

She ran at guards, the metallic clang of sword against sword reverberating against the stone walls. She ducked as a guard slashed at her, rolling clear of a downward attack. She swiped at his feet, catching him in the ankle. Blood poured from his foot as he stumbled forward onto the point of her sword.

Matt rushed the guards, his axe raised precariously above his head. He brought it crashing down into the group of guards but missed entirely, embedding the blade into the wall. Matt tugged on the handle, trying to pull it free, but it refused to budge. He looked up at the guards, his head snapping back as a knuckeguard smashed into his face.

Twilana caught Matt as he fell backward. Placing him on the ground gently, she hopped to her feet, slashing at the front guard. He ducked, her sword missing his face by inches. She spun on her heel and raised her foot into his chest, knocking him backward into the guards behind him. She let loose a barrage of vicious blows, hacking and slashing at the group. They dropped to the floor one by one in a crumpled heap at her feet.

Matt looked up at Twilana, a slight smile on his lips. She nodded and elbowed the axe stuck in the wall, knocking it free. Twilana returned his smile as it clanged to the floor. She turned and bolted down the hallway as he crawled over and retrieved the axe.

"Hurry," she shouted to Matt and Aaron.

Aaron took off down the hallway behind Twilana, helping Matt to his feet. They broke into a run, chasing after her, trying to close her considerable lead. A voice rose from behind them, echoing off the cramped quarters of the hallway.

"Master!"

Three heads turned in unison. Despite looking far more unkempt than the last time he saw the man, Aaron immediately recognized Hsai. His face was dirty and blood dripped down his cheek from a cut below his eye. He held a bow in front of him, an arrow nocked tightly on the string, aimed directly at Aaron's head.

"I'm afraid I can't let you leave, sire," Hsai said, stepping towards Aaron on unsteady legs. Beads of sweat formed on his forehead and rolled down his face, mingling with the blood. His robes had been tattered and charred, exposing a large gash in his chest. "You abandoned us in our time of need. Our soldiers are dying because of your cowardice."

Twilana sprinted back toward Aaron, worried about the crazy look in Hsai's eyes. He pulled the bowstring tighter, shifting the arrow from Aaron to her.

"Do not try it, woman," he said.

Twilana stopped in her tracks, questioning whether she would be able to reach him before he could loose the arrow. She was fast, but could she outrun an arrow? She was tired, hungry and had been in several fights in the last couple of hours. She wouldn't take the risk.

Clutching the axe, Matt raised his hands up, showing Hsai that he proved no threat. "I don't know who you are," Matt said, "but I think we can talk about this."

Hsai's eyes went wide with anger, the words spewing from his mouth. Tiny flecks of spittle flew from his lips as he spoke. "There is no talking. This... *person* was supposed to help us. We waited for his return, when he would bring respect and dignity back to our people. But he left us when our time of redemption came."

Aaron watched as Hsai delivered his diatribe. He slowly lowered his hand toward his waist, placing his fingers on the butt of the pistol. He hoped Hsai's insane rambling would keep him distracted long enough to grab the weapon. He wasn't so lucky.

Hsai's eyes flicked toward Aaron as he pulled the pistol from his waistband. He shifted the bow to Aaron as he raised the gun. Aaron pulled the trigger and a flash exploded from the barrel, the lead pellet racing down the hallway.

Hsai's chest exploded in a spray of blood as the pellet struck him. His muscles contracted, his hand twitched and his fingers released the bowstring. The arrow shot through the air, headed straight toward Aaron.

Without thinking, Matt stepped into the path of the arrow, blocking Aaron from its danger. Squeezing he eyes shut, he moved his arms in front of him, the axe parallel with his body. Matt heard a sharp *tink* of metal on metal and slowly opened his eyes to find both Hsai and the arrow lying harmlessly on the floor.

Matt turned to find Aaron staring at him, a huge grin splitting his face. Twilana gaped wide-eyed behind them. Aaron chuckled. "That was pretty damn cool."

Matt inhaled deeply, his entire body shuddering. He placed the head of the axe on the floor and leaned against it. Steadying himself on the handle, he looked up at his friends. "Let's get out of here."

CHAPTER 42

Escaping from Puyoa City was easier than sneaking into it. Since both armies were so busy fighting each other, neither army paid any attention to the three people skulking around the castle in the darkness. Though Aaron, Twilana, and Matt were armed well enough to protect themselves, no one came close enough to necessitate using the weapons.

Twilana led the group into the forest, instructing Aaron to stay in front and use his torch to light the way. The torch threw off little light as it sputtered and spat, threatening to go out at any time. Twilana stayed close behind him, clutching her sword tightly. She didn't like the idea that Hisaki was still out there and could send soldiers after them so she hoped the cover of the forest would hide them well enough. After all, given the lump on the back of his head he would have when he woke up, he had every reason to want them dead.

Matt felt a chill run through his body. He began to sweat despite the cool autumn air. Placing his hand on his forehead, he wiped the perspiration from his brow, feeling the fever creeping back into him. The battleaxe he carried grew heavy in his grip, his fatigue forcing him to drag the axehead on the ground for most of the way. His arm throbbed as the axe bumped and lurched over rocks and tree roots but he grew so accustomed to the pain that he barely noticed it.

Twilana looked up at the sky, trying to track their movements by the alignment of the stars. It was a skill all Janian soldiers were taught, one of their basic survival skills, and she was good at it. But each time she tried, she grew more frustrated. The star's locations were unfamiliar to her, preventing her from finding a single constellation that she knew. She couldn't even tell which direction was north. Shaking her head, she urged Aaron to press on.

They came upon a clearing as the sun started to peek over the horizon. Deciding that wandering aimlessly in the forest did them no good, Twilana stopped, grabbing Aaron's arm.

"We need a plan," she said. "Where do we go from here?"

Matt dropped the handle of the axe, letting it flop to the ground. He shuffled over to a boulder and slowly lowered himself onto it. Sweat dripped from his forehead as he wrapped his arms across his chest. His skin filled with goosebumps and he wished he had the foresight to steal a shirt from one of the fallen guards before they escaped the castle. He looked up at the sun, shielding his eyes from the light and stared at the silhouette of a majestic mountain off in the distance.

Aaron looked at Twilana and smoothed his hair. His shoulders drooped and he leaned his back against a tree, staring at the ground. He rubbed his eyes, releasing a loud sigh. Matt looked up at his reaction, knowing that he was hard at work devising a scheme.

"I'm not entirely sure," he said, looking up at Twilana. "But Hsai said something about a volcano. A shrine that no one ever visits anymore."

"A shrine?" Matt asked. He slapped at a bug on his leg, tracking it with his eyes as it flew away. "To who?"

"To me."

Matt turned to Aaron, his head cocked to the side. Aaron sighed, not wanting to go into detail about his ordeal. He saw how Matt was treated and thought regaling them with tales of being bathed by a pair of beautiful women and the sumptuous dinners of roasted duck wouldn't do much to help his morale.

"It's…it's not important. What matters is what he said." Looking up, Twilana noticed the volcano hovering over the countryside. Though long dormant, it showed signs of life, sporadically belching plumes of smoke into the air. She peered at the craggy surfaces of its hillside, examining it for caves or tunnels or portals of swirling blue and purple light.

"Well, we have nothing else," Twilana said. "Let's get moving." She shuffled the sword from one hand to the other and stepped carefully into the forest.

*   *   *   *   *

They walked through the forest for hours, getting turned around a few times along the way. The thick canopy of leaves and branches blocked their view of the mountain, throwing them off course. Aaron and Twilana also had to take turns helping Matt over the more arduous territory. Matt's fever returned, sucking the energy out of him. As they reached the base of the volcano, he bent over, struggling to catch his breath. He leaned against a boulder and coughed, which burned his dry throat.

Twilana looked up at the volcano, squinting in the early afternoon sun. She climbed over a few of the rocks to stand on a large boulder. Feeling her way along the side of the mountain, she wrapped her fingers around the protruding rocks, lifting herself off her feet. Dropping back to the boulder, she examined the volcano some more, believing it was craggy enough to allow them to climb to the top.

"Rest up," she shouted over her shoulder. "We have quite a bit of climbing to do."

Matt lowered himself to the ground, resting his arms on his knees and looked up at Twilana. "Climbing?" His breath was wheezy and broken. "No one said anything about climbing."

Twilana pointed to a rocky shelf near the summit of the volcano. Beyond the shelf sat a dark oval which Twilana took to be a cave leading deeper into the mountain. "I'm betting that's where we need to go. Since I don't see any roads leading up there, that means we climb."

Matt closed his eyes and hung his head, the resolve draining from his body. He sat in silence for a few moments before he looked up at Twilana. "OK, let's get this over with." He pushed himself from the ground and walked over to the rocky wall. Leaning his axe against the wall, he groped around the rocks, looking for a few decent hand holds. He looked up and planned his route to the top, spotting a large escarpment about halfway between the ground and the cave. At least there was a place to stop and rest if he needed to.

An arrow hit the wall next to Matt's hand, bouncing off the stone. He watched as it clattered to the ground, staring at it for a moment before turning back to the forest.

A group of soldiers burst through the trees, a platoon of archers taking position all along the treeline. The archers were in perfect formation, each one down on one knee. Their arrows were strung back on their bows, aimed directly at the volcano. Or, more specifically, at Aaron, Matt and Twilana.

Matt stared down the shafts of dozens of arrows. He raised his finger and pointed toward them. "We have company." His voice was calm, as if the threat of death no longer bothered him. Matt shielded his eyes from the mid-day sun and examined the soldiers, looking at the details of their armor. He realized that the legion was comprised of both Chinese and Japanese soldiers. Seems they were able to put aside their differences, banding together to fight a common enemy. Matt felt an odd sense of pride at having so thoroughly pissed off two groups of people that they both wanted him dead.

Aaron and Twilana turned toward the forest, spotting the archers. Aaron stood in horror as they released their bowstrings, sending a wave of arrows into the air. Twilana grabbed Aaron's wrists and dropped to her knees, pulling him behind the boulder.

The arrows flew through the air like a hive of angry bees. Matt reached over, snatched the handle of his axe and dropped to the ground next to Twilana. The arrows ricocheted off the volcano wall, toppling harmlessly into the dirt.

"What now?" Aaron asked, his back against the boulder and arms covering his head.

"I say we rush them and take them by surprise," Matt replied, lifting the axe above his head menacingly. Twilana reached up and eased his arm down.

"That's a terrible idea," she said. "They will kill us before we get three steps toward them. But we need to fight back. We should let them come to us. We can hold our ground here." Twilana grasped her sword with two hands. Matt raised his arm again, a smile stretched across his face. After all the torture these people inflicted on him, he was ready and happy to give some of it back to them.

Aaron looked at him. "Hold it there, tough nuts. You can barely stand on your own." He reached over and grabbed the axe from Matt's hand. "I don't think you should be fighting anything."

"Then what am I supposed to do?" Matt whined, his voice

rising an octave

"Get around the side of the mountain," Twilana said. "Find cover. Once we're done here, if we live, we'll find you."

Dejected, Matt turned and duck-walked around the back of the hillside, careful to stay below cover and out of sight of the archers.

Twilana looked at Aaron, her sword primed for action. "You ready?"

He smiled, his head bobbed in a strong, pronounced nod.

They leapt to their feet in unison, raising their weapons in preparation for the battle. A wall of flame erupted before them, the heat so intense it forced them to regain cover behind the boulder. Aaron shielded his face from the fire as Twilana examined the sudden blaze.

The flame wall extended ten feet in both directions, long enough to keep them completely out of view of the advancing army. It burned cleanly and evenly, unlike the sputtering flame of a bonfire. This inferno burned as if being fed a steady supply of fuel. There was no odor of gas or smoke, just a pure, solid heat emanating from the blaze.

A creature swooped down from the sky, landing in front of Twilana. Her eyes widened as she stared at the tall man. A dingy white tunic hung on his large, muscular chest. His clear blue eyes and long, blonde hair shimmered in the light cast by the fire. The man could have easily been mistaken for a body-builder or a Swedish movie actor, were it not for the large, feathered wings protruding from his back.

His arms hung at his sides, one hand clutching a sword made of fire. He turned his thin, strong face to Twilana, bowing his head slightly. He extended his free hand to her gently. "Come with me."

Twilana had been through a lot in the past two days and with everything she's gone through, she wasn't about to blindly trust a winged man with a flaming sword. She stepped forward, angling the sword with the man's neck. Her lips curled into a snarl, her words dripping with venom as she spoke.

"I don't know who you are, but you need to back away from us."

"My name is Sauriel," the man said, his face revealing no hint of fear. He placed two fingers on the blade steadied on his neck and softly pushed it to the side. "I am here to help you."

Sauriel twitched his hand, extinguishing the flaming sword. He slid the hilt into a sheath attached to his belt. "This," he began, motioning to the wall of fire, "is my doing. I created it to protect you from the attack. But it won't last much longer. We must move quickly."

Aaron stared up at Sauriel, his axe lying uselessly next to him. He backed up and scanned the side of the volcano, searching for Matt but finding no trace of him. Sauriel looked down at him, reading the confusion on his face.

"Your friend is safe and waiting for us. I will take you to him."

Aaron's eyes shifted to the top of the mountain and found Matt's head peeking over the side of an outcropping, looking down at them. Turning to Twilana, Aaron placed a hand on her shoulder.

"I think we can trust him," he said. Though he had no reason to believe it, he did.

Twilana looked at him, her face slowly beginning to relax. She sighed and slid the sword between her belt.

Sauriel smiled, extending his hands to them. Aaron and Twilana each grasped a hand, gripping tightly. With a mighty flap of his wings, they were airborne, quickly ascending the volcano wall.

It took them less than a few seconds to reach the top of the volcano. Sauriel gently lowered his passengers onto the rocky ledge. Twilana released Sauriel's hand and dropped to the ground, looking around for Matt. Aaron fell much less gracefully, skidding along the dirt and rocks, kicking up a cloud of dust. Sauriel landed next to him and helped him to his feet.

Matt walked from the mouth of the cave, smiling at Aaron's unfortunate arrival. Composing himself, he brushed the hair from his face, and looked up at Sauriel. "Where are we going now?"

Ignoring the question, Sauriel walked into the cave, quickly disappearing in the darkness. A minute passed. Then two. Through the darkness, blue and pink spots began to grow and spin, coalescing into one, large sphere. The light from the sphere emphasized Sauriel's silhouette. He cocked his head slightly and looked at them.

"We are going bowling."

CHAPTER 43

Welcome To Rodrigo's Bowling Alley exclaimed the pink and blue neon sign running the length of the wall.

Or it would have, if half of the letters hadn't been burned out or broken. As it were, the sign proclaimed *We come o R drig s Bo ling Alley.*

Sauriel motioned to a tiny, plastic booth. Aaron and Twilana slid into opposing sides as Matt attempted to sit next to Aaron. Sauriel grabbed his shoulder. "You should come with me," he said, leading him to the back of the building. Aaron watched as they disappeared around a corner. He placed his elbows on the Day-Glo orange table, resting his chin in his hands. A wide yawn escaped his mouth and he felt his eyelids growing heavier. Twilana, on the other hand, was riding a wave of adrenaline, her knees shaking furiously under the table. After a moment, she slid from the booth and began to pace the floor.

"OK," she said to herself. "This just got really weird."

Aaron's eyes slowly opened and he glared at Twilana. He heard her words, but his mind interpreted them as one, long, incomprehensible syllable. He laid his head on the table, happy to finally have a moment of peace.

He was fast asleep in a matter of seconds.

*　　*　　*　　*　　*

Sauriel had the foresight to alert Raphael that he was on his way, allowing him to prepare for their arrival. Raphael turned the kitchenette of the bowling alley into a makeshift emergency room. Stainless steel surgical tools, bandages, and medications of all kinds were neatly laid out on the serving counter.

Raphael anxiously awaited Sauriel and his patient. He leaned against an old refrigerator, his hands clasped as his waist. His face was turned up in an expression of worry, his dark-brown eyes reflecting his concern. As the head medical officer of the Angelic High Military, Raphael assisted on numerous emergencies pertaining to angels, cherubs and seraphim. But he never had the chance to care for a human before. As his first time, he was downright apprehensive, worried that he would make a mistake. What if he misread the physiology books he power-studied when he heard of Matt's condition? What if his patient died in his care? It would make no difference to the universe, but it still made Raphael uneasy. A bead of sweat formed on his brow. He grabbed the loose fabric of the cord securing his tunic and wiped it away, spotting Sauriel and Matt as they entered the room.

"Sit, sit," Raphael said, pointing to the stainless steel countertop. Matt raised himself onto the counter as Raphael rummaged through his supplies. He pulled out a clean, white rag and handed it to Sauriel. "Can you please wet this with warm water?" Sauriel nodded, taking the rag and holding it under the tap.

Raphael turned back to Matt. He cut the crusty bandage around his arm, pulling it away from the wound. Matt howled in pain as the stiff, blood-drench cloth pulled at his damaged flesh.

"Sorry," Raphael said with a frown, his eyebrows raised. "So sorry." Matt grunted his acceptance of the apology, biting his cheek to get through the pain.

Satisfied with the wetness and warmness of the rag, Sauriel offered it to Raphael, moving himself to the back of the room and out of the way. Raphael gently wiped the dirt and grime from the wound on Matt's shoulder. Matt watched as the strange winged man stared at his chest, trying to think of a time he was in a more uncomfortable situation. Luckily for him, nothing came to mind. Matt cleared his throat, addressed the angel. "Everything look OK?"

Raphael nodded, his eyes never leaving the wound. "Yes, this one looks fine. It just needs a little…" Raphael's words trailed off. Placing his hands together, he rubbed his palms furiously. A pure white light emanated from his hand as he held it over Matt's shoulder. Matt's body was engulfed in a warm, peaceful feeling and his nerves tingled. When Raphael removed his hand, all that was left of the wound was a cleanly healed scar.

"How did you do that?" Matt asked excitedly.

Raphael ignored Matt's question. Reaching down, he grabbed Matt's wrist, slowly unraveling the bandage around his hand. Matt flinched as the scabbing stuck to the bandage tore away from the wound.

Dropping the wrapping on the floor, Raphael turned Matt's hand over and examined his palm, dabbing away the dirt and grime with the wet rag.

"It looks worse than it is," he said. "But I think I have just the thing."

Laying Matt's hand on the table, Raphael walked over to his utensils and lifted the lid from a cardboard box. Rifling through its contents, he withdrew a black square of fabric. Raphael pinched the corner of the fabric and flicked his wrist, allowing it to unravel into a long, black glove.

"Slip your hand in here," he said, pulling apart the open end, holding it out to Matt.

Matt cautiously raised his hand and slid it into the glove. "What is it?"

"*Manos Dei*," Raphael responded. "The Hand of God. Works wonders on hand injuries."

Sauriel watched as Raphael tended to Matt's injuries. His brain screamed as Gabriel's voice flashed in his head. *Michael wishes to see you right away.*

Wordlessly, Sauriel turned and exited the kitchenette, grabbing a soft-baked pretzel on his way out. He munched on the pretzel as he wound his way through the bowling alley and descended the stairs to the storeroom.

Reaching the bottom of the hallway, Gabriel greeted Sauriel with a nod of the head. He was dressed in his battle fatigues, old and worn out, showing the wear and tear of being on the front lines. His sword hung sheathed on his hip, a bow and quiver slung between his wings.

Behind him stood Michael, hunched over a rickety wooden table, staring at a pile of old maps. His uniform was almost an exact copy of Gabriel's, only differing in color. Michael had worked his way up the ranks of the Angelic High Military, and so was awarded the honor of a dark blue tunic, which was also adorned with the

Wings of Generals. He looked up as Sauriel entered, his face morphing into a cold scowl.

"What in His name happened out there?"

"Sir?" Sauriel responded sheepishly. He was taken aback by Michael's tone. Like most of the troops in the Angelic High Military, Sauriel heard rumors of Michael's temper, but never witnessed it for himself. Now, he found himself on the receiving end of a tirade.

"Your orders were to gather the travelers and bring them to us, not start a war that would destroy two empires!" he slapped the table, knocking over a stack of papers. Michael's gaze dropped to the mess, his head shaking from side to side. "We don't have the resources to send someone in to fix your mistakes, either"

Sauriel felt the urge to correct Michael, to defend himself, stating that he had no involvement with the battle. And also that, by the end of things, the Chinese and Japanese had worked together, which would be the stepping stone to bringing the two civilizations together. But instead he chose to remain silent, opting not to further enrage the General.

"We are out of time," Michael continued. Pushing the papers aside, he arranged and flattened the map. The paper was decorated with swatches of green, varying in shades. Thin, black squares dotted the sheet, lined up in neat, little rows. Michael's finger jabbed an area in the center of the map, nearest the largest square.

"This is our entrance point," he said. Gabriel leaned forward, examining the page. "Our Intel tells us it's lightly guarded, but it will be dangerous regardless."

I watched as Gabriel nodded his agreement. Even if he felt that the idea was a bad one, he would never voice his opinion. After all, Gabriel is a soldier. His job is to follow orders, not comment on them.

"I'm glad you could make it, Metatron," Michael said, his eyes never leaving the maps.

Though I had only been in a room for a couple of minutes, it surprised me that it took so long for the angels to notice my presence. We Grigori are ubiquitous in nature, able to be everywhere at once. By focusing our concentration, we can narrow our existence into one area, making our presence known. But angels are just one step down from omniscience. As soon as my focus became more definite, it would have resonated in their being, alerting them. It's difficult to sneak up on an angel, so it was quite a shock to realize that, after nearly ten minutes of watching them, they finally acknowledged me.

Of course, they did have pressing matters to attend to.

I bowed to Michael and Gabriel and extended my hand to Sauriel. He shook it tightly as I turned back to Michael to deliver my update.

"They've yet to find the Ocularium," I began. "It was a good thought to keep it off all personnel records. At the very least, we can maintain our contact with the angels out in the field and can call them in if necessary. Lucifer and Lauren are holed up in your office, most likely deciding where to attack next."

Sauriel looked at me with a furrowed brow. "What could they want with the Ocularium?"

I shrugged and shook my head despondently. "It's only a guess, at this point but we assume that it has to do with the Leviathan. With Jehoel being gone as long as he has, I fear that Lucifer was able to extract the knowledge of its whereabouts from him. Which is why I believe he is looking for the Ocularium."

Michael wiped his hand down his face, a twitch I've witnessed in times of frustration. "Then our only option is to overtake him before he finds it." He flipped through the maps, pulling one from the bottom. Using his finger, he traced a line from one end of the map to the other. "Our best entrance point is here..."

I slowly backed away as Michael and Gabriel worked on their new plan. Though I wished I could have been there to lend my help and knowledge, plotting attacks is not my place. I turned and climbed the stairs, leaving the soldiers to their war.

CHAPTER 44

I found Aaron and Twilana relaxing in the Day-Glo orange booth, each with a mug of beer in front of them. Though their eyes showed exhaustion, they seemed livelier than they had in days.

"How are the two of you faring?" I enquired as I approached.

Aaron looked up and stared at me through squinted eyes. The sight of a disheveled old man must have confused him. Extending my hand, I took the time to introduce myself, hoping that this would put him at ease.

"It's a pleasure to meet you, Aaron," I said. "My name is..."

Aaron jumped from his seat and grabbed my hand, shaking it furiously. "I know who you are," he said, an ecstatic grin on his face. He wrapped his arms around me and hugged me tightly. It was now my turn to be confused.

He released me, and I stepped back cautiously. Aaron continued.

"I grew up watching your HBO specials. I love your "Stuff" skit."

Realizing the connection, I bowed my head and smiled. George Carlin was a vulgar comedian and satirist who hailed from the world where Aaron lived. Having seen some of the "specials", I had to laugh at the association, seeing the similarities in our appearances.

"No, no," I said, setting the record straight. "I am not Mr. Carlin. My name is Metatron. I am the head of the Order of

Grigori."

Twilana stared up at me as Aaron seated himself disappointedly. "What's the 'Order of Gregory'?" she asked.

I motioned to the booth and she slid over, allowing me room to sit. "No, dear," I replied. "The Order of Grigori. We are a socialized race, entrusted with the observance and chronicling of universal events."

"What does this have to do with us?" Aaron asked.

I sighed, hoping to avoid this portion of the conversation. Though I could tell them how they became involved, I felt that duty was better left to the angels. But since he asked, I wasn't about to leave them in the dark.

"You stumbled upon a nexus," I began. "A bridge between realities. Since your fishing expedition, you have been traveling between dimensions, bouncing from one world to the other."

"How do we get home?" Twilana asked. "And what's the deal with the guys with the wings?"

"They are members of the Angelic High Military," I said.

Aaron looked at me incredulously. "Angels?"

I nodded. "Yes. But before they can send you home, they need your help.

My words did not sit well with Aaron. He shot to his feet, the sudden movement spilling their beers. As the foamy liquid spread across the tabletop, he slammed his hands on the table and leaned into me, anger seething from his words.

"I'm done doing favors for strangers," he said. "All I'm willing to do now is take my friend and go the hell home." He straightened his back, his eyes searching the bowling alley. "Where is Matt? What have you done with him?"

Twilana touched his hand, a gentle gesture that calmed him slightly. She pointed behind him, diverting his attention.

Matt walked toward us, smiling and full of energy. His injured arm was covered in a long black glove. He wore a new t-shirt that proclaimed *Jesus Is My Homeboy*. He waved as Aaron looked up at him.

Aaron returned the smile, happy to see that Matt was doing better. Aaron rushed toward him, grabbing and lifting him off the floor in an enthusiastic bear hug. Matt winced, pushing himself free from Aaron's grip "Watch the arm, dude."

Aaron released Matt, slapping his back in apology. He slid

to the far end of the booth, allowing Matt room to sit beside him. Matt spotted me and I could see the confusion spread across his face. A sense of recognition flashed in his eyes.

"I am not who you think I am," I said, rising from my seat. Turning to Aaron, I continued. "I will deliver the message of your impatience to my associates." I bowed, leaving them to themselves.

"Wasn't that...," Matt began, pointing at me as I left. Aaron shook his head, cutting off his words.

Twilana patted Matt's hand, smiling. "I'm glad to see that you are recovering," she said. Matt watched as her eyes swirled into a light shade of green. He smiled at the sincerity of her statement.

Matt's face became serious as he turned to Aaron. "I don't like this, man. I think this was a big mistake."

Aaron leaned in close, placing his elbow in the puddle of beer. He spoke silently, disguising his conversation in a whisper. "Me neither. Those 'angels'? I don't think we can trust them."

"Not that," Matt said. "Well, I don't trust them either." He gestured around the room. "I'm talking about the fact that we're stuck in a bowling alley."

"What is this 'bowling alley' thing, anyway?" Twilana asked. She searched her new surroundings for anything familiar, but found none. She had never seen neon lights fashioned in the shape of words, never smelled the aroma of burnt nachos, or experienced the pleasure of having her feet stick to the floor in puddles of stale beer. She had never seen anything like this place on Janus and she wasn't sure what to make of it.

"It's a game that we have back home," Aaron explained. "You roll a ball down a straight-a-way and knock over pins at the other end." He pointed to a large-waisted, flannel-shirted woman rolling a ball down a straight-a-way. Twilana watched as the ball struck the pins, leaving only two standing. The woman released a vulgar expletive that rhymed with 'sother-ducker.' Twilana's face pinched as the visual example left her more confused than before.

"But what's the point?"

"There is no point," Matt said. "People do it as a way to pass the time. Some people manage to make a profession out of it, but that's about it. It's mostly for lonely housewives who want to get away from their families once a week, or men who use it as an excuse for cheating on their wives."

Aaron's eyes flicked from Twilana to the other end of the

room. He spotted Sauriel walking with two other men. Men dressed in military fatigue-styled tunics. Men with wings growing from their backs. Sauriel said something to the men, pointing in their direction as he spoke. Two heads popped up and looked at them.

"Guys," Aaron said, his whisper becoming more of a hiss. "I have a bad feeling about this place."

CHAPTER 45

I made my way down to the kitchenette, looking for a little something to eat. Though Grigori have no need for physical sustenance, I do enjoy the taste of an ice cream sundae now and then. Passing the threshold to the tiny cooking area, I found Raphael packing away his medical supplies. Michael hovered over him, his face expressing a mixture of concern and irritation. Gabriel stood at the far end of the room, his arms gesticulating wildly. He must have been explaining something to Michael, something he didn't want me to hear because as soon as he saw me, his eyes went wide and his arms dropped to his side. Michael turned toward me, seeing what had caused Gabriel to suddenly go mute and eyed me suspiciously.

Ignoring them, I padded over to the freezer. As I poked through the food, I could feel all eyes in the room on me. Turning carefully, I examined the three angelic faces.

"Yes?"

Michael stepped forward, forcing his face to hide all the frustrations he was suffering. He politely asked me what I was up to. Grabbing a carton of ice cream from the freezer, I walked over to the counter, scooped myself a significant serving, and explained my conversation with the travelers.

"What right do you have to speak with them?" Gabriel growled at me. "You have no authority in this manner."

Raphael's face bunched uncomfortably. Grabbing his box of tools, he toed past me. He raised his eyebrows to me as he disappeared from the room and left me alone with the General and his muscle.

"I wasn't trying to take away any control," I replied, spooning a helping of ice cream into my mouth. I allowed it to melt on my tongue before continuing. "They've been through a near equivalent of Hell. I felt it prudent to explain what they had just experienced. Not only prudent, but polite as well."

Gabriel opened his mouth to respond but Michael raised his hand, silencing him. "What information did you get from them?" Michael asked me.

I was confused by his question. "I wasn't plying them for information. I merely wished to check on them."

Michael frowned and turned back to Gabriel. "Go speak with them. Find out what you can."

Gabriel nodded and hurried off. I watched as he disappeared down the alley. Alone with Michael, I inquired as to his motives.

"That is none of your concern, Metatron," he said, brusquely. "You've done your job. Let me do mine." He walked off down the corridor to the basement.

A strange feeling brewed in the pit of my stomach. The kind of feeling one gets as the precursor to a terrible event. For someone who was charged with notating the happenings of the universe, I felt completely lost. I pushed my bowl of Rocky Road to the side, my hankering for ice cream now gone.

CHAPTER 46

Matt grew bored as they sat around the uncomfortable booth. He drummed his fingers on the table and stared at the giant metal bars that dropped from the ceiling and cleared the pins from the lanes. Little by little, his eyelids drooped, the fatigue catching up to him. He was jolted awake as Aaron pushed himself from the booth and headed toward the restroom.

"Come on," Matt said to Twilana as Aaron disappeared around the corner. He grabbed her hand and dragged her from the booth.

Matt ambled into the pub and pulled two stools from the bar, settling himself on one. He waved down the bartender. The chunky, black-shirted man approached, greeting them with a throaty belch.

"Two beers, please," Matt said.

The bartender nodded, scratched his beard, and reached under the bar, revealing two semi-clean mugs. He pulled a long-handled tap and filled the mugs as Matt and Twilana sat in silence, waiting for their drinks. Aaron burst through the door, holding a bright pink ball and wearing a childishly excited grin.

"Are you guys coming? I got a lane. You just need shoes. We're at ten. I'm starting without you." He disappeared as quickly as he arrived.

Matt watched the door close slowly and shook his head. He turned back to the bartender.

"And a couple shots of whiskey."

The bartender placed the mugs filled with a small amount of yellow liquid topped with a mountain of white foam on the counter. He filled two small shot glasses with a light brown whiskey and put them on the bar next to the mugs. Matt quickly picked up one of the shot glasses, placed it to his lips and drained it. Twilana reached for the second glass, but Matt swooped in and grabbed it, downing it. He grabbed one of the mugs, took a sip and slipped off the bar stool, motioning to Twilana to follow him.

Matt held the door as Twilana sauntered through the threshold. Before Matt could follow, the bartender shouted, "You need to pay."

"Open a tab," replied Matt. "I'm sure I'll be back." The bartender shrugged and turned his attention to the television bolted to the wall.

They found Aaron celebrating his second consecutive strike with a strange sort of dance that made him look like he was being electrocuted while in the middle of an epileptic seizure. Matt sat in the Day-Glo orange booth and sipped his beer. Aaron waved Twilana to the lane, handed her a ball, and encouraged her to roll. Matt couldn't help but think how Aaron's excitement over the sport was borderline creepy.

* * * * *

Aaron passed hours bowling and was going into his thirty-second frame. Matt passed the hours drinking beer and wondering if he still had lips. Twilana began to understand bowling a little better and, at Aaron's prodding, played for quite some time. But after twenty four frames, she had enough and chose to help Matt run up his bar tab.

Picking up his nineteenth spare of the night, Aaron looked up at Matt and Twilana. Matt's head rested on his hand, staring off into space, his eyelids drooping. Twilana laid her head on the table and slept silently. In all fairness, though, this wasn't due to the boredom of bowling; she was pretty hammered by that point.

"Come on, guys," Aaron prodded. "This game is no fun with only one person."

"This game is no fun with any number of people," replied Matt, grabbing his mug. He swirled the beer around the bottom of it before downing it.

Aaron joined them in the too-small booth, sweat dripping from his brow. His shirt had grown dark in patches from the ball-rolling exertion of the past two and a half hours.

"I don't know how you're having a good time," Matt continued. "This place is more boring than my Aunt Edna's family reunions."

"Well, at least it's better than being attacked by seven-foot lizard people or being tossed into the middle of an Asian civil war." Aaron picked up Twilana's mug and took a sip, grimacing as the warm beer hit his taste buds.

Twilana lifted her head from the table. "I'll take the seven-foot lizard people any day," she said groggily before dropping her head with a thud.

"It's not even about that," Matt said, sloshing the beer as he placed the mug on the table. "Have you even looked around this place?"

"Yeah, it's a bowling alley," Aaron replied. "So what?"

"Have you seen any doors? Windows even?"

"Most bowling alleys don't have windows," he said, matter-of-factly.

Matt rolled his eyes, shaking his head in frustration. "You know what I mean, ass. Have you seen a way out of this place?"

Aaron scanned the room, looking for an exit of any kind. "Come to think of it, I haven't."

"Just my point. It would seem that we are trapped in a giant bowling alley."

Aaron considered the observation for a moment. "That's impossible," he said dismissively. "Look at all of these people. If they can get in here, they have to be able to get out."

Matt looked up at a portly gentleman who happened to be passing the table. He wore a sleeveless t-shirt that was white at the time of purchase, and faded blue jeans, the knees fraying away to holes. His "John Deere" baseball cap seemed to be more an extension of his mullet rather than placed on top of it. Though Matt was slightly frightened by the man, he gathered the courage to speak to him.

"Excuse me, sir?" The appellation was more of respect for a stranger than of the perceived status of the man. The man grumbled over to the table with a polite smile. Matt could see that his once white t-shirt was stained yellow from equal parts sweat and nacho cheese.

"Wha' kin I do yuh fer?" The man asked. Though a

distance of four feet separated them, Matt smelled the unmistakable odor of regurgitated whiskey. Gulping back a heave, he continued. "Well, me and my friend here were wondering what else is around here."

The man raised his arms to motion around the building, giving Matt a clear view of the forest of hair growing from his armpits. "Well, y'got the snack shop over thur, the bar behin' me wit' a TV showin' the NASCAR races, and onna other side is the Ms. Pac-Man machine. Watch out fer that one," he warned, leaning in close enough to make Matt's eyes water, "I done lost so much money to Ms. Pac-Man that she should start callin' herself a hooker." The man reared back and released a massive howl at his joke. Matt jumped at the sudden outburst. He smiled graciously, afraid to insult the behemoth of a man.

"No," Aaron chimed in. "What he means is, what's outside the bowling alley?"

The amused look on the man's face turned to utter confusion at the question. "Outside the bowlin' alley? Whatchoo mean 'outside the bowlin' alley'? We got everything we need right hur. Beer. The ladies." The man tipped his head to something in the distance and winked. Aaron turned to see a very large woman in a too-tight tank top and cut-off jeans blush with giddiness. Her cheeks turned a bright-orange, matching both the color of her eyeshadow and the mop of hair on her head. A shudder rippled through Aaron's body at the thought of the woman as a sexual object.

"And we got alla bowlin' yuh could wan'," the man finished. "What more could yuh need?"

"See," Matt said, regaining his composure, "we were looking to get some tacos, play a little billiards, maybe catch a movie. Where might we go to do that?"

The man scratched his head, causing his cap to tilt from side to side. "Gee, boyo, I couldn't help ya thur. See, we're parta a league hur, so our days are pretty much full o' bowlin'." He paused to release a small burp. "Com'a think of it, we need a sub for one'a our guys. He got sick the other day and couldn't make it. Maybe one'a youse could fill his spot."

Aaron felt a wave of triumph rush through his body and shot Matt an 'I-Told-You-So' look. Matt's theory of a 'Bowling Alley Universe' had been incorrect. Aaron prodded the man for more information to cement his victory. "Really? That's too bad. Where is he now?"

"Right over thur," replied the man, tilting his head to the side. Matt and Aaron looked in the direction and found a skinny man bundled in a ragged blanket. His head was soaked with sweat, his eyes slits in his face, and an old bucket sat next to his chair. "Old Ray musta ate something that didn't agree wit' 'im. Been tossin' his cookies fer three days now. I tol' that blamed fool not ta eat all those hot dogs after the 'frigerator broke down."

Aaron's internal victory celebration ground to a halt. Turning back, he saw Matt wearing the expression he had been just a few seconds earlier. Feeling some confidence that he still may be right, Aaron asked for more information. "Why doesn't he just go home? Surely he would be more comfortable there."

"Nah. Ray's fine right where he is." Another burp. "So whadda ya say? Either'a you fellas feel like subbing?"

Matt turned his glare from Aaron back to the man and resumed his original tone of respect. "No, no. We are already on a team."

"Suit yerselves." The man turned and walked away, leaving Matt triumphant and Aaron dumbfounded.

"Shit. Maybe you're right," Aaron conceded.

Matt pushed his empty beer mug to the side and grabbed Twilana's, draining it in a single swig. "Tell me about it," he said, all of his hopes plummeting to the floor.

CHAPTER 47

"A bowling alley universe," mumbled Matt into his beer. "A strip club universe I could take, but a bowling alley universe?"

Twilana awoke a few hours after Matt and Aaron made their disheartening discovery. They took turns filling her in between trips to the men's room and refilling their beers. Twilana had many questions about their whereabouts, but most of them really had to do about the game of bowling itself. She watched the patrons, examining the way they threw the balls down the lane, only to have them reappear through the loud machine a minute later. As her mind devised a plan of escape, she spotted Gabriel peering around a corner, watching them. It was the third time he had looked their way. "We're being watched," she said, cocking her chin toward the far wall.

Aaron turned drowsily as Gabriel disappeared behind the wall. "What's that all about?"

"Perhaps that Metatron guy and those angels are holding us prisoner," she said.

"Well, I can't think of any place more torturous than a bowling alley, that's for sure," Matt remarked.

Twilana raised her eyebrow. "Wait here," she said and pushed off from the table, rising to her feet. She approached the concession stand and reached over the counter, pulling three Styrofoam cups from the stack next to the soda machine. Snatching up a handful of spoons from a tray of plasticware on top of the counter, she headed back to the table, placing her collection of disposable utensils in front of Matt and Aaron before hurrying off again.

"What's she up to?" Aaron asked. Matt shrugged wordlessly, raising his beer to his lips. He watched as Twilana headed toward a cigarette vending machine, grabbing the box of matchbooks sitting atop the machine. She looked around the area, her eyes landing on two more boxes of matchbooks on the floor. She scooped them up and stacked the boxes together. Twilana scanned the room, finding a nearby supply closet.

She twisted the doorknob. It was locked. She crouched down and peered around for something she could use to pick the lock but oddly, the floor was free of debris. Sighing dejectedly, she rose to her feet. Her gaze floated around the bowling alley, her mind working to create a plan B. She spotted a chubby man on a stool behind a cash register and an idea came to light.

Twilana walked to the booth, placing the boxes she held on the table next to the cups and spoons.

"What *are* you doing?" Aaron asked. Shooting him a quick glance, she answered with a wink and sauntered over to the man.

Leaning on the counter, Twilana worked up her most saucy, seductive smile. She waited for the man to acknowledge her, but he was, at the moment, fully engaged with in his handheld video game.

"Hi," she crooned, grabbing the man's attention.

"Hello," he replied, pushing his glasses up on the bridge of his nose. "Can I help you?"

"I hope so," she said, glancing at his nametag, "Morty." She twirled a length of hair between her fingers.

The man cleared his throat. He could have been attractive, had he known the secret of Proactiv. His hair also could have used a little attention, looking like he just rolled out of bed. Three days ago. Without showering. His clothes, however, were at the height of fashion. In the '80s. And a couple of days on a treadmill wouldn't have hurt him either.

But other than that, he was fairly good looking. Which is why he could understand how this beautiful woman would be interested in him.

Morty pressed a button on the video game and placed it on the counter. Rising to his feet, he smiled. "Anything for you, pretty lady." He did his best to be charming. He needed to take a few more lessons.

Twilana batted her eyes. "I was wondering…" She allowed the thought to trail off. "No. It's silly."

Her coyness amused Morty and he flashed her a very toothy grin. Apparently he did not have an education on the proper use of a toothbrush. Dental hygiene aside, he placed his elbows on the counter and leaned closer to her. "It's not silly. What can I do for you?"

"I was wondering if you had keys to that room over there." She raised her arm and pointed to the storage closet. She gave the gesture a little twirl, to add some extra flirtation.

Morty's smile widened, showing a few holes where teeth should be. Apparently he did not have very good dental coverage, either. "Of course I have keys." He jingled a set of keys hanging from a belt loop. "I have keys to every room in this place. I *am* a supervisor, after all."

Twilana gave him a look, feigning shock. "Really?" She smiled, scrunching up her nose and narrowing her eyes. "I like a man with power." A throaty giggle finished the exchange.

Lifting his elbows, Morty lumbered from behind the counter. He removed the keys from his belt loop, cocking his head at Twilana. "Show me which room you want to check out, toots." Another toothy grin.

She cringed at the nickname but ignored it, deciding that it was wiser to keep up the façade than punch Morty in the throat. So she smiled and headed toward the storage closet, swaying her hips dramatically as she walked. She could almost feel Morty's eyes burrowing a hole through her derriere.

Twilana led Morty past Matt and Aaron. Matt was stifling a laugh while Aaron shook his head amusedly. She rolled her eyes and ignored them.

She came to a stop beside the closet and leaned against the doorframe. "Here it is, sweetie," she remarked with a playful grin.

Morty beamed and fumbled with the keys. He dropped them, picked them up, chuckled, and fumbled again. After moments of searching, Morty found the correct key and slipped it into the keyhole. As he did so, Twilana pinched a bundle of nerves on the back of his neck, causing him to collapse, the key stuck in the doorknob.

Twilana turned the key and the knob simultaneously and

swung the door open. Bending down, she wound her hands under Morty's armpits, restraining her gag-reflex at the dampness of Morty's shirt. She dragged him into the closet and closed the door. She groped around in the darkness for a light switch, finding a dangling string in the center of the room. A quick tug allowed Twilana just enough light to see.

The room was a standard storage area. Rusted metal shelves lined each wall. Most of the shelves were dented or bent, the result of being forced to hold too much. On each shelf were cans of chemicals, bottles of chemicals, and puddles of chemicals that had leaked from various cans and bottles over the years.

Squinting in the semi-lightness, Twilana read the labels on the containers. Latex paint. Glass cleaner. Liquid wax. She noted that many of the cleaning supplies had never been opened and wondered just how clean the bowling alley could be. She winced at the thought.

Her eyes fell upon a white, plastic container. She read the label. *Weed-B-Gon*. Picking it up, Twilana shook the container, gauging the amount it held. Satisfied, she continued to rummage around the closet.

A gray, cubical box sat on the floor next to the door, the word 'RYOBI' embossed across the top. Twilana grabbed it, tucked it under her arm, and left the room, leaving Morty snoring on the cement floor.

Four tear-soaked eyes greeted her at the table. Matt had doubled over with stomach pains from a fit of intense laughter as Aaron's final chuckles had finally begun to dissipate. She not-so-gently placed the bottle and the box on the table, its sudden thud announcing the end of the hilarity.

"Not one word," she demanded with no other explanation.

Shooing Aaron, Twilana sat in the plastic booth. She separated the cups, placing them side by side. Grabbing the boxes of matchbooks, she slid one in front of Matt and Aaron.

"Make yourselves useful and scrape the match heads into this cup."

They opened the boxes and did as they were told, scraping silently. A few minutes had passed before the curiosity got the best of Matt.

"So, what are we doing here?"

205

Twilana grabbed the box, snapped the yellow plastic hinges and lifted the lid. She pulled out a power drill and squeezed the trigger. A soft 'whir' accompanied the spin of the chuck.

"Getting us out of here."

She fished around the inside of a box, sifting through the collection of drill bits that were haphazardly tossed in after the last person used the drill. Finding a large bit, she slid it into the chuck and tightened it. Placing the drill on the table, she rose from the booth and toed to the nearest ball rack. Her eyes scanned the racks, reading the engraved numbers on each of the balls. Grabbing a purple one, for no other reason than it matched her eyes, she rolled it around in her hands. Satisfied with its weight, she rushed up the tiny steps and dropped the ball on the table.

It only took Twilana thirty seconds to drill a suitable hole in the ball. Then about ten minutes more to crush the foam core in the center of the ball and shake it free. The most time was spent scraping the match heads, which took both Matt and Aaron a combined total of ninety minutes and four beers. However, in all fairness, after the first two beers, the scraping was much harder to focus on.

When they finished, Twilana grabbed each of their cups and swished them around. Content with the amount of scrapings, she picked up the container of weed killer and unscrewed the cap. She tipped the weed killer over the empty cup, filling it about a third of the way.

Recapping the weed killer, Twilana picked up a spoon from the table and began to shovel match head scrapings into the liquid, stirring slowly after each addition. Aaron realized that Twilana hadn't answered Matt's question earlier and decided to dig a little deeper into her plan. "How is this going to help us get out of here?" he asked, sipping the last of his beer.

Mid-scoop, Twilana raised her eyes, her face blank considering possible answers. Should she explain her plan and have them inundate her with millions of questions? That would be annoying, especially when she needed to concentrate. She could keep ignoring their questions, but then she runs the risk of them continually asking what her plan was, which would be annoying. She decided to answer in a 'keep things cryptic but reassure them that everything will work out fine' tactic.

"It just will."

Aaron released a loud sigh that expressed both his frustration with being kept in the dark and his anticipation to learn what Twilana was doing. Twilana realized the double meaning of the sigh, and smiled to herself.

Adding the final scoop to the liquid, Twilana stirred it for a good half minute. Lifting the spoon, she shook a clump of pasty, red goop plop back into the cup. She looked at Matt.

"Hold the ball steady."

Matt wrapped his hands around the purple sphere, a dull pain thudding through his hand. For the first time of the night, he realized how much better he was feeling. His body still ached and he felt a straining in his chest when he inhaled, but after all he'd been through, he was happy to just not be engulfed in pain any longer.

Twilana carefully spooned the red goop into the freshly drilled hole, pushing the paste down as far at the spoon would allow. She instructed Matt to shake the ball slightly so that the goop would drop down into the inner cavity of the ball. They alternated filling and shaking until the cup was empty. Twilana then slid a few tiny nails she found at the bottom of the drill case into the hole, and filled it with pieces of Styrofoam torn from the cup. Once the work was done, Twilana decided it was time to share her plan with her companions.

"What we have here, gentlemen, is a bomb."

Though Matt and Aaron's interest in Twilana's project had waned significantly since she started, the final word of her statement brought their attention right back.

Aaron placed his elbows on the table, eyes wide, and leaned in to listen to her clarification.

"You just built a bomb in an hour and a half with shit you found in a bowling alley?"

Twilana's pride swelled up at the succinct summarization of what she had accomplished. A wry smile spread on her face. "Well, it was really quite simple. Most people don't even realize how explosive some ordinary household items really are."

"So, how do we use it?" Matt asked.

Twilana continued. "All we have to do it toss the ball down the alley…"

Before she got the chance to finish her instructions, Matt grabbed the ball and hopped down the two steps leading to the bowling lanes. Pushing a rather large gentleman to the side, he tossed the ball down the lane. As it rolled toward the pins, he crouched down, covering his head. Twilana, Aaron, and the angry bowling patron watched as the ball veered into the gutter and harmlessly disappeared behind the pins.

"What you go and throw a ball down my lane for?" the portly gentleman asked.

Matt peeked his eyes out from under his arms, expecting to see a gaping hole in the wall of the building and flaming debris flying in all directions. But all he found was an irate fat man.

Erecting his body, Matt brushed off his pants, cleared his throat, and said "I'm sorry. I thought this was my lane." He hurried up the steps, not worrying if the lie had successfully placated the man.

"What the hell? Nothing exploded. Your bomb didn't work."

Twilana shook her head. "It would have worked if you did it right. It's an impact bomb. You have to *hit* something in order for it to go off."

She turned to Aaron. "Can you please..?" Aaron nodded and rose from the seat, making his way to the ball return.

He grabbed the purple ball as it erupted from the mechanism and slipped his fingers into the holes. Sauntering to the lane, he held the ball at eye level, lining up his shot. He took three steps, swung his arm, and released the ball.

Twilana watched the ball as it rocketed down the lane. "You'll want to take cover now," she said to Matt, pulling him under the table.

The ball struck the pins and an explosion ripped through the building. A wave of flame spilled from the ball, engulfing the pins, the mechanical arm, the neon lights and the wall itself. Smoke billowed as concrete and metal tore from the structure and flew in every direction from the blast. A cloud of dust spread through the bowling alley, covering everything it touched in tiny particulates of cement.

As the fire died down and the dust settled, Aaron looked around at the fallout of the explosion. Pure white light poured in through the newly created hole.

Matt and Twilana crawled out from under the table and made their way to Aaron's side. Matt examined the hole. "Nice spare."

"It would have been a strike if you didn't suck."

Twilana smiled at the derisive friendship of her traveling mates. "Come on, you two" she said. "Let's see what's out there." She stepped onto the polished alley toward the hole in the wall.

CHAPTER 48

The blast shook the foundation of the building and Michael's eyes widened with confusion. He looked up at Gabriel, watching as he stared up at the ceiling. The dumbfounded look on his face told Michael that Gabriel was just as confused as he was. They raced from the kitchenette out onto the main floor of the bowling alley, finding the travelers running down the bowling lane toward a massive hole in the wall.

Michael slapped Gabriel on the chest, fanning the dust away from his face with his other hand. "Stop them!" he shouted.

Gabriel looked at Michael and nodded. Placing his hand on the hilt of his sword, he flapped his wings and lifted his body into the air. The sword burst into flames as he pulled it from its scabbard. With the speed of an eagle, Gabriel took off toward the travelers.

Twilana heard Michael's shouting through the ringing in her ears. Her head snapped around and she spotted Gabriel barreling toward her. She let her instincts to take over and rolled to the side, dodging Gabriel's attack. A spittle of flame rained down on her as he passed overhead. She brushed the sparks away and pivoted on her heels

Gabriel swung around and hovered in the air for a moment. His face contorted into a grimace as he looked down at her. He spotted Michael as he rushed toward them, his flaming sword in hand.

Aaron watched as the angels descended on them. His heart

pounded in his chest and he could feel the sweat rolling down his back. He broke into a run but his feet lost traction on the highly polished wood. He stumbled to his knees and reached out, grabbing Matt's shirt. As Aaron fell, he pulled Matt's center of balance down and they both crashed to the floor.

Twilana dropped to a knee, her eyes steadied on Gabriel. She watched as the angel drew back his sword and flew straight toward her. She braced herself as he picked up speed, drawing closer to her position.

Gabriel's arm flexed as he swung the sword. Forcing her legs out from beneath her, Twilana dropped to the floor, landing flat on her back. Gabriel's sword swiped over her face, barely missing her. As he glided over her, she punched upward, hitting his neck, striking a bundle of nerves. His body tensed and his wings went immobile. Slamming into the floor, Gabriel skidded a few yards, his sword clattering down the lane.

Twilana loped across the floor and grabbed Gabriel's sword as Michael swooped in front of the hole, blocking their escape. His sword in flames, he urged them to advance, taunting them with his eyes. Aaron raised his head from the floor and spotted Michael. He froze in fear as the angel's eyes bore down on him.

"You'll not be going anywhere," Michael said, stepping toward them.

Twilana grasped the sword with both hands. As she stared at Michael, she could feel the anger inside her growing, bubbling to the surface. In the past two days she had fallen into a dimensional portal, been a prisoner, had her life threatened numerous times, and she lost count of the number of people she's had to kill. She didn't want any of those things to happen but someone was always there forcing her hand. She was hungry, tired, and just wanted to go home. And she wasn't about to let some guy with wings and a bad attitude get in her way.

Michael smiled wickedly as Twilana stepped toward him. He placed the tip of his sword to the floor and the room rumbled as a giant crack opened in the floor. Michael thrust the sword deeper into the floor and the crack widened, spreading towards Twilana. She shifted her weight and leaped out of its path but her foot slipped and she fell to the ground. The crevice passed beneath her, swallowing her. She reached out, just barely grabbing the side of the chasm, her body dangling above the widening void.

Aaron watched as Twilana disappeared into the floor. He pushed himself up to his hands and feet, crawling awkwardly towards the crevice. He flopped to the ground and shot his hand over the edge, grabbing Twilana's wrist. He held her tightly, bracing himself on the floor, trying to keep her from falling farther into the hole. But each time he felt he had enough traction, the slick floor showed him otherwise as he inched closer and closer to the edge. Looking up, Aaron watched as Michael lumbered toward them, flaming sword in hand, anger etched into his face.

"I don't want to kill you," Michael said, "but I will. You are an important part of Lucifer's plan, and I cannot let you leave here until I figure out how he intends to use you."

Aaron watched in fear as Michael raised his sword above his head, the flaming tip aimed for Aaron's back. Looking down the lane, he spotted Matt struggling rising to his feet.

Matt balanced himself against the slippery floor. His head snapped back and forth, his eyes searching the room. He carefully stepped down the bowling lane, away from Michael and the massive crevice.

Matt rushed the last few feet from the bowling lane onto the platform. Reaching out, he lunged for the ball return and grabbed a ball in each hand. Shaking his head, he considered the ridiculousness of his plan, wondering if he could make it work. He pushed the doubt out of his mind, knowing if he failed, his friends would be dead. He turned back to Michael and walked confidently toward the lanes.

"Hey, jerkoff," Matt shouted. Michael lifted his gaze to him am his sword hovered over Aaron's back.

Wordlessly, Matt rolled one ball down the lane, then the other. Michael watched as the colorful spheres inched their way toward him. He threw his head back and laughed. Taking one step to the side, the balls meandered past him harmlessly. He looked up at Matt, the fury in his eyes replaced with irritated amusement.

"Did you really think that would work?"

Aaron looked down at Twilana. She placed her feet on the wall of the crack, pulling her knees into her chest. She nodded to him. Summoning all of his strength, he pulled his arm backward, wrenching Twilana from the crevice as she kicked off from the wall. The momentum sent her flying up, over the edge of the hole.

Twilana landed on the floor in front of Michael, plunging the flaming sword into his stomach.

Michael looked down at the hilt sticking out of his body. Angrily, he swung his sword at Twilana. She ducked out of the way and punched him in the ribcage. He stumbled backward and Twilana lifted her foot to deliver a roundhouse kick to his chin.

Michael dropped to his knees and tipped over onto his side. His sword clattered from his hand. Tilting his head he watched as the trio bolt for the hole. He sat up, spotting Sauriel and Raphael as they emerged from the basement stairwell. They looked around the room, shocked at the chaos they found.

"Get them you idiots!" Michael shouted, pointing to the gaping hole in the wall.

The order snapped them from their reverie. Sauriel flapped his wings, taking to the air. He rushed toward the travelers, trying to block their escape but he only managed to get a few feet before they disappeared into the light.

CHAPTER 49

Sauriel stopped in mid-air as the trio disappeared into the light. He lowered himself to the floor, folding his wings behind his back. Turning, he looked at Michael and Gabriel lying on the floor. It was a rare sight to see the General and his right-hand man defeated. He knew the likelihood of catching the travelers was slim, and that he would be better served helping his commanding officers. Sauriel also knew that this decision would earn him a reprimand from Michael but he didn't care.

Gabriel rolled over to his side, pushed himself up on one arm. His head buzzed from the impact, the neck tingling where Twilana struck him. He shook his head, turned to find Sauriel standing in front of the hole, the travelers nowhere to be seen.

Sauriel pointed to Gabriel. "Help him out," he shouted to Raphael. Raphael took to the air and rushed to Gabriel's side. He placed his hand under Gabriel's elbow, steadying his weight while he pulled himself up. Raphael grabbed Gabriel's chin, twisting his head from left to right, examining the contusions on his face. He checked his pupils for signs of a concussion, satisfied that Gabriel's worst injury was to his pride.

Sauriel knelt over Michael's unmoving body. He placed both hands on the hilt of the sword in his belly and pulled it slowly, inching the blade from the wound. Raphael joined them, kneeling on the floor beside Michael. Rubbing his hands furiously, the white glow shone from between his fingers. He watched as the blade emerged from Michael's stomach. The flame of the sword cauterized the wound, reducing the bleeding but left the skin of Michael's belly bubbling and festering. Raphael moved his glowing hands over Michael's wound, but Michael pushed him to the side and rose to his feet. He looked from Raphael to Sauriel to Gabriel, the disappointment evident on his face. Shaking his head, Michael bent over and picked up his sword.

"General," Gabriel said pitifully. "Are you OK?"

Michael pushed his way past the angels, avoiding eye contact. He mumbled softly to himself as he walked off.

"You are all worthless."

CHAPTER 50

Matt landed flat on his stomach. The fall scratched his face and knocked the wind out of him. He lay on the hot concrete for a moment before lifting himself up on his arms and sitting back on his knees. He pushed to his feet and took two large steps backward. Looking up, he shielded his eyes from the sun and watched as Aaron and Twilana appeared from the swirling vortex in the sky. They spun and tumbled in mid-air before crashing to the concrete at Matt's feet. He reached down and offered them both hands, helping them up.

They dusted themselves off as Matt's eyes swept the large glass and metal buildings, feeling a sense of familiarity about the city. It was remarkably unremarkable, unlike the last few places they visited. No anthropomorphic alligators. No sadistic despot out to destroy half of Asia. It seemed a lot like his own, beloved New York City, but much cleaner. The roads well maintained and free of potholes. The air smelled fresh, lacking the permeating aroma of hot garbage and urine.

It was this that gave him his first hint that something was off.

Looking to his left, Matt spied a newspaper stand a few yards away. He rushed over and browsed the titles on the shelf. Though many of the title logos were familiar, the names were all unknown to him.

Seraphim Quarterly. Wing and Flyer. Angels.

He picked up a copy of *The New Eden Post* and stared at the front page story. The headline referred to the disappearance of the Angelic High Military's general in arms, featuring a picture of the angel that tried to kill them in the bowling alley. The caption beneath the photo proclaimed the angel's name to be Michael.

Matt held up the newspaper to Aaron and Twilana. "Out of the frying pan, huh?" he said, thumbing through the pages.

"Wonderful," Aaron said. "We try to get away from them and land right in their backyard. What are the odds of that?"

"Pretty good, apparently," Matt said, his voice dripping with sarcasm.

A small squeaky voice rose from behind the rows of magazines.

"This ain't a library, bub. You gonna pay for that or what?"

Matt looked up to find a baby-faced man staring back at him. The man pushed his ascot cap back on his head, allowing him a clearer view to grimace at the deadbeat customers.

Placing the newspaper back on the stack, Matt felt an odd sense of comfort. Even beyond the universal barriers, some things never changed. He gave Babyface a quick smile before turning back to Aaron and Twilana.

"According to that newspaper, those guys from the bowling alley are the military here," Matt said. "Their HQ got overrun, and they were forced to hide out. If we find their HQ, we find the guys who wanted them out."

"Why do you keep saying 'HQ'?" Aaron said.

"And then what?" Twilana asked, ignoring the remark. "We just walk into the lion's den and ask 'Can you send us home now? Why would they even help us?'"

Matt considered her question for a moment, shrugging his shoulders.

"I really don't think we have a better option," Aaron said, settling the debate. "If we find these guys, we may be able to trade the location of the angels for a trip home."

"I don't like it," Twilana replied. "Can we really just give up the angels like that? Aren't they supposed to be the good guys?"

"They just tried to kill us," Matt said, his patience finally breaking. "Do you really consider that 'good'?"

As they argued, Aaron looked up at the city. He was impressed with the architecture of the buildings, marveling at the post-modern futurism the city portrayed. One building caught his attention, the golden accents shining brightly in the mid-day sun. Tilting his head back, he bathed in the beauty of the tower. His eyes traced the letters adorned the crest of the building, barely missing their importance.

Reaching back, Aaron tapped on Matt's shoulder, pointed up to the letters. Matt's eyes widened as he realized the significance, his mouth curling into a curious smile.

AHM.

"They couldn't be that stupid," he said, turning to Aaron and Twilana. "To just advertise like that?" Without waiting for an answer, he turned and broke out into a sprint toward the building.

Matt pushed himself through the building's revolving door, riding it around a second time for no other reason than just because. As he stepped into the building, his shoes sloshed in an inch-deep puddle of water. He looked up and watched as the water flowed from an exposed copper pipe jutting from the center of a broken fountain. The marble was crushed, shards of stone scattered throughout the room. Matt nudged a stone face with his foot and the lifeless eyes spun to look at the other side of the room.

Aaron and Twilana caught up to him, stunned at the damage surrounding them. Aaron stepped over pieces of marble and looked down at a heavy metal door lying on the floor. The edges of the door were torn and twisted, appearing to have been blown off its hinges. He squatted down and lifted the corner of the door, revealing a lifeless body. The man's eyes were pale and cloudy, frozen in fear. The water permeated his body, his flesh bloated and distended. Even Aaron could tell that his wings were bent at unnatural angles. He breathed a pitiful sigh and slowly lowered the door onto him.

"Maybe the angels *are* the good guys," Aaron said aloud. "Just look at this place. Who would have done this?"

Matt shook his head as he rifled through the remains of the solitary desk in the room. He grabbed a mint from the desktop and unwrapped it, placing it in his mouth. "I'm at the point where I don't care. All I wanna do is go the hell home."

"Maybe we can help you with that."

Three heads snapped up in unison, eyes landing on a tall, dark haired man standing on the railing a few floors up. He leaned forward, arms spread out wide, and slid from the golden bar. He fell a few feet before two large, black wings erupted from his back. He flapped them a couple of times, pivoting his body in mid-air and landed gently on his feet.

"So you are the trio that has Michael in such a tizzy," Nathaniel said, his wings folding behind his back. He straightened his t-shirt and ran a hand across his head to fix his hair.

Twilana stared at the angel, finding something different about him. Despite the clothing he wore, a striking difference to the military fatigues of the angels they met earlier, he had a different air about him. He didn't bother trying to come off as friendly or welcoming. With the way he looked at them, his face taut and hard, it seemed as if he didn't care about frightening people. It looked like he, in fact, preferred it.

"We don't want any trouble," Twilana said. She held her hands up, palms out, showing him that they meant no harm.

Nathaniel took a bold step forward, folding his arms across his chest. "I believe you. In fact, I was waiting for you."

Matt tilted his head, his eyes narrowed. "How could you have known we were coming?"

Nathaniel threw his head back releasing a loud laugh, startling Matt. When his laugh subsided, he looked at Matt with a wide smile. "Buddy, you're all the angels can talk about."

Twilana looked at Aaron and watched as his face melted into a look of uncertainty. He shrugged, unsure of how to proceed in the situation. Luckily, Matt was willing to handle things.

"You said you could help us," Matt said. "Can you get us home?"

"I never said I could help you," Nathaniel replied. "But I know someone who can."

"Take us to him," Matt responded.

Nathaniel stood his ground, arms over his chest. His eyes passed between the three faces staring at him, studying them like a dissected frog in a high school science class. His intention was to intimidate them, to make them feel like they had no choice in his decisions, but at the end of it all, there was only one outcome; that which Lucifer desired.

But they didn't need to know that.

Exhaling, Nathaniel's eyes fell on Matt. "Fine. Come with me. He turned and walked down a hallway at the rear of the building. Matt rushed to keep up with him.

Aaron stepped next to Twilana, his elbow brushing hers. He turned to her as she looked up at him and watched the color in her eyes swirl to a misty gray.

"Yeah, I don't like this either," he said. Slipping his hand into hers, they stepped after Matt and Nathaniel.

Nathaniel led them to the back of the atrium to a small, rickety elevator, hidden away from the rest of the building. He pressed the button on the wall and the doors slid open. As they piled into the tiny elevator, Aaron felt that it would have been cramped with four regular people, but the addition of Nathaniel's large wings made it downright suffocating.

As Nathaniel pressed the button labeled *28*, Matt spotted the engraved number *6*, smiled to himself at the extra *66* scrawled next to it in black marker, enjoying the demonic humor. The doors closed and the elevator car shot upward.

A few seconds later, the doors opened. Standing outside the elevator was a well-dressed man in a three piece suit, smiling deviously.

"Good morning, lady and gentlemen," the man said. "I don't think we've been formally introduced."

CHAPTER 51

Michael's telepathic message went out to every nearby angel, alerting them of his plans. He ordered every available soldier to join him at the bowling alley so he can go into further detail. Many of them were involved in important missions on other worlds and were unable to abandon their posts. But the others he recalled on the principle of a Universal Emergency. He was also forced to call in the reserves of lower tier angels and cherubim to bolster his ranks. He waited for his army to arrive at the bowling alley, going over his plan with Gabriel and Sauriel. When they arrived, he realized his forces consisted of twenty five Angelic soldiers, each one undisciplined and lacking the experience he required for the task at hand.

"This is it?" he said, examining his army. Most of the soldiers were fresh faced, barely trained in the proper use of a flaming sword, and there wasn't a single one old enough to remember his exile of Lucifer. He shook his head and paced the floor.

I leaned in to Sauriel. "Why didn't he call them in when Lucifer first attacked?" I whispered. He looked at me and shrugged, turning back to Michael. I couldn't grasp the fact that Michael would allow himself to be run out of his own headquarters by an onslaught of Demons yet call in the full force of his army to chase after three, powerless humans. A sharp *SHHHH* snapped me out of my thinking. I looked up to find Gabriel staring at me, a finger to his lips. His eyes flashed with annoyance.

"Troops," Michael began. "Your mission today is of the utmost importance. We have reason to believe that three off-worlders have joined forces with our fallen brothers, Lucifer and Nathaniel. These three have already viciously attacked Gabriel and myself...."

It was hard to tell who was more surprised at Michael's words, me or Sauriel. There's no denying that the travelers were trying to escape, but Michael and Gabriel technically attacked *them*, forcing them to defend themselves. I wondered why Michael chose to skew the truth in such a manner.

Michael continued. "And now they have disappeared, most likely to alert Lucifer of our presence. Since they are a vital component of Lucifer's plans to over-throw our power, they must be stopped. By any means necessary. You all have your orders. Dismissed."

As the army of angels dispersed, I watched Sauriel rush to Michael's side. Though I couldn't hear what they said, I could tell the gist of the conversation from Michael's anger. He flicked his wrist, dismissing Sauriel. He turned and walked away, his face wrenched in disappointed anger. He looked at me and I read the silent apology in his face.

CHAPTER 52

"Well, technically," Aaron said, "we haven't been formally introduced to anyone."

"Except for the Metatron guy," Twilana added.

Lucifer smiled. "Ahh, Metatron. I haven't seen him in ages. How is the old man? You know what? It doesn't matter. You probably know of me as I have many names, but I prefer to go by Lucifer. But you can call me Lou. And I really should apologize to you."

"Apologize?" Matt asked. "For what?"

"For all of this. It was never my intentions to drag you into this mess. But I must be honest with myself, I'm glad you did get mixed up in it. See there's something very important that I need, and only the two of you," he leveled his index fingers at Matt and Aaron, "can help me get it."

"What can we help *you* with?" Aaron said. "We just want to get home."

"And I want to send you home." Lucifer grasped his hands in front of his chest, giving him the appearance of a television evangelist. He spoke solemnly and without a hint of malice. He was very convincing for the Prince of Lies. "See, our two desires are interconnected. I cannot get what I want without sending you home, and sending you home gives me exactly what I want." His mouth twisted into a one-sided smile.

"You haven't answered my question," Aaron said. "What do we have to offer you?"

Lucifer smiled with the other half of his mouth. He clasped his hands at his waist and looked at Nathaniel. "Will you bring our guest in, please?" he said. His eyes shifted back to Aaron. "I'd like you three to follow me." Without waiting for a response Lucifer spun on his heels and walked down the hallway.

Aaron stepped forward and turned, meeting Matt face to face. "I don't like this, man. It's bad enough that the angels tried to kill us. Now we're dealing with Lucifer. We can't trust anything he says."

"What other choice do we have?" Matt asked, wiping his forehead with the back of his hand. He questioned why he was sweating so badly. The building's air conditioning kept the room cool and he hadn't had a fever since the angel rubbed his chest with light. It took him far too long to realize that the reason he was sweating was an anxious fear of the decision in front of him.

Twilana stepped in closer, listening to their conversation. "He has a point," she said, looking at Aaron. Aaron turned to her, eyes wide, mouth wider.

"How can you say that? This is insane!"

"It's not insane," Twilana added. "It is your only chance to go home."

"Yours too," Matt said.

Twilana closed her eyes and shook her head. "No. Not me. If I go back to Janus, I will be arrested and put to death. There's nothing for me there." Her breath caught in her throat. She chocked it back, inhaling deeply through her nose. "Not anymore."

Aaron looked at her, his eyes belying his sympathy. From behind her, the *click clack click* of expensive designer shoes rang through the hallway. Aaron turned to find Lucifer standing at the edge of the hall, his arms folded across his chest.

"You coming?"

Aaron nodded. Looking back at Twilana, he placed his hand in hers and gave it a reassuring squeeze. He tugged her arm, leading her toward Lucifer. Matt watched as they left.

"How come no one wants to hold *my* hand?" he mumbled under his breath before joining them.

"So maybe I haven't been all that forthcoming with you," Lucifer said as he led the trio down the hallway. "You've asked me a straight-forward question, which I've dodged for far too long. Tell me...do any of you know about the 'Apocalypse'?"

Aaron looked at the back of Lucifer's head, his eye drawn to the blinking blue light in his Bluetooth headset. "You mean the end of the world?"

Lucifer turned his head slightly, looked at Aaron quickly over his shoulder. "Ahh, see, that's a bit of a misnomer. The literal translation of 'Apocalypse' is 'a revelation of something hidden'. Some believe it to be the meaning of life. Others feel it is when the kingdom of Heaven throws its doors open to everyone."

"So what do you think it is?" Matt shouted from the rear. He dragged his hand along the polished silver railing as they walked, looked down at the damaged lobby below. He watched a thin trickle of water spurt from a broken pipe of the fountain.

Lucifer clapped and rubbed his hands together. "Well, I have a few ideas. Most of which involve me proving the Angelic Military wrong. See, the funny thing about 'Revelations' is that they are fluid. Malleable. It all depends on the last man standing and what they want to reveal."

"And you want to prove that the angels…" Aaron began.

"Are full of shit." Lucifer finished. He stopped shortly and faced Aaron. "Have you heard of the Leviathan?"

Aaron scoffed at the notion. "Have I heard of…?" He looked at Matt. "He asks if I've heard of *Leviathan*." Aaron turned back to Lucifer. "Of course I have. It's one of Ernie Hudson's best works."

"After *Ghostbusters*," Matt added.

Aaron nodded, pointing to Matt. "True."

Lucifer's smile vanished as he closed his eyes. He pinched the bridge of his nose, his face contorting as if someone had jammed needles under his fingernails. "No, not the movie *Leviathan*. THE Leviathan. A key component in the Apocalypse? Devourer of sinners?"

Aaron stared at him, shrugged his shoulders.

"No? Nothing?" Lucifer shook head, turned back to the doorway. "What are they teaching in schools these days?" he mumbled to himself. He walked in silence, allowing Aaron, Twilana, and Matt to follow. He quickly rounded a corner, his eyes burrowing into the door at the end of the hall.

As they reached the door, Aaron's voice chimed in. "But again, what does any of this have to do with us?" Lucifer's hand paused on the doorknob. He turned, the smile peeking through his lips.

"See, it's the Leviathan I need." He slowly pushed the door open. "And the Leviathan is on your world."

CHAPTER 53

Michael watched as his army of angels and seraphim exited the bowling alley. His plan was sound, strong enough to overtake the Angelic High Military building and reclaim their headquarters. The thought of Lucifer occupying his office made him nauseous, but the idea of Lucifer actually coming closer to his endgame... He spent millennia preventing Lucifer from bringing about the end of the world. He wasn't about to let up now.

"Do you think this is wise, sir?" Gabriel asked, pacing back and forth behind Michael. He had not left Michael's side since the skirmish in the bowling alley, concerned that some undiagnosed wound would incapacitate him at an inopportune moment. But now, Gabriel wondered if that wound was mental, a harsh blow to the head clouding his judgment, and he was witnessing the effects of it.

Michael had grown used to ignoring Gabriel when he began to prattle on. Gabriel was a loyal angel, but he never really had much to add to a conversation. His ideas were dense and short-sighted; Michael kept him around for his skills in battle, not his intellectual prowess. But at that moment, Gabriel's words grated on Michael's nerves, and he had no time to deal with Gabriel's whining.

Looking over his shoulder, Michael glared at Gabriel. "Never question my orders," he replied, a stern look in his eye. Michael leaned on the Day-Glo orange table and pored over the maps one final time. He was sure he knew the AHM building inside and out and had provided his troops with the perfect entry points to choke Lucifer off from his goal. But he needed to be certain that he hadn't made a mistake. "Why don't you make yourself useful and fetch me a new sword?"

Gabriel nodded. "Yes, sir." He turned toward the corridor leading to the basement of the bowling alley and picked up a black duffel bag, unzipping the flap. He rifled through the weapons they were able to grab before the evacuation and wrapped his fingers around the hilt of a sword. He turned it over in his hand, examining the leather wrapping around the handle. He flicked his wrist to the side and a spear of flame erupted from the end. The flame had a good balance to it. A steady, reliable feed. He flicked his wrist again, satisfied that Michael will be pleased with the weapon. Or, if not pleased, at least Gabriel won't get yelled at. He rushed back up the stairway and returned to Michael's side. He placed the sword on the table next to the maps.

Michael picked up the sword and slid the hilt into his belt. He folded the maps onto themselves and turned to the hole in the wall. He stared at the bright, white light, allowing it to wash over his body for a time. He closed his eyes and inhaled deeply, anticipating the coming battle with Lucifer. Envisioning his fallen brother's defeat in his mind. Opening his eyes, he exhaled and turned to Gabriel.

"It's time." His wings burst from his back, extending to their fullest. He flapped once, his body lifting clear off the floor. A few more flaps and Michael was rocketing toward the hole in the wall, disappearing into the bright, white light.

CHAPTER 54

The door slowly swung open, revealing Lauren seated at an old, cluttered desk. She sat back in the chair, feet propped up on a stack of crinkled, dog-eared papers. She filed her nails, examining their clean, smooth edges. Lauren looked up at the door as it swung inward, the breeze it created blowing the papers to the floor.

"Hello, brother," she giggled, swiveling in the chair. She placed her elbows on the desk and cupped her chin in her hands. As Twilana spotted the woman, her eyes narrowed in anger. She pushed past Lucifer, bounding into the room. She reached for her belt, grasping at the sword before she realized that she had left it in the bowling alley. Her fury got the better of her and she hopped up onto the desk. Lauren leaned back in the chair, out of the reach of Twilana's first swing. Lauren raised her hand and an invisible force knocked Twilana across the room. She collided into the wall, falling among a shower of leather-bound books and a cloud of dust.

Aaron rushed into the room, kicking the books as he flew to Twilana's side. He grabbed her arm and pulled her up from the floor. Twilana wiped the dust from her eyes, leaping toward Lauren again. Aaron tightened his grip, spinning her around, pulling her into his arms. He held her by the waist, struggling to subdue her.

Lauren shot from the chair, a ball of fire forming in her palm. Lucifer stepped forward, into the path between the crazed women. He looked at Lauren, shaking his head. She flapped her hand and extinguished the fireball, lowering herself back into the seat. Lucifer turned to Twilana, spreading his arms warmly.

"There's no trouble here," he said, his car salesman smile returning. "Whatever happened between you and Lauren is all in the past. Everything here is copacetic."

Twilana lunged forward one final time, almost pulling Aaron to the floor in the process, but he was able to maintain his balance. Twilana began to calm down and slowly stopped struggling against Aaron's hold.

Matt strolled into the room, picking up a book from the pile on the floor. He looked at the cover. *The History of the Golden Sphere of Ancaarta*. He flipped through the pages. The book looked more like a personal journal rather than a history book; handwritten pages, notes scrawled in the margins, a rough sketch of some kind of tool or symbol. He snapped the cover shut and dropped the book back onto the pile.

"Good," Lucifer said. "Now that we're all cool, let's get down to business." He clapped his hands again for emphasis. His eyes shifted to the door as it swung open wider. "Ah, fantastic! Our final guests are here!"

Lucifer waved his hand to the door, beckoning Nathaniel to enter. He tromped into the room, his big, black boots shaking the floor as he walked. A body was slung over his shoulder, a broken wing hung limply from its back. Behind him he dragged a second body by its clothes, a frail old man, his head covered in stringy white hair. Aaron looked down at the second figure, realizing who it was.

"How did Metatron get here?" Aaron asked.

Lucifer looked up at Nathaniel as he released my tunic, dropping me to the floor. I'll admit, things got a little hazy here, seeing as how I was unconscious for some of this, but based on the observations from other Grigori and the surveillance recovered from the building, this is an accurate retelling of the events. "Found him sneaking in the service entrance." Nathaniel turned and lowered the body on his shoulder into a cracked leather couch in the corner.

Lucifer chuckled a deep, throaty laugh. His body shook as a maniacal joy overtook him. "This is perfect! I couldn't have planned it better myself!" Lucifer stepped over to me and crouched down beside me. He slapped my face one, then twice to wake me. Placing his hand on my chest, he released a wave of telekinetic energy into me. My eyes snapped open and I sat straight up, gasping for air. Lucifer shot to his feet and stepped back, giving me space to breathe.

"Where am I?" I asked, searching the room. The place seemed familiar, as well it should. I was in my office, surrounded by all of my things. Papers sat on my desk as I left them, more or less. Though it looked like I was going to have to repair my bookcase.

Matt walked to me and extended his arm. I took his hand and he helped me to my feet. I brushed the dust from my tunic and felt a blazing pain in my head. Placing my hand on my forehead, I felt a tender lump. I turned to Nathaniel. "Did you have to hit me so hard?" He shrugged and sat on the corner of my desk.

Lucifer placed his hands on each of my biceps. "Now that you're here, Metatron, I need you to get me into the Ocularium."

I shook my head, trying to hide the fear in my eyes. I failed. "I…I can't do that."

The pressure on my arms increased as Lucifer's grip tightened. He pulled me closer, his face inches from mine.

"You can…" he said. Flames emerged from the corner of his eyes and his tongue split into a fork. "And you will."

I could feel my body begin to tremble. The heat coming off his skin grew unbearable, beads of sweat started to trickle down my face. I swallowed hard, freeing my Adam's apple from the headlock Lucifer's words had it in. I nodded my head before I even realized what I was doing.

Realizing I just signed the contract, Lucifer relaxed, his eyes and tongue returning to their normal state. He released my arms and stepped back. "Wonderful!"

I scanned the room, realizing all eyes were focused on me. Stepping backward, I slowly made my way toward the rear of my office, down the tiny corridor packed with file boxes. I placed my hand on the wall carving, closed my eyes and centered my concentration. A moment later, the door slid to the side, revealing the Ocularium.

Lucifer squealed with delight at the sight of the hidden room. He rushed down the corridor, knocking over the awkwardly stacked boxes, littering my office floor in a sea of paper. He pushed past me into the room, torn between the ecstasy of nearing his endgame and disappointment at the meager accommodations where it would take place.

Leaning through the doorway, Lucifer flapped his hands at the group. "Come, come! All of you. Nathaniel, bring Jehoel in here."

Nathaniel grabbed Jehoel's arms and lifted him from the couch. Winding his arm under his chest, he carried the unconscious angel like a sack of potatoes, Jehoel's feet dragging behind him. Matt and Aaron exchanged uneasy glances, finding the situation to be frighteningly bizarre.

"He means you, too," a gruff voice said from behind them. Matt turned to find Lauren, arms crossed, foot tapping on the hardwood floor, glaring at him. Matt turned and walked through the corridor, losing his balance as a sheet of paper slipped from under his foot. His hand shot out to the wall, catching himself before he fell.

Lauren placed her hand on Aaron, giving him a gentle shove. Twilana's face tensed and she raised up on her feet toward Lauren. "Touch us again and I will suck your eyeballs from their sockets," she hissed. Twilana added a "bitch" just for good measure. Lauren laughed at her threats but urged Aaron on without touching him.

The tiny room felt cramped being occupied by so many people, but not as cramped as it had just hours before. Lucifer tromped around the room, getting a feel for its energy. He barked orders like an uptight wedding planner, looking at Nathaniel, motioning to the Oculus in the center of the room. "Lean him against that. Tie him up if you have to."

Nathaniel nodded, propping Jehoel's body on the glowing red sphere. He unbuckled his belt, pulling it from around his waist and secured Jehoel's arms making him look like he fell asleep hugging the Oculus.

Lucifer continued directing his pawns. "Lauren, you come over here, on the other side. I need you closer to the Oculus." He dashed over to Matt, grabbing his arm and led him to a point in the far corner of the room. "And you are going to go…"

"Wait, wait, wait," Matt said, throwing his hands up. Matt braced his feet, pushing against Lucifer's cajoling. "What is going on here? What's with the unconscious guy? What is this place?"

Lucifer slapped Matt's arms playfully and circled around him so that they were face to face. "This, my friend, is your ticket home. I promised you I would send you back, and that's what I intend to do. But we just need to perform one little ritual first."

"Ritual?" Aaron stepped forward, his face twisted in confusion. "What kind of ritual?"

Lucifer sighed and dropped his chin to his chest. He stepped toward Lauren, looked up at Aaron, speaking slowly to punctuate his words. "As I've said, I want to find the Leviathan. Thanks to Jehoel here," he slapped Jehoel on the back, "I know where to find it; your world."

As Lucifer spoke, Jehoel's body heaved and his head lifted. He looked around the room through swollen eyes, his face a mass of bruises. Lucifer looked down at him and smiled. "Oh, look. He's awake." He chuckled curtly.

Jehoel looked up at Lucifer as he continued his speech. "Jehoel here was entrusted to guard the Leviathan until the Apocalypse had been initiated. The two of them are psychically linked. But the death of Jehoel will sever that link, allowing the Leviathan free reign again. Imagine how much pent up rage the poor creature has after being kept captive for a few millennia?"

Matt stepped forward, grasping the severity of what's about to come. "So what is this? Some kind of blood ritual?"

Lucifer narrowed his eyes, bobbed his head noncommittally. "Something like that."

"Uh uh. No way," Aaron proclaimed, stepping backward through the door. "I didn't sign up for that. We aren't going to sacrifice anyone to the devil to open up some doorway."

Lucifer nodded, folding his hands behind his back. "I get your hesitance. But two things. One, you aren't sacrificing someone *to* the devil. You're sacrificing someone *with* the devil. Big difference."

Lucifer's eyes glowed a bright red and the door behind Aaron slammed loudly. Aaron's head snapped around at the noise before turning back to Lucifer and watched him stepping threateningly toward him. "And two, no one said you had a choice. Nathaniel?"

Nathaniel's long black wings flapped to life and he closed the length of the room in a flash. He wrenched Twilana's arm around her back, the fingers of his other hand wrapped around her throat. He pulled her off the floor, her feet dangling in midair. She choked and sputtered, struggling to breathe. Aaron watched in horror as her face blanched.

"Let her go!" Aaron shouted. "She has nothing to do with this."

"Give me your consent," Lucifer said. His voice was flat and calm despite the flames sputtering from his eyelids. "I need you to say yes."

Aaron fought with his morals, unsure of what to do. If he said yes, he would condemn a stranger to death. If he said no, he would condemn his friend to death. Either way, someone would die. But there was only one choice to make that he could live with.

"Fine. We'll help you."

Lucifer nodded. Nathaniel lowered Twilana to the floor, just enough that her feet were on the ground and she could breathe. He held on to her arm and throat, ensuring that Aaron and Matt followed through with their promise.

Lucifer raised his arm, pointing to the corner. Waving his hand, he ushered Aaron to his spot. He looked at Matt and flicked his wrist to the opposite end of the room. Matt walked to the spot silently, arms hanging powerlessly at his sides.

Matt placed his back to the wall and looked around at the tiny room. Directly in front of him, Lauren held onto the glowing red ball, a semi-conscious angel tied to the pedestal with a twelve dollar belt. His best friend of twenty years stood across from him, his nerves no doubt as rattled as his own. Near the exit was an old man dressed in a long dirty shirt. The man's body shook with fear as he watched the scene, helpless to do anything about it. Next to him was a tall, winged man who threatened to snap the neck of his new friend. And at the far end of the room stood Lucifer, the self appointed Prince of Darkness, a creature Matt thought was a myth until a few minutes ago.

Matt watched as Lucifer extended his arm and a dark mist emanated from his hand. The mist swirled and solidified, transforming into a long, black sword speckled with tiny, twinkling dots. Grasping the hilt of the sword, Lucifer strode to the Oculus and grabbed Jehoel's hair with his free hand. He pulled his head back and placed the blade against the angel's throat. He looked into Jehoel's eyes and smiled.

"Are you ready for the end of the world?"

CHAPTER 55

Sparks flew from the Oculus, raining down around Lauren in a shower of red and purple. She closed her eyes and turned her head, shielding her face from the onslaught. The air split above the Oculus, revealing a portal of swirling purple light. A harsh wind blew across the room, forcing Lauren to clutch the orb tighter.

"Stay focused!" Lucifer shouted to her. He turned back to Jehoel, the black sword hovering just above the angel's throat. Lucifer recited the words of the ancient spell that would transfer control of Jehoel's power to himself. He closed his eyes and tilted his head back to the ceiling. His mouth spoke the words from a language lost for thousands of years. Electricity crackled between him and Jehoel. He placed the tip of the sword against Jehoel's skin.

Lucifer lowered his head and turned his eyes to Matt, shouting over the ruckus of the vortex. "Come closer!"

Matt bent his head lower, bracing himself against the wind. Though he was only a few steps away, the force against him made the walk more difficult. Matt reached the Oculus and Lauren extended her hand to him. He looked at it uneasily.

"Take it," Lucifer shouted. Matt closed his eyes and reached up, wrapping his fingers around Lauren's. Lucifer turned to Aaron. "Now you!"

Aaron walked toward Lauren, reaching for her hand. When he touched her, Lauren's body tensed and her head flopped back. Bright, white light beamed from every orifice of her face, extending straight through the floating vortex. The vortex widened, increasing the strength of the windstorm. I raised my hand to protect by face against the gale-force winds. Beside me, Nathaniel flapped his wings, negating some of the pressure of the storm, but I noticed his feet braced against the floor, trying to maintain his footing.

Through tearing eyes, I stared at the portal, mesmerized by the beauty of it. I had never seen a Hellfire-induced nexus before. I have seen many portals in my time, but never one of this size or intensity.

Aaron struggled to free his hand from Lauren's, using her incapacitated state to escape, but her tense body caused her hand to contract and her grasp tightening around his fingers. Lucifer watched as Aaron used his free hand to pry Lauren's fingers from his. Without missing a beat, he raised the sword and placed the point against Aaron's neck. His eyes shifted to Lucifer, watching as he shook his head in warning.

A massive roar bellowed through the room from beyond the nexus. Lauren responded with a shrill scream that mingled with the bright light flowing from her mouth. Matt looked up and watched as a long, pink tentacle appeared from the vortex. It hung in the space between worlds, thrashing from left to right. Slowly, it snaked its way down into the Ocularium, the triangular head exploring the room. Matt stared at the tentacle as it rolled over the occulus, the suction cup-like appendages making nauseating sucking sounds as it felt its way around the sphere. Matt realized he'd seen this thing before, way down at the bottom of the Arthur Kill beneath the Outerbridge Crossing.

An explosion ripped through the Ocularium, blasting away the wall behind Nathaniel. Rubble flew in every direction. Nathaniel was knocked from his feet, giving Twilana the chance to roll free from his grip. I reached down and pulled her away as Nathaniel slammed face-first to the floor. She jumped to her feet and rushed to Aaron's side. Grabbing his hand, she tugged at Lauren's wrist, trying to separate them.

"No!" Lucifer shouted, his head snapping around to discover a trio of angels dressed in heavy golden armor floating outside the gaping hole in the wall. The angels were armed each with a battle axe, a golden spear, and a flaming sword. The angel with the axe rushed the room and flung the weapon at Lucifer. He released Jehoel's hair, allowing the angel's chin to crash against the Oculus. Spinning to face the axe, he flicked his wrist, deflecting it with a wave of Hellfire. The axe crashed harmlessly against the wall. Lucifer slashed at the angel as he flew toward him. The angel juked, the tip of the Blade narrowly missing him. He tried to swoop around to take another shot at Lucifer but misjudged his speed and collided with Lauren. They tumbled to the floor, the impact freeing her from her catatonic state. Matt and Aaron's hands slipped from hers and, free from her grip, they rushed towards the exit.

"Can you get us out of here?" Twilana asked as they ran past. They held their heads low, trying to stay below the madness. I turned to the door, placing my hands on the intricate wood carvings. Closing my eyes, I concentrated, using my powers to open it but it refused to budge.

"No," I said, turning back to them. "He must have done something to it."

"Great," Matt muttered. "So we've come all this way just to get killed by a bunch of angels and the Leviathan."

The other two angels had Lucifer cornered. The angel with the sword slashed at him, catching him just above the waist. His sword scorched Lucifer's charcoal grey suit. Lucifer looked down at the damage, flames shooting from his eyes. He grunted and lunged at the two angels. Lucifer's sword cleaved through the angel's spear. He spun around, the blade rising in an upward arc into the second angel's head, slicing his helmet clean in half. It clattered to the floor revealing a deep gash in the angel's face. He dropped to his knees and fell sideways, blood pooling around his head.

The angel with the two spear halves flapped his wings and jumped, away from Lucifer. He hovered in the air, dropping the useless half of the spear. Raising the pointed end to Lucifer, he leaned forward, but the tentacle wrapped around his waist. The angel's eyes went wide with fear. Placing his hands of the slimy tentacle, he tried to wriggle free, but the tentacle constricted, crushing him. He winced in pain, turning the point of the spear and stabbed the tentacle. Thick, purple blood dribbled from the wound and a roar echoed from above them. Lucifer watched as the tentacle retreated into the vortex, dragging the screaming angel with it.

Nathaniel regained his footing and rushed to Lucifer's side.

"Was this supposed to happen?" he asked, watching the vortex as the tentacle returned, slapping the floor with a violent *thud*. Lucifer shook his head and turned to the hole in the wall to find a second wave of angels entering the room.

"No," he replied, grasping the hilt of the sword in both hands. He stepped toward the oncoming angels, bracing for their attack. "I didn't get the chance to finish the ritual. It hasn't bonded to me."

Nathaniel flapped his wings and circled in midair, crashing on top of the angel leading the charge. The angel smashed into the floor, his nose exploding in a gush of blood. Nathaniel turned to find Lucifer clashing swords with two other angels.

Lauren struggled to her feet, kicking the angel beside her. She looked up at Lucifer and watched as he fought two angels at once. Raising her arm, she pointed at one of them and released a stream of Hellfire. It struck him in the back and he slammed into the wall. Lucifer slashed at the second angel, splitting his chest. He looked over at Lauren and smiled.

"Don't let them get away," he shouted, pointing to Aaron and Matt before engaging an additional squad of angels. Lauren turned to the travelers, her face contorting into a wicked grin. She walked toward them, flexing her fingers at her side. Twilana stepped in front of her, her fists clenched. Without hesitation, she swung at Lauren, hitting her in the jaw. Lauren's head snapped to the side and she stumbled sideways. Regaining her balance, she extended her finger and pointed at Twilana. Twilana side-stepped the blast of Hellfire and grabbed Lauren's finger, pulling it back until she heard a sickening crunch. Lauren screamed in pain and dropped to her knees, clutching her hand to her chest. She looked up at Twilana.

"You'll pay for that, bitch." She screamed again as she pulled the finger, setting the break. After a second, Lauren held her hand up, bending the finger as if nothing happened.

Twilana stepped backward and smirked. She waved her fingers in a "Come on" gesture. Lauren slowly rose to her feet when a voice boomed throughout the room.

"Lucifer!"

All heads turned to the hole in the wall. Michael floated in midair, resplendent in his gold and silver armor. A flaming sword crackled in his hand, his wings beat rhythmically. His head titled to the side, spotting Aaron and Matt.

"Ah. And the traitors as well. I should have known I would find you here with him." He turned to the angels fighting Lucifer and pointed to the travelers with his sword. "You capture them. Lucifer's mine."

The two angels nodded, lifting into the air. One swooped down at Twilana, barely missing her as she juked to the side. The other landed in front of Aaron and Matt. Matt balled his fist and lunged at the angel but he backhanded him in the face, sending him reeling to the side. The angel reached out, grabbed Aaron by the throat and shoved him against the wall.

Matt rolled on his shoulder and placed his hand on the floor. As he pushed himself up, he spotted the golden battle axe lying a few feet away. Reaching out, he grabbed it and leapt toward the angel. The axe head slammed down on the angel's arm, severing it just below the elbow. The angel screamed, blood gushing from the stump. Aaron slid down the wall to the floor.

Lauren rose to her feet, her eyes never leaving Twilana. A golden arrow flew past her, clattering against the floor to her side. Turning, she spotted a quartet of angels heading her way The archer raised his bow and aimed a second arrow at her. Lauren pointed at him, knocking the bow upward. The arrow launched harmlessly into the ceiling. She extended her fingers and wiggled them. The angel screamed as his wings pulled from his back, the ragged stumps gushing blood all over the floor. With a twitch of her wrist, the angel flew backward through the hole in the wall, his screams fading as he plummeted to the street below.

The remaining three angels circled around her and Twilana, their feet firmly planted on the floor. The women stood back to back, watching as the angels approached, brandishing an array of weapons.

"Think we can take them?" Twilana asked, wiping sweat from her eyes.

"What's this 'we' junk?" Lauren responded. "You just broke my finger."

"Yeah, well, once they're done with me, they'll be coming after you. Us working together is mutually beneficial."

Lauren considered her words. She didn't like the idea, but she couldn't disagree with it. Lauren nodded a truce and raised her hands. A jet of flames rose from the floor, engulfing one of the angels. Lauren giggled as his body charred and spit before her, his lifeless form flopping to the floor.

Michael's sword struck Lucifer's, the flames sputtering as the two blades clashed. Lucifer clenched his fist and punched at Michael. The angel leaned back, evading the attack. Lucifer reeled and tumbled forward, giving Michael the opportunity to bring his knee to Lucifer's chest. He gasped for air as he dropped to his knees. Michael stepped closer to Lucifer, the flames of his sword burning bright. Lucifer swung his leg wide to sweep Michael's feet from under him. Michael jumped backward, swinging his sword low, slicing Lucifer's thigh.

"You'll never win, Lightbringer," he said as Lucifer pressed against the wound in his leg. "You never do."

Blood dribbled through Lucifer's fingers. A flash erupted from his palm and a moment later, the bleeding stopped. Wiping the blood from his hand on his suit jacket, he looked up at Michael, clutching the sword in both hands.

"Not this time. Never again." He jumped to his feet and dashed toward the angel, sword primed above his head. Behind him, a second tentacle appeared through the portal, feeling around the floor. The tentacle rolled over a fallen angel and wrapped itself around the body. It lifted the soldier up into the air and disappeared into the ether.

I watched in horror as more and more tentacles appeared, each one whipping back and forth in the center of the room. Looking up at the portal, I shrank in fear as the head of the Leviathan poked its way through the nexus. Rows of sharp teeth gnashed and drool slobbered down the side of its mouth. Its glowing green eyes looked straight at the Oculus and Jehoel still strapped to it. A tentacle wove its way across the floor, wrapping around Jehoel's waist. The angel struggled to break free as the Leviathan lifted him from the ground and shoved him into its mouth. As the razor-sharp teeth slashed and flayed his flesh, the screams of the angel reverberated through the room.

"Oh, my," I said as the Leviathan lumbered toward us.

CHAPTER 56

The angels converged on the Leviathan, weapons slashing and hacking at the creature's thick hide. With each injury, the monster released a howl of pain as viscous, purple blood oozed from its wounds. But this did not stop it; the attack barely slowed it down. Its tentacles thrashed around the room like bullwhips and it inched forward, knocking the angels off their feet. It reached out, grasping an angel in its powerful grasp and devoured him.

Lucifer's plan to control the Leviathan was sound. The telepathic bond Jehoel shared with the beast kept it docile. Had he finished the ritual and killed Jehoel, the link would have been transferred to Lucifer. However, with Jehoel dying before the ritual could be completed, the Leviathan regained control of itself. And now all it wanted to do was feed.

Matt looked at me with fear in his eyes. "What do we do?"

I stared at him blankly. From years of studying significant events of the universe, I have learned a vast amount of knowledge, picking up a few tricks on life. My position as a Grigori has always prevented me from sharing these secrets with others. However, given our situation, I was willing to forego my title and provide them with the answer to save the universe. But, for once, I had no solution to the problem at hand.

Michael and Lucifer crossed swords, their battle growing more vicious with each attack. Michael surpassed the passion of following his duties; he was making this fight personal. He hated Lucifer for the years of aggression he had shown the AHM throughout the years. It was evident that Michael wanted to end their feud once and for all.

I watched as their swords clanged in the air. Lucifer thrust at Michael, dodging the angel's counter-attack. Michael slashed, his blade colliding with Lucifer's, a shower of sparks falling to the floor. My eyes fell upon Lucifer's sword. Having been so wrapped up in the events, I failed to recognize the Blade.

"The sword!" I proclaimed so loudly I nearly startled myself. A trio of heads turned toward me, their eyes all expressing the same level of confusion. I pointed to Lucifer across the room.

"The sword Lucifer has. It has the power to destroy the Leviathan."

"Wonderful," Matt said, rolling his eyes. "We just have to get it away from Satan as he's engrossed in a wicked swordfight with an archangel. Sounds easy enough."

A pair of angels swooped down and slammed into Matt's back, knocking him to the floor. The battle-axe flew from his grip and he drew his hands up in front of his face, breaking his fall. A foot stomped onto his back, causing his arms to crumple and his face to smash into the stone floor. Gabriel stood on top of him, the tip of his flaming sword placed against his neck. Matt could feel the heat from the blade on his skin and shivered.

"By order of the Angelic High Military," Gabriel said, "and the power granted to me by Him Himself, you are all under arrest."

I approached Gabriel, hands pressed together, pleading with him. "You can't do this now. This isn't a time for a petty grudge. We need to end this…"

"I *am* ending this, Metatron." Gabriel turned his head to me, his eyes shooting daggers. His mouth was twisted into a frown. "And there is nothing petty about my orders."

Twilana wrestled an angel to the ground, punching him in the face. She brushed the hair from her forehead and looked up, spotting Gabriel standing over Matt. Rolling from the unconscious angel, she crouched down and grabbed the battle-axe from the floor. She straightened her knees and sprung upward, burying the head of the axe into Gabriel's back. His eyes shot open and his jaw dropped. A trickle of blood ran down the corner of his mouth. He stumbled forward, falling to the floor, head flopping to the side. I stood over his lifeless body, horrified by the sight.

Matt rolled onto his side, a sharp pain shot through his

leg. Sliding his hand into his pocket, he felt the familiar shape of the Janian light grenade. He shook his head and chuckled to himself, happy with the Japanese' inability to perform a proper search.

Aaron extended his arm to Matt to help him to his feet.

"How do we get the sword away from Lucifer?" Aaron asked.

Michael turned to Matt and Aaron. Anger flashed in his eyes as he spotted Gabriel's lifeless body on the floor. Ignoring Lucifer, he took to the air and raced toward us.

Nathaniel's body collided with Michael's, sending them crashing to the ground. Michael pushed himself to his hands and knees. Nathaniel was on his feet in moments and delivered a brutal kick to Michael's ribs. The angel dropped to the ground and Nathaniel grabbed his wing, twisting it. Michael screamed in pain as Nathaniel knelt down and punched him in the cheek.

"OK, well, there's one occupied," Matt said. "What about Lucifer?"

Twilana bent down and pulled the axe from Gabriel's back, bolting toward Lucifer. He turned, ducking under the axe blade. Twilana skidded on the floor, twisting her body to strike again. Lucifer lifted his sword and blocked the attack.

"Are you kidding me?" he growled, shoving the blade forward. She stumbled backward, swinging the axe in a wide arc. "Do you really think you can match me?"

"Don't need to." Twilana swung the axe upward, catching Lucifer in the wrist. His hand separated from his arm, still clutching the Blade. Twilana dropped the axe, letting it clatter to the floor. She leapt into the air, grabbing the sword by Lucifer's hand still clutching the hilt. She gracefully landed on the floor and pried Lucifer's fingers from the handle.

"I just need the sword."

Lucifer eyed her wearily. He looked over her shoulder and spotted Lauren fighting with two of Michael's angels. Lucifer released a shrill whistle, catching her attention.

"Time to go, dear sister." He turned and dove through the hole in the wall, dropping to the street below.

A flash of Hellfire erupted from Lauren's hands, pushing the angels back. She ran for the hole and jumped after him.

Twilana spun on her heels and raced back toward Aaron

and Matt. The Leviathan bawled as Michael's remaining angels attacked it, fighting it back into the corner. In a fit of rage, the Leviathan swiped at them, tentacles thrashing sharply. The angels retreated, looking back to search the room for Michael. They found him wrestling with Nathaniel. The angels turned to each other and nodded, hastily flying from the room.

"You two get to the portal," Twilana said, her fingers flexing around the handle of the sword. "I'll take care of the beast."

"I can't let you do this, Aaron said. His voice cracked as he struggled to hold back a flood of emotion. He inhaled deeply, feeling his throat burn. "You can't sacrifice yourself for us."

She placed the tip of the Blade on the floor and stepped toward him. Her eyes were stern, swirling through a spectrum of blues. "Now's not the time to get chivalrous. There's no way you can handle this thing." She swallowed hard, her throat bulging. "Besides, there's no need for you to die here. *You* have the opportunity to go home. I have nothing left."

They stared at each other. Aaron felt his heart pounding in his chest. His arms shook. He wanted to say something but his brain froze.

Matt reached out and grabbed Aaron's arm. "She's right," he said. Aaron looked at him. He closed his eyes, dropping his chin to his chest. Matt walked past him and wrapped his arms around Twilana, hugging her.

"Thank you," he whispered, her blue hair brushing against his lips. "For giving us a chance." He stepped back, flipping the light grenade in his fingers. "This should give you an edge. At least let you get close to it."

She stared at him and smiled.

"Come with us," Aaron said. "If you stay here, you won't make it. Come with us and…" She raised her hand to cut him off.

"We can't allow this beast to run wild here. And besides, there's nothing for me on your world, either."

"There's me." Aaron looked at Twilana, watching as her eyes swirled between shades of gray and red. He leaned in close to her, taking her hand in his. He reached up to her face, brushed a strand of hair from her cheek. She grabbed the back of his neck and pulled him closely.

They kissed, their embrace drowning out the chaos around them. Twilana placed her hand on Aaron's chest and pushed him away. She looked down at her hand, feeling the thumping of his heart. "Don't forget about me." Spinning on her foot, she sprinted toward the Leviathan.

Nathaniel twisted Michael's arm, forcing him against the floor. He could feel his strength fading. His battle with the angels had worn him down, and wrestling with an archangel was no easy task. Michael took advantage of Nathaniel's fatigue, pushing himself up on his knees and slamming the back of his head into Nathaniel's face. He reeled backwards, his grip on Michael's wrist loosened. Reaching out, Michael grabbed an axe that had fallen to the floor. He flapped his wings, taking to the air and chased down the travelers.

Twilana raced across the room, weaving between the throngs of fallen angels. Michael threw the axe at her, sending it flying end-over-end. She jumped to the side and the axe sailing safely past her and ricocheting off the stone floor. Michael cursed, flapping his wings harder to close the gap between them.

Matt pressed the red button on the light grenade. Kneeling down, he slid the bomb across the floor. It bounced off the pedestal of the Oculus and came to a rest a few feet from the Leviathan.

"Cover your eyes!" he shouted to Twilana, placing his hands in front of his face.

A blinding flash of white light filled the room. Michael pitched sideways, his pupils burning from the blast. He plowed headfirst into the stone and fell to the ground, unconscious.

The Leviathan lurched from side to side, blinded by the flash, knocking a group of angels to the ground with its massive body. Twilana continued toward the beast, the sword held tightly in her fist. She leapt as a tentacle swung toward her, her agile body easily clearing the attack. She landed on her feet, not missing a step.

As Twilana drew nearer to the Leviathan, she swung the sword, slicing the monster's hide. The beast reared back, roaring in pain. Twilana ignored it and slashed again, catching it in the eye.

She jumped onto the Leviathan's head and ran down its neck, along its back. Looking at Matt and Aaron, she smiled.

"Get to the portal!" she shouted.

Aaron stared at her as she dropped to her knees. Rotating the Blade in her fist, she aimed the point of the sword at the Leviathan's back. Her eyes remained fixed to Aaron's, her resolve hardening.

"Now!"

Aaron mouthed "thank you" and bowed his head. Matt tugged his arm, pulling him toward the nexus. He leapt onto the Oculus, jumping straight up into the abyss. The swirl from the windstorm grabbed him, carrying him up into the portal. With one final look at Twilana, Aaron inhaled and climbed onto the Oculus, jumping into the nexus behind Matt. A wave of blue and pink sparks splashed out behind him as he disappeared.

Twilana watched as they disappeared. Closing her eyes, she thrust the Black blade into the Leviathan's hide.

Blood oozed as the wound bubbled, releasing wisps of smoke as they popped. The Leviathan bucked back and forth, trying to throw her off. Twilana tightened her grip on the sword and inched her body backward. She dragged the sword through the beast's flesh, opening the wound further.

The Leviathan slowed, its strength draining from its body. Tentacles flailed flaccidly, making a final, fruitless gesture to swat at Twilana. She ducked low to avoid them. The Leviathan stopped moving, releasing a long bellow of pain. Its tentacles dropped the ground, unmoving, as the beast's threnody dissipated through the room.

Peeling her fingers from the hilt of the sword, Twilana sighed. She looked down at the gaping wound in the Leviathan's back, watched as the blood dribbled down its sides. She felt a sudden swell beneath her knees. Her eyes moved toward the creature's hide and watched as it puffed and bloated.

She rushed slid down the Leviathan's side as its corpse distended. The sudden inflation knocked her to the ground. She leapt to her feet and watched as the body enlarged like an old party balloon. Turning, she ran toward the portal, the wet sounds of the Leviathan's dead body nauseating her.

The Leviathan exploded in a flash of bright, purple light, blowing Twilana off her feet. The light engulfed her, wrapping her in warmth. Despite the ominous situation, she felt completely at ease. She closed her eyes and relaxed, thoughts of her life on Janus flooding her mind.

CHAPTER 57

The universe had had enough disorder for one day and it needed to correct itself, a stiff shudder spreading out across all of reality. But this wasn't a sort of fearful shudder. More like willing oneself to throw up after feeling very sick. And if a giant, universal puke was going to fix things, then that's what the universe was going to do.

But the damages had taken its toll. The edges of the Universe began to curl like a sticker on a kindergartener's notebook, revealing the tiniest bit of its dark underbelly. For years, order reigned across the galaxy; a place for everything and everything in its place. There had been a few moments, brief, passing glances where chaos took center stage, but it had been beaten back into the corner for a timeout each time. However, this latest transgression was the final straw. The constant breaching of the time/space continuum had weakened the delicate balance of reality, causing microscopic tears in the fabric of space. These microscopic blemishes weren't severe enough to cause any harm by themselves, but if they failed to be corrected, they would begin to multiply. And if someone with enough chutzpah and no scruples were to come along and take advantage of them, who knows what would happen.

CHAPTER 58

Matt felt his body floating, his arms and legs completely weightless. Opening his eyes, he was instantly assaulted by a wave of definite blackness. He rubbed his eyes, hoping that he'd merely been temporarily blinded by the light grenade. But as he moved his hands and blinked wildly, all he could see was a permeating nothingness.

Panic welled in his chest. All at once, he imagined how he would have to adjust living as a blind man. Thoughts of learning to read Braille and getting a guide dog flooded his mind when a tiny, green dot caught Matt's attention from the corner of his eye. Turning, he squinted at the object, surprised to finally see anything besides black. The light darted back and forth, moving erratically. It grew larger, exposing more and more of its detail. Matt quickly realized that he was facing the green, fishy shape he and Aaron discovered days ago.

Seeing the glowing fish filled Matt with an overwhelming dread, suddenly realizing that he hadn't breathed since he awoke. The light from the fish illuminated his surroundings and he looked over to see Aaron floating next to him. Looking up, Matt spotted the sun hanging over the choppy water. He didn't know how he got under the river, but he knew he needed to get out. He grabbed Aaron's wrist and swam toward the surface, dragging Aaron through the grimy water. His chest heaved as he rocketed upward.

Matt's head crested the water and he took a deep breath, inflating his lungs. Lifting Aaron, he slid his arm around his chest, holding his head above the water. They bobbed in the river and Matt relished every deep breath he took. His legs burned and his arms tingled. With his free hand, he slapped Aaron's face, hoping to revive him so he could swim on his own.

Aaron coughed and heaved a spray of water. He reached up and wiped the wet hair from his face, looked up at the sky. He turned to look at Matt, uncomfortably conscious that Matt's arm was wrapped around his chest. "What the hell are you doing?"

Matt laughed and pushed away. The sun shone down on the river, casting a yellowing hue as it reflected off the water. Relaxing his body, Matt floated on his back, floating gently along the surface. He felt the sun on his face and a cool breeze blew across his skin. He had felt these things countless time before but never seemed to enjoy them as he did at that moment. Matt sighed, feeling a familiar burning sensation in his lungs, an aftereffect of almost drowning. Again. He didn't mind the pain this time. It meant that he was alive.

Righting himself in the water, Matt spotted a familiar red and white object floating a short distance away. He splashed Aaron and, ignoring the waves of pain in his legs, kicked his way toward to the boat.

Grasping the tiny ladder, Matt pulled himself up. He took two steps and flopped down on the red pleather bench. Looking down, he saw that everything was exactly as they left it; wallets, cellphones, empty beer bottles. Aaron climbed up the ladder and stepped onto the bench before settling himself on the edge. His head hung limply to his chest and his hands were folded between his knees.

"Do you think it's over?" Aaron asked, looking up from the debris lying on the floor of the boat. "Do you think we saved the universe?"

Matt shrugged. "I don't think *we* saved anything."

Aaron frowned as his thoughts flashed to Twilana. She stayed behind to battle a beast, just to send them home. He looked out over the river, staring at the tiny specks of buildings that lined the shore. "But everything feels right, at least. I just wish things could have ended differently"

Matt nodded. "Me too, man." He reached down and pulled two beers from the cooler. Handing one to Aaron, he gave him a playful jab in the shoulder. Aaron smiled, cracked the beer cap and took a swig.

Leaving Aaron to his sadness, Matt slid into the driver's seat. Turning the key, the engine revved to life and he spun off, pointing the boat toward the shore. A spray of water erupted behind the boat as Matt gunned the accelerator, intent on getting home and taking a well-deserved nap.

EPILOGUE

Months passed since Lucifer's attack on the Angelic High Military but the effects of the battle lingered. I paced the length of the Ocularium, contemplating the events. Having been witness to so many important occurrences throughout the universe, seen wars and death, births and new beginnings, I had grown accustomed to the atrocities intelligent beings can commit. But this was different. This time I was a part of the events and that made me uneasy. I constantly wondered if I could have done anything differently. Wondered if I *should* have done anything differently, abandoned my oath as a Grigori and acted. Looking through the clear plastic sheet that covered the hole in my wall, I stared out at the city, transfixed by the glittering wonder of it all. Shaking my head, I strolled back into my office.

Leaning over my desk, I gathered a sheaf of papers and tucked them into my briefcase. I looked up at the clock, knowing I was early but anxious to get moving. Stepping from my office, I sauntered to the elevator. The sweet sounds of Muzak Bryan Adams comforted me on my ride down. The elevator *ding*ed and I stepped from the car, passing the security desk. I looked over and found a strange face. Wes had worked in the AHM security office for nearly 30 centuries and all that was left of him was a pile of ashes and his half-melted nametag. I nodded to the unfamiliar security guard, a simple polite gesture to hide the fact that I haven't remembered his name.

I stepped around the statue, a large structure that replaced the fountain. It served as a memorial to the fallen. The craftsmanship was beautiful, capturing the likeness of the day's hero. The features of Twilana Salizar stared out from the white marble, her hand raised high in triumph, holding the Onyx Blade of Belial. The artist chose to make the blade out of true onyx, providing a beautiful juxtaposition to the white stone. She stood atop the fallen remains of the Leviathan, its tentacles wrapping halfway up her leg. All around the base were the names of the angels that lost their lives that day, and those that had gone missing. My eyes fell upon one name in particular.

Gabriel. Though I didn't know the angel, or necessarily like what I knew about him, he didn't deserve the ending he got. None of them did.

I turned from the memorial, pushing my way through the revolving door for the last time.

*   *   *   *   *

"Archangel Michael, Prince of Light, Angel of Protection, Strength and Truth, Ruler of the Sun, how do you plead?"

Michael stood from his chair before the tribunal, facing the charges against him. His singular goal to find and destroy the travelers coupled with his quest for revenge against Lucifer was looked upon poorly by the higher ups. He was deemed to have not acted in the best interests of New Eden and the rest of the universe. He was immediately arrested and brought to trial for his crimes; Wrath, Vanity and Greed.

"Not guilty, sirs," he said. His arms were shackled, hanging uselessly in front of him. His hair had grown a few inches, the stubble on his face a few days old. His clothing was stained and rumpled. I had never seen Michael in such an unkempt state.

A long, white sheet separated the room. Three dark silhouettes bled through the sheet, the forms of three people seated in high-backed chairs. The Tribunal was the law of New Eden, relied upon to find and deliver justice among the angels. The Tribunal's power rested in their anonymity, which was the purpose behind the theatrics. "Archangel Michael, given the evidence we have seen today, the sworn statements from many of the event's witnesses, including that of an ordained and respected of the Grigori, it is our ruling that the charges before you stand. Your actions needlessly threatened those in your charge. Furthermore, we find the death of Lieutenant General Gabriel to be the result of your negligence, and as such, move to strip you of all rank and titles."

Michael leaned back as the Tribunal spoke, each word hitting him like a punch in the gut. "But sirs, you don't understand! I recognized the danger and acted…"

"Silence!" The Tribunal's voice boomed through the room, fluttering the crinoline sheet. "You had the chance to plead your case. According to angelic law, the severity of your crimes calls for a severe punishment, which in this case includes death. But due to your years of faithful service, we have decided to grant leniency, and hereby exile you from New Eden, sending you to live the rest of your days on the inhabited planet of Earth. You will lose access to the use of your powers as well as the privilege of Angelic telepathy. Do you understand our decree?"

"Yes, sirs." Michael's chains rattled as he spoke, his head drooping to the side.

"Guards, you may remove the prisoner." A pair of angels flanked Michael, each grabbing an elbow. They escorted him through the double doors at the front of the room. As they passed, Michael's eyes met mine and anger flashed across his face. I imagine that were it not for the guards, he would have risked the wrath of the Tribunal and come after me.

After the sentencing, I walked the streets of New Eden for a few hours. My nerves were still on edge from Michael's silent threat, but I was happy to have some closure to the experience. The city had an amazing calming effect, allowing me to get lost in the hustle of other people's lives. Yet somehow my mind refused to stop racing. I thought about Twilana and the sacrifice she made. About Aaron and Matt and the ordeal they went through, hoping they managed to find their way home. With the destruction of the Ocularium, I was unable to tune into their whereabouts. Unable to follow up with them.

I also thought about Lucifer and Lauren. And about Nathaniel. They disappeared before the battle ended but I was sure they would turn up. They always did. But what kind of trouble would they bring with them next time?

In the end, it wasn't my worry. After millennia as the ranking Grigori, I retired my post, deciding it was time to move on. I still had a number of good years left and felt they would be better spent concentrating on me instead of living through the milestone events of everyone else. Though my recent experience rattled me to the bones, it made me realize one important thing; I wanted to live for myself.

Unfortunately, I had no idea where to start. Maybe I'd write a book…

Twilana's tale of survival continues in…

The Relentless Pursuit
Of The Cosmic Awareness

MICHAEL GARY WIRTH

CHAPTER 1

Twilana's eyes watered as a cloud of dust enveloped the room. Tears rolled down her cheeks and pain engulfed her eye sockets but she refused to blink. Refused to look away from Aaron. In the short time she'd known him, this strange man that fell into her life through some fluke, cosmic accident, she developed deep feelings for him. There was a connection with him that she'd never felt with anyone else. The burning in Twilana's eyes intensified but she knew it wasn't just from the dust. They burned with the fear of loss. She knew that she would never see him again and that pain hurt her deeply. But she at least took solace in the fact that he was returning home. Safely. And that he'd have his life ahead of him.

Her eyes flicked to Matt, Aaron's friend and travelling companion. A man that she had considered a friend as well. One that'd she'd risk her life for.

"Go!" she shouted. Through the chaos and smoke, she watched as Matt grabbed Aaron's arm and pull him toward the vortex. Twilana trusted Matt's logic, that he would not make an emotional decision. And as she watched Aaron disappear into the swirling purple miasma of the beyond, she was thankful for that trust.

Twilana squeezed her eyelids shut and a torrent of tears dribbled down her cheeks. Inhaling deeply, she swiped the back of her hand across her face, leaving wet streaks on her skin. The flood of emotions filling her chest made her uncomfortable, being forced to face feeling that he'd never faced before. Being Captain in the

Janian military never afforded her many opportunities to care for somebody else. She'd dealt with death plenty of times and lost people she'd never see again. But this was different.

She balled her fist and shook her head, pushing the emotions to the side. Looking down, she watched as the beast undulated beneath her feet. She felt the sword in her hand, the heavy onyx blade that shone with the light of a million twinkling stars, and tightened her grip on the hilt. Lifting the blade above her head, she spun the sword in her hands, leveling the point at the creature. The Leviathan: a mythical being whose presence summoned the end of the world. Given the last couple of minutes, Twilana had to believe that there may be some truth to the myth. Not that she was going to simply stand by and let it happen.

Closing her eyes, she threw her head backwards and jammed the sword into the Leviathan's back. Thick, pink blood oozed from the wound as the monster shrieked in pain. Dropping to her knees, she dragged the blade through the flesh of the Leviathan's back, splitting its hide as she inched her was backward. Blood sprayed from the gash, bathing everything in a warm, pink goo.

The Leviathan released a piercing threnody as it bucked wildly. Twilana slid down its side, her boots kicking up a spray of blood as she landed on the floor and stepped back as the creature entered its final death throes. Her head hung limp as she listened to the wet slapping sounds of the Leviathan's dying tentacles all around her. The exhaustion of the past week finally caught up to her. Her body ached. Her soul ached. Her heart ached.

Turning from the bloody, pulsating corpse, Twilana looked up, her gaze meeting Metatron's. His gentle face stared at her, his eyes showing a mixture of relief and pity, knowing that, for her at least, the victory was bittersweet. She could feel her cheeks tingling from the trail of tears. All she wanted to do was scream out to relieve the pressure in her chest but as she opened her mouth, all that escaped was a yawn. Metatron smiled at the revelation of her humanity.

Seeing Metatron's smile eased Twilana's nerves. Her heartbeat slowed as she returned his smile, vowing to herself to find some place small, warm, and quiet to fall asleep for a few days. But a rumble in the floor disrupted that fantasy. She turned toward the body of the Leviathan and saw the quivering in its lifeless flesh. Slightly at first, almost imperceptibly but as she stared at it, the shaking became more pronounced, more intense. Placing her hand on its hide, she felt waves flowing throughout its body. She had no idea what was causing it but she turned from the Leviathan's corpse and sprinted across the room.

Twilana pumped her legs as hard as she could to put as much distance between her and the Leviathan. Behind her, a warm blast of air and a flash of bright, pink light ripped through the room. Her body grew heavy as the light engulfed her. Her muscles fought against her will, dragging her down. She dropped to her knees as every cell in her body grew cold, the light sapping all warmth from the room. Looking up at Metatron, she watched as his mouth moved. He was shouting to her but no sound passed his lips. He raised his hand, reaching out to grab her. She tried to lift her arm but the light had her trapped, unable to move. She watched helplessly as a grimace of fear spread across Metatron's face.

The light became brighter, washing away the details of the room around her. Metatron's face seemed to dissipate, disappearing slowly from reality. As the light grew brighter, Twilana suddenly realized that it wasn't Metatron that was disappearing. It wasn't the Occularium fading from reality.

It was her.

Twilana bolted upright in her bed, sweat pouring down her face and chest. Her stomach roiled and her throat contracted. Leaning over the side of the bed, she retched, a splash of vomit erupting from her gullet. Her chest heaved a few times, forcing the contents of her stomach up her throat. She sat upright for a minute, staring at the wall across from her, waiting for another wave of sickness. Satisfied that it was over, she wiped the bile from the corner of her mouth and lay back in the bed.

The same dream plagued her every night for weeks. But it was more than a dream. It was a memory. A recollection of the event that changed everything.

Feeling a chill run through her body, she wrapped the bearskin blanket around herself and rolled over onto her side. She closed her eyes but images from the dream continued to flash through her brain. She knew she wouldn't be going back to sleep. Hopping out of the bed, she dropped the blanket and grabbed her clothes, the dirty, ragged uniform of her military days. It had long since outlived its usefulness but Twilana couldn't bear to part with it.

But sentimental attachment was only part of the reason she kept the uniform; she had no skills to sew new clothes. The dark blue outfit had been repaired many times over, cuts and tears sewed up with whatever she could find. The outfit looked terrible but as she slipped into it, it made her feel good. Powerful. Like her old self.

Crouching down, she grabbed her dagger. Like her clothing, the dagger was cobbled together from whatever material she could find, repaired numerous times over the last few months. But one thing had always remained the same about the weapon. Wrapping her fingers around the cold black hilt, she dragged the edge across her fingertips, feeling its sharpness. The old stone she found had been quite useful, retaining its edge for quite some time, but she knew that she would need to find a new one soon. She pulled on the vines that attached the stone to the hilt.

Looking down at the handle, she remembered her dream, remembered the pain of leaving Aaron and Matt. Every time she looked at the weapon, she was reminded of that moment. The sight of the blade was directly attached to that memory. Besides the clothes on her back, the hilt was the only piece that remained of her time on that world.

It was the handle of the Onyx Blade of Belial.

CHAPTER 2

Ducking low, Twilana emerged from the mouth of the cave into the clearing. She righted herself and inhaled deeply, the sweet scent of the jungle air filling her lungs. A cool breeze brushed over her skin, flittering her hair. Twilana smiled, the air seeming to chase away the remnants of last night's dream.

The sun peeked over the horizon far off in the distance, casting a few thin tendrils of light through the trees. Twilana looked out into the semi-darkness and reveled in the tranquility of the morning. With the sun came the heat; beads of sweat formed on her forehead. Wiping them away, she slipped the dagger into her belt and stepped from the rocky outcrop. She lowered herself down the sloping hill and quickly surveyed her surroundings, listening to the crinkling of the leaves as they rustled in the breeze.

The air was heavy with moisture. Twilana tugged at her shirt, fanning the sweat that dripped down her chest. This type of humidity was new to her; the buildings on Janus all contained self-sustaining bio-systems, each carefully maintained to create a comfortable climate. All of her life, she was surrounded by air conditioners, heating units and dehumidifiers, making sure that she never suffered from unsightly perspiration. Even though she'd gotten used to it over the past few months, that didn't mean she liked it.

She stepped into the morning light. Skulking slowly between the trees, she kept her eyes focused on the ground, searching the dirt for a trail of animal prints that may lead to her breakfast. The humidity wrapped itself around her, causing her clothes to cling to her body. She was fanning the sweat on her chest again when she spotted a line of paw prints leading over a small hill. She knelt next to the tracks and examined them.

Rising to her feet, she made her way around the tall trees surrounding her, pushing aside the curling vines that dropped from the branches. The area was awash in large, green, bushy leaves sprouting from the treetops. Bright yellow moss grew along the sides of the trees and down to the ground, feeding on the damp bark and jungle detritus. Every so often a breeze would shake the leafy canopy overhead, sending a flurry of leaves tumbling down to the jungle floor. Up above, puffs of flowers dotted the branches, breaking the monotony of green with balls of blue, pink, and purple. Reaching up, Twilana plucked a pink flower from the tree. Tilting her head back, she held it above her mouth and squeezed the nectar from the pistil. The juice flowed over her tongue, its sweetness invigorating her.

Pausing for a moment, she listened to the rustling of leaves, catching the undertones of something else. She turned her head and listened to the wind, holding her breath to hear better. Finding the source of the noise, she dropped to her knees and crawled over a large, peeking down on a stream beneath her.

A scrawny brown fawn stood at the edge of the stream, its pink tongue lapping up the cool, clear water. Twilana watched the drinking deer, transfixed by the ripples of water that erupted from beneath the animal's mouth.

Sliding the dagger from her belt, Twilana inched her way toward the edge of the rock, moving cautiously to stay as silent as she could. She grabbed the underside of the rock and rolled herself over the side, landing on a mound of moss directly beneath it. The muted thud sounded like a clap of thunder to her, forcing her to pause, breath held as she waited for the deer to bolt off into the brush. The deer lifted its head and sniffed the air a few times before turning back to the stream to continue its drink.

Gripping the handle of the blade, Twilana stepped closer to the fawn, slowly placing her feet in the soft, loamy dirt, moving like a cat on shag carpeting. Steadying her breathing, she pivoted the blade in her hand, resting the cool stone against her forearm. She shifted her weight to her front foot, bracing, waiting for the perfect moment to pounce.

An orange blur passed before her, taking her aback. She turned her head and blinked rapidly. When she looked back toward the stream, the deer was gone. She spotted the fawn farther downstream, kicking and bucking as a tiger stood on its flank, its jaws clenched tightly around its neck. A heart-wrenching wail escaped the deer's mouth as its flailing grew weaker and weaker. Thick red blood oozed from its throat, draining the life from its body.

"Oh no, you don't," Twilana muttered under her breath. Spinning on her front foot, she lunged at the tiger, swiping the blade at its hind quarters. The tiger roared in pain as the stone slashed its thigh. It kicked at Twilana, hitting her square in the chest. She flopped to the ground with a thud, the blade tumbling from her hand.

The tiger stepped back from the deer and limped toward Twilana. It sniffed at the air as it drew closer to her, fires of anger burning in its big, blue eyes. Twilana looked up at the tiger, its low, throaty growl prickling her skin, questioning the intelligence of her attack. Her hand frantically patted the ground beside her, searching for her weapon.

Twilana's fingertips brushed the cold stone of the hilt of the knife. She rolled onto her belly and lunged for the blade as the tiger pounced on her, its massive paws pinning her shoulders to the ground. Grasping the blade, she reached back and slashed at its face. The blade tore open the animal's cheek and blood trickled down its maw. The tiger roared again as it stepped back from Twilana, giving her the chance to hop to her knees and turn toward the beast. Twilana leaped and buried the knife into the tiger's leg. It growled viciously, pawing at her. Tears formed in her eyes as the razor-sharp claws raked across her ribcage. She twisted the blade and the tiger's roar grew more pained as it pushed her back with its massive paw.

Twilana tumbled to the dirt, the pain in her chest almost unbearable, her vision blurry with tears. She wiped her eyes clear and forced the pain to the side, struggling to rise on shaky legs. She clutched the blade tightly, the tips of her fingers turning white. The tiger circled around, limping on its injured foot, huffing loudly. It sprang, but Twilana ducked out of its way. The tiger fell to the ground, kicking up a wave of leaves and dirt. She jumped onto the tiger's back, jamming the knife into its side. It reared up on its hind legs, throwing her into a growth of bushes and weeds.

Shaking her head, Twilana lifted herself up on her elbow and waited for the tiger to attack. She watched as it looked back at her, curl its lip and growl. It huffed loudly through its nose before turning to the woods and loping off between the trees, disappearing in the tall grass.

Twilana lay back on the dirt, a deep, throaty laugh breaking the silence. Her shoulder hurt, her side throbbed and she'd lost her breakfast. She sat up in the grass and wrapped her arms around her knees. Despite all of the bad luck she faced that morning, she somehow felt more alive than she had in months.

Pushing herself to her feet, Twilana felt a strange pulsing in her hand. Cradling it against her chest, she massaged the back of her hand to calm the nerves. A moment passed before she realized that her hand wasn't tingling because of an injury; the pulsing came from the blade.

Twilana held the weapon in front of her and watched as tiny vibrations moved through the hilt. She turned, facing the stream and noticed that the strength of the vibrations increased, growing more pronounced. Giving the blade a confused look she took a step backward. The vibrations weakened. She shook her head and smiled to herself, contemplating the strangeness of the blade. She stepped forward again and, as expected, the vibrations returned. Twilana sighed, dropping her arms to her side and tromped through the tall grass. With each step, she felt the trembling of the blade grow stronger but she ignored it. She was hungry, she was tired, and her ribs hurt like hell. The hilt of the blade was crafted by some sort of ancient, magical demon. She stopped trying to understand it a long time ago. At this point, its only purpose was to help her hunt.

A sudden pulse shot up Twilana's arm, so strong and abrupt that it caused her drop the knife. She bent over to grab it, rifling through a clump of dried grass. As she grasped her blade, a strange object caught her attention. Dark black, spotted with thousands of twinkling white dots. She reached through the grass and picked it up, holding it up to the light to examine it.

Her breath caught in her throat as she realized she was holding another shard of the Onyx Blade.

CHAPTER 3

The fluorescent light flickered over Lauren as she leaned against the stainless steel countertop, staring at the long strand of red hair she twirled between her fingers. Bored and disinterested, she contemplated her current situation. She looked down and scowled at the blue polo shirt she wore. The stiff polyester made her skin made her itch and just felt downright gross. She hated having to wear that shirt but she had no choice. According to Section III, Paragraph B, Sub-section 2 of the Employee Handbook, *"Arthur Treachers employees are to dress in a manner that reflects the company culture and, as such, all manner of dress shall be in the form of a blue Polo shirt (to be provided by your manager) and khaki pants"*. How the notion of "blue polo" and "khaki" reflected the nature of fried fish Lauren hadn't a clue. She tugged at the shirt and continued to snap the wad of pink chewing gum between her teeth.

"Would you stop that, please?"

Lauren grunted, her attention placed firmly on the strands of hair between her fingers and the chewing gum. Lucifer reached up and pulled her hand away from her hair.

"And stop that while you're behind the counter. The last thing I need is for someone to complain about hair in their food."

"Sir, yes sir," Lauren said, mocking him with a salute. Sighing exasperatedly, she strolled over to the register, leaning her elbows on the counter.

Lucifer was dressed as the model associate. Khaki pants neatly pressed and wrinkle free. Blue polo shirt tucked into his pants, secured by a shiny black belt. His hair, though well-coiffed, had lost the sheen he was used to, but he managed to adjust well to the new look. Even his nametag, which introduced him as "Lou", was pinned proudly to his chest at a perfect 90 degree angle.

"What, are you bored?" Lucifer asked, straightening his back. He shifted down the counter, pulling a sleeve of drinking cups from the shelf. "Because if you want, you can count all this stuff for me." He bent over to get a look at the cups in the back of the shelf, eyeballing each one and taking a mental count. Looking down at the inventory spreadsheet clipped to his brown clipboard, he checked a box next to the entry for *Medium Cups* and scribbled a legible *94* on the line for *Count*.

"Yeah, OK," Lauren groaned. "Like you'd let anyone take the reins of your precious inventory."

"You're right," Lucifer growled, placing the clipboard on the countertop. "I won't let anyone do this. You know why? Because I believe in doing things right. Meanwhile all you seem to do is mope. Do you think I like being here? Having to hide away from everything? Not to mention this." He pointed to his nametag where, beneath his name, exclaimed 'Assistant Manager'. "You think I *like* being an 'Assistant' Manager in a place like this? Hell, there's no reason I shouldn't be a District Manager. But I deal with it because I know. We just need to give it time and when we return to New Eden, things will be different."

The fall from power was the most frustrating part of their exile for Lucifer. Back home in New Eden, he enjoyed a lofty position of being the head of the underworld, a virtual kingpin of the vices and sins of the city. If someone needed a fix, had some itch that needed to be scratched, Lucifer was sure to profit from it in one way or another. But when he tried to release the Leviathan in the middle of the Angelic High Military building, a plan that failed spectacularly, he and Lauren had been forced to hide out on this backwards-ass planet, blending in with the population by getting low paying, low profile jobs.

While Lucifer eventually grew into his new role, Lauren hated it with every fiber of her being. She pushed up from the counter and turned to Lucifer, leaning her hip on the dented stainless steel. Though she couldn't stand what they were reduced to, she trusted Lucifer completely. He took her in when she was at the lowest point of her life and showed her what it was like to have someone care for her. He told her they needed to lay low so she would do what he asked. But that didn't mean she wouldn't have a little fun with him in the meantime. She blew a large pink bubble with her chewing gum, letting it pop loudly. Her smile widened as Lucifer gave her a side-long glare.

"Go clean out the grease traps," he muttered. Lauren's smile faded. She turned and skulked back to the kitchen, picking clumps of gum off her lips.

ABOUT THE AUTHOR

Shortly after receiving his Bachelor's Degree in Visual Communications, Michael Gary Wirth realized that his passion didn't lie in the arts but in writing. Looking to make writing his full-time profession, he self-published his first sci-fi novel, *The Non-Linear Flow of the Universal Tides*. He has since turned his attention to other works, such as a sequel to *Non-Linear Flow* as well as a number of other genre spanning titles. When he isn't guiding his characters through battles with demons, bowling alley alternate dimensions, and saving the entirety of space-time, he enjoys his downtime with his beautiful wife, Lauren, and his stinky but cute cat, Pepe. For more information on his upcoming stories, visit his website at www.MichaelGaryWirth.com